THE FALL OF GONDOLIN

J.R.R. Tolkien

Edited by Christopher Tolkien

With illustrations by Alan Lee

WILLIAM MORROW
An Imprint of HarperCollinsPublishers

To my family

First published by HarperCollins*Publishers* 2018
This William Morrow paperback edition published 2024

Library of Congress Cataloging-in-Publication Data is available.

ISBN 978-0-06-337639-7

23 24 25 26 27 LBC 5 4 3 2 1

CONTENTS

MAP OF
BELERIAND
AND THE LANDS
TO THE NORTH

ILLUSTRATIONS

On the preceding pages of this book there will be found a map, and at the end genealogies of the House of Bëor and the princes of the Noldor. These are taken from *The Children of Húrin*, with some minor alterations.

PREFACE

In my preface to *Beren and Lúthien* I remarked that 'in my ninety-third year this is (presumptively) the last book in the long series of editions of my father's writings'. I used the word 'presumptively' because at that time I thought hazily of treating in the same way as *Beren and Lúthien* the third of my father's 'Great Tales', *The Fall of Gondolin*. But I thought this very improbable, and I 'presumed' therefore that *Beren and Lúthien* would be my last. The presumption proved wrong, however, and I must now say that 'in my ninety-fourth year *The Fall of Gondolin* is (indubitably) the last'.

In this book one sees, from the complex narrative of many strands in various texts, how Middle-earth moved towards the end of the First Age, and how my father's perception of this history that he had conceived unfolded through long years until at last, in what was to be its finest form, it foundered.

The story of Middle-earth in the Elder Days was always a

shifting structure. My *History* of that age, so long and complex as it is, owes its length and complexity to this endless welling up: a new portrayal, a new motive, a new name, above all new associations. My father, as the Maker, ponders the large history, and as he writes he becomes aware of a new element that has entered the story. I will illustrate this by a very brief but notable example, which may stand for many. An essential feature of the story of the Fall of Gondolin was the journey that the Man, Tuor, undertook with his companion Voronwë to find the Hidden Elvish City of Gondolin. My father told of this very briefly in the original Tale, without any noteworthy event, indeed no event at all; but in the final version, in which the journey was much elaborated, one morning out in the wilderness they heard a cry in the woods. We might almost say, 'he' heard a cry in the woods, sudden and unexpected.* A tall man clothed in black and holding a long black sword then appeared and came towards them, calling out a name as if he were searching for one who was lost. But without any speech he passed them by.

Tuor and Voronwë knew nothing to explain this extraordinary sight; but the Maker of the history knows very well who he was. He was none other than the far-famed Túrin Turambar, who was the first cousin of Tuor, and he was fleeing from the ruin – unknown to Tuor and Voronwë

---

* To show that this is not fanciful, in his letter to me of 6 May 1944 my father wrote: 'A new character has come on the scene (I am sure I did not invent him, I did not even want him, though I like him, but there he came walking into the woods of Ithilien): Faramir, the brother of Boromir.'

– of the city of Nargothrond. Here is a breath of one of the great stories of Middle-earth. Túrin's flight from Nargothrond is told in *The Children of Húrin* (my edition, pp.180–1), but with no mention of this meeting, unknown to either of those kinsmen, and never repeated.

To illustrate the transformations that took place as time passed nothing is more striking than the portrayal of the god Ulmo as originally seen, sitting among the reeds and making music at twilight by the river Sirion, but many years later the lord of all the waters of the world rises out of the great storm of the sea at Vinyamar. Ulmo does indeed stand at the centre of the great myth. With Valinor largely opposed to him, the great God nonetheless mysteriously achieves his end.

Looking back over my work, now concluded after some forty years, I believe that my underlying purpose was at least in part to try to give more prominence to the nature of 'The Silmarillion' and its vital existence in relation to *The Lord of the Rings* – thinking of it rather as the *First Age* of my father's world of Middle-earth and Valinor.

There was indeed *The Silmarillion* that I published in 1977, but this was composed, one might even say 'contrived' to produce narrative coherence, many years after *The Lord of the Rings*. It could seem 'isolated', as it were, this large work in a lofty style, supposedly descending from a very remote past, with little of the power and immediacy of *The Lord of the Rings*. This was no doubt inescapable, in the form in which I undertook it, for the narrative of the First Age was of a radically different literary and imaginative nature. Nevertheless, I knew that long before, when *The Lord of the Rings* was finished but well before its publication, my father had expressed a deep wish and conviction that the First Age and the Third Age (the world of *The Lord of the Rings*) should be treated, *and published*, as elements, or parts, *of the same work*.

In the chapter of this book, *The Evolution of the Story*, I have printed parts of a long and very revealing letter that he wrote to his publisher, Sir Stanley Unwin, in February 1950, very soon after the actual writing of *The Lord of the Rings* had reached its end, in which he unburdened his mind on this matter. At that time he portrayed himself self-mockingly as horrified when he contemplated 'this impracticable monster of some six hundred thousand words' – the more especially when the publishers were expecting what they had demanded, a sequel to *The Hobbit*, while this new book (he said) was 'really a sequel to *The Silmarillion*'.

He never modified his opinion. He even wrote of *The Silmarillion* and *The Lord of the Rings* as 'one long Saga of the Jewels and the Rings'. He held out against the separate publication *of either work* on those grounds. But in the end he was defeated, as will be seen in *The Evolution of the Story*, recognizing that there was no hope that his wish would be granted: and he consented to the publication of *The Lord of the Rings* alone.

After the publication of *The Silmarillion* I turned to an investigation, lasting many years, of the entire collection of manuscripts that he had left to me. In *The History of Middle-earth* I restricted myself as a general principle to 'drive the horses abreast', so to speak: not story by story through the years in their own paths, but rather the whole narrative movement as it evolved through the years. As I observed in the foreword to the first volume of the *History*,

> the author's vision of his own vision underwent a continual slow shifting, shedding and enlarging: only in *The Hobbit* and *The Lord of the Rings* did parts of it emerge to become fixed in print, in his own lifetime. The study of Middle-earth and Valinor is thus complex; for the object of the study was not stable, but existed, as it were, 'longitudinally' in time (the author's lifetime), and not only 'transversely' in time, as a printed book that undergoes no essential further change.

Thus it comes about that from the nature of the work the *History* is often difficult to follow. When the time had come, as I supposed, to end at last this long series of editions it occurred to me to try out, as best as I could, a different mode: to follow, using previously published texts, one single particular narrative from its earliest existing form and throughout its later development: hence *Beren and Lúthien*. In my edition of *The Children of Húrin* (2007) I did indeed describe in an appendix the chief alterations to the narrative in successive versions; but in *Beren and Lúthien* I actually cited earlier texts in full, beginning with the earliest form in the *Lost Tales*. Now that it is certain that the present book is the last, I have adopted the same curious form in *The Fall of Gondolin*.

In this mode there come to light passages, or even full-fledged conceptions, that were later abandoned; thus in *Beren and Lúthien* the commanding if brief entrance of Tevildo, Prince of Cats. *The Fall of Gondolin* is unique in this respect. In the original version of the Tale the overwhelming attack on Gondolin with its unimagined new weapons is seen with such clarity and in such detail that the very names are given of the places in the city where the buildings were burnt down or where celebrated warriors died. In the later versions the destruction and fighting is reduced to a paragraph.

That the Ages of Middle-earth are conjoint can be brought home most immediately by the reappearance – in their persons, and not merely as memories – of the figures of the Elder Days in *The Lord of the Rings*. Very old indeed was the Ent, Treebeard; the Ents were the most ancient people surviving in the Third Age. As he carried Meriadoc and Peregrin through the forest of Fangorn he chanted to them:

In the willow-meads of Tasarinan I walked in the Spring.
Ah! the sight and the smell of the Spring in Nan-tasarion!

It was very long indeed before Treebeard sang to the hobbits in Fangorn that Ulmo Lord of Waters came to Middle-earth to speak to Tuor in Tasarinan, the Land of Willows. Or again, at the end of the story we read of Elrond and Elros, sons of Eärendel, in a later age the master of Rivendell and the first king of Númenor: here they are very young, taken into protection by a son of Fëanor.

*

But here I will introduce, as an emblem of the Ages, the figure of Círdan, the Shipwright. He was the bearer of Narya, the Ring of Fire, one of the Three Rings of the Elves, until he surrendered it to Gandalf; of him it was said that 'he saw further and deeper than any other in Middle-earth'. In the First Age he was the lord of the havens of Brithombar and Eglarest on the coasts of Beleriand, and when they were destroyed by Morgoth after the Battle of Unnumbered Tears he escaped with a remnant of his people to the Isle of Balar. There and at the mouths of Sirion he turned again to the building of ships, and at the request of King Turgon of Gondolin he built seven. These ships sailed into the West, but no message from any one of them ever came back until the last. In that ship was Voronwë, sent out from Gondolin, who survived shipwreck and became the guide and companion of Tuor on their great journey to the Hidden City.

To Gandalf Círdan declared long after, when he gave him the Ring of Fire: 'But as for me, my heart is with the Sea, and I will dwell by the grey shores, guarding the Havens until the last ship sails.' So Círdan appears for the last time on the last day of the Third Age. When Elrond and Galadriel, with Bilbo and Frodo, rode up to the gates of the Grey Havens, where Gandalf was awaiting them,

Círdan the Shipwright came forth to greet them. Very tall he was, and his beard was long, and he was grey and old, save that his eyes were keen as stars; and he looked at them and bowed, and said: 'All is now ready.' Then Círdan led them to the Havens, and there was a white ship lying . . .

After farewells were spoken those who were departing went aboard:

> and the sails were drawn up, and the wind blew, and slowly the ship slipped away down the long grey firth; and the light of the glass of Galadriel that Frodo bore glimmered and was lost. And the ship went out into the High Sea and passed on into the West . . .

thus following the path of Tuor and Idril as the end of the First Age approached, who 'set sail into the sunset and the West, and came no more into any tale or song.'

*

The tale of *The Fall of Gondolin* gathers as it proceeds many glancing references to other stories, other places, and other times: to events in the past that govern actions and presumptions in the present time of the tale. The impulse, in such cases, to offer explanation, or at least some enlightenment, is strong; but keeping in mind the purpose of the book I have not peppered the texts with small superimposed numbers leading to notes. What I have aimed at is to provide some assistance of this nature in forms that can be readily neglected if desired.

In the first place, I have in the 'Prologue' introduced a citation from my father's *Sketch of the Mythology* of 1926, in order to provide a picture, in his words, of the World from its beginning to the events leading finally to the foundation of Gondolin. Further, I have used the List of Names in many cases for statements a good deal fuller than the name implies; and I have also introduced, after the List of Names, a number of separate notes on very varied topics, ranging from the creation of the World to the significance of the name Eärendel and the Prophecy of Mandos.

Very intractable of course is the treatment of the changing of names, or of the forms of names. This is the more complex since a particular form is by no means necessarily an indication of the relative date of the composition in which it occurs. My father would make the same change in a text at quite different times, when he noticed the need for it. I have not aimed at consistency throughout the book: that is to say, neither settling for one form throughout, nor in every case following that in the manuscript, but allowing such variation as seems best. Thus I retain *Ylmir* when it occurs for *Ulmo*, since it is a regular occurrence of a linguistic nature, but give always *Thorondor* for *Thorndor*, 'King of Eagles', since my father was clearly intending to change it throughout.

Lastly, I have arranged the content of the book in a manner distinct from that in *Beren and Lúthien*. The texts of the Tale appear first, in succession and with little or no commentary. An account of the evolution of the story then follows, with a discussion of my father's profoundly saddening abandon-ment of the last version of the *Tale* at the moment when Tuor passed through the Last Gate of Gondolin.

I will end by repeating what I wrote nearly forty years ago.

It is the remarkable fact that the only full account that my father ever wrote of the story of Tuor's sojourn in Gondolin, his union with Idril Celebrindal, the birth of Eärendel, the treachery of Maeglin, the sack of the city, and the escape of the fugitives – a story that was a central element in his imagination of the First Age – was the narrative composed in his youth.

Gondolin and Nargothrond were each made once, and not remade. They remained powerful sources and images – the more powerful, perhaps, because never remade, and never remade, perhaps, because so powerful.

Though he set out to remake Gondolin he never reached the city again: after climbing the endless slope of the Orfalch Echor and passing through the long line of heraldic gates he paused with Tuor at the vision of Gondolin amid the plain, and never recrossed Tumladen.

The publication 'in its own history' of the third and last of the Great Tales is the occasion for me to write a few words in honour of the work of Alan Lee, who has illustrated each Tale in turn. He has brought to this task a deep perception of the inner nature of scene and event that he has chosen from the great range of the Elder Days.

Thus, he has seen, and shown, in *The Children of Húrin*, the captive Húrin, chained to a stone chair on Thangorodrim, listening to Morgoth's terrible curse. He has seen, and shown, in *Beren and Lúthien*, the last of Fëanor's sons seated motionless on their horses and gazing at the new star in the western sky, which is the Silmaril, for which so many lives had been taken. And in *The Fall of Gondolin* he has stood beside Tuor and with him marvelled at the sight of the Hidden City, for which he has journeyed so far.

Finally, I am very grateful to Chris Smith of Harper-Collins for the exceptional help that he has given to me in the preparation of the detail of the book, especially in his assiduous accuracy, drawing on his knowledge both of the demands of publication and the nature of the book. To my wife Baillie also: without her unwavering support during the long time the book has been in the making it would never have been made. I would also thank all those who generously wrote to me when it appeared that *Beren and Lúthien* was to be my last book.

PROLOGUE

I will begin this book by returning to the quotation that I used to open *Beren and Lúthien*: a letter written by my father in 1964, in which he said that 'out of my head' he wrote *The Fall of Gondolin* 'during sick-leave from the army in 1917', and the original version of *Beren and Lúthien* in the same year.

There is some doubt about the year, arising from other references made by my father. In a letter of June 1955 he wrote '*The Fall of Gondolin* (and the birth of Eärendil) was written in hospital and on leave after surviving the Battle of the Somme in 1916'; and in a letter to W.H. Auden of the same year he dated it to 'sick-leave at the end of 1916'. The earliest reference of his that I know of was in a letter to me of 30 April 1944, commiserating with me on my experiences of that time. 'I first began' (he said) 'to write The History of the Gnomes* in army huts, crowded, filled with the noise of

---

* For the use of *Gnomes* for the people of the Elves named the Noldor (earlier Noldoli) see *Beren and Lúthien* pp.32–3.

gramophones'. This does not sound like sick-leave: but it may be that he began the writing before he went on leave.

Very important, however, in the context of this book, was what he said of *The Fall of Gondolin* in his letter to W.H. Auden of 1955: it was 'the first real story of this imaginary world.'

My father's treatment of the original text of *The Fall of Gondolin* was unlike that of *The Tale of Tinúviel*, where he erased the first, pencilled manuscript and wrote a new version in its place. In this case he did indeed extensively revise the first draft of the Tale, but rather than erase it he wrote a revised text in ink on the pencilled original, increasing the multiplicity of change as he progressed. It can be seen from passages where the underlying text is legible that he was following the first version fairly closely.

On this basis my mother made a fair copy, notably exact in view of the difficulties now presented by the text. Subsequently my father made many changes to this copy, by no means all at the same time. Since it is not my purpose in this book to enter into the textual complexities that all but invariably accompany the study of his works, the text that I give here is my mother's, including the changes made to it.

It must however be mentioned in this connection that many of the changes to the original text had been made before my father, in the spring of 1920, read the Tale to the Essay Club of Exeter College at Oxford. In his introductory and apologetic words, explaining his choice of this work in place of an 'Essay', he said of it: 'It has of course never seen the light before. A complete cycle of events in an Elfinesse of my own imagining has for some time past grown up (rather, has been constructed) in my mind. Some of the episodes have been scribbled down. This tale is not the best of them, but it is the only one that has so far been revised at all and that, insufficient as that revision has been, I dare read aloud.'

The original title of the tale was *Tuor and the Exiles of Gondolin*, but my father always later called it *The Fall of Gondolin*, and I have done the same. In the manuscript the title is followed by the words 'which bringeth in the Great Tale of Eärendel'. The teller of the tale in the Lonely Isle, on which see *Beren and Lúthien* pp.30–31, was Littleheart (Ilfiniol), son of that Bronweg (Voronwë) who plays an important part in the Tale.

It is in the nature of this, the third of the 'Great Tales' of the Elder Days, that the massive change in the world of Gods and Elves that had taken place should bear upon the immediate narrative of the Fall of Gondolin – and is indeed a part of it. A brief account of those events is needed; and rather than write one myself I think it far better to use my father's own condensed, and characteristic, work. This is found in the 'Original *Silmarillion*' (also 'A Sketch of the Mythology'), as he himself called it, which can be dated to 1926, and subsequently revised. I used this work in *Beren and Lúthien*, and again in this book as an element in the evolution of the tale of *The Fall of Gondolin*; but I use it here for the purpose of providing a concise account of the history before

Gondolin came into being: it also has the advantage of itself deriving from a very early period.

In view of the purpose of its inclusion I have omitted passages that are not here relevant, and here and there made other minor modifications and additions for the sake of clarity. My text opens at the point where the original 'Sketch' begins.

After the despatch of the Nine Valar for the governance of the world Morgoth (Demon of Dark) rebels against the overlordship of Manwë, overthrows the lamps set up to illumine the world, and floods the isle of Almaren where the Valar (or Gods) dwelt. He fortifies a palace of dungeons in the North. The Valar remove to the uttermost West, bordered by the Outer Seas and the final Wall, and eastward by the towering Mountains of Valinor which the Gods built. In Valinor they gather all light and beautiful things, and build their mansions, gardens, and city, but Manwë and his wife Varda have halls upon the highest mountain (Taniquetil) whence they can see across the world to the dark East. Yavanna Palúrien plants the Two Trees in the middle of the plain of Valinor outside the gates of the city of Valmar. They grow under her songs, and one has dark green leaves with shining silver beneath, and white blossoms like the cherry from which a dew of silver light falls; the other has golden-edged leaves of young green like the beech and yellow blossom like the hanging blossoms of laburnum which give out heat and blazing light. Each tree waxes for seven hours to full glory and then wanes for seven; twice a day therefore comes a time of softer light when each tree is faint and their light is mingled.

The Outer Lands [Middle-earth] are in darkness. The growth of things was checked when Morgoth quenched the lamps. There are forests of darkness, of yew and fir and ivy. There Oromë sometimes hunts, but in the North Morgoth and his demonic broods (Balrogs) and the Orcs (Goblins, also called *Glamhoth* or people of hate) hold sway. Varda looks on the darkness and is moved, and taking all the hoarded light of Silpion, the White Tree, she makes and strews the stars.

At the making of the stars the children of Earth awake – the Eldar (or Elves). They are found by Oromë dwelling by the star-lit pool, Cuiviénen, Water of Awakening, in the East. He rides home to Valinor filled with their beauty and tells the Valar, who are reminded of their duty to the Earth, since they came thither knowing that their office was to govern it for the two races of Earth who should after come each in appointed time. There follows an expedition to the fortress of the North (Angband, Iron-hell), but this is now too strong for them to destroy. Morgoth is nonetheless taken captive, and consigned to the halls of Mandos who dwelt in the North of Valinor.

The Eldalië (people of the Elves) are invited to Valinor for fear of the evil things of Morgoth that still wandered in the dark. A great march is made by the Eldar from the East led by Oromë on his white horse. The Eldar are divided into three hosts, one under Ingwë after called the Quendi

(Light-elves), one after called the Noldoli (Gnomes or Deep-elves), one after called the Teleri (Sea-elves). Many of them are lost upon the march and wander in the woods of the world; becoming the various hosts of the Ilkorindi (Elves who never dwelt in Kôr in Valinor). The chief of these was Thingol, who heard Melian and her nightingales singing and was enchanted and fell asleep for an age. Melian was one of the divine maidens of the Vala Lórien who sometimes wandered into the outer world. Melian and Thingol became Queen and King of woodland Elves in Doriath, living in a hall called the Thousand Caves.

The other Elves came to the ultimate shores of the West. In the North these in those days sloped westward in the North until only a narrow sea divided them from the land of the Gods, and this narrow sea was filled with grinding ice. But at the point to which the Elf-hosts came a wide dark sea stretched west.

There were two Valar of the Sea. Ulmo (Ylmir), the mightiest of all Valar next to Manwë, was lord of all waters, but dwelt often in Valinor, or in the Outer Seas. Ossë and the lady Uinen, whose tresses lay through all the sea, loved rather the seas of the world that washed the shores beneath the Mountains of Valinor. Ulmo uprooted the half-sunk island of Almaren where the Valar had first dwelt, and embarking on it the Noldoli and Quendi, who arrived first, bore them to Valinor. The Teleri dwelt some time by the shores of the sea awaiting him, and hence their love of it. While they were being also transported by Ulmo, Ossë in jealousy and out of love for their singing chained the island to the sea-bottom far out in the bay of Faërie whence the Mountains of Valinor could dimly be seen. No other land was near it, and it was called the Lonely Isle. There the Teleri dwelt a long age becoming different in tongue, and learning strange music from Ossë, who made the sea-birds for their delight.

The Gods gave a home in Valinor to the other Eldar. Because they longed even among the Tree-lit gardens of Valinor for a glimpse of the stars, a gap was made in the encircling mountains, and there in a deep valley a green hill, Kôr, was built. This was lit from the West by the Trees, to the East it looked out onto the Bay of Faërie and the Lonely Isle, and beyond to the Shadowy Seas. Thus some of the blessed light of Valinor filtered into the Outer Lands [Middle-earth], and falling on the Lonely Isle caused its western shores to grow green and fair.

On the top of Kôr the city of the Elves was built and was called Tûn. The Quendi became most beloved by Manwë and Varda, the Noldoli by Aulë (the Smith) and Mandos the Wise. The Noldoli invented gems and made them in count-less numbers, filling all Tûn with them, and all the halls of the Gods.

The greatest in skill and magic of the Noldoli was Finwë's elder son Fëanor.* He contrived three jewels (Silmarils)

---

* Finwë was the leader of the Noldoli on the great journey from Cuiviénen. His eldest son was Fëanor; his second son Fingolfin, father of Fingon and Turgon; his third son Finarfin, father of Finrod Felagund.

wherein a living fire combined of the light of the Two Trees was set, they shone of their own light, impure hands were burned by them.

The Teleri seeing afar the light of Valinor were torn between desire to rejoin their kindred and to dwell by the sea. Ulmo taught them craft of boat-building. Ossë yielding gave them swans, and harnessing many swans to their boats they sailed to Valinor, and dwelt there on the shores where they could see the light of the Trees, and go to Valmar if they wished, but could sail and dance in the waters touched to light by the radiance that came out past Kôr. The other Eldar gave them many gems, especially opals and diamonds and other pale crystals which were strewn upon the beaches of the Bay of Faërie. They themselves invented pearls. Their chief town was Swanhaven upon the shores northward of the pass of Kôr.

The Gods were now beguiled by Morgoth, who having passed seven ages in the prisons of Mandos in gradually lightened pain came before the conclave of the Gods in due course. He looks with greed and malice upon the Eldar, who also sit there about the knees of the Gods, and lusts especially after the jewels. He dissembles his hatred and desire for revenge. He is allowed a humble dwelling in Valinor, and after a while goes freely about, only Ulmo foreboding ill, while Tulkas the strong, who first captured him, watches him. Morgoth helps the Eldar in many deeds, but slowly poisons their peace with lies.

He suggests that the Gods brought them to Valinor out

of jealousy, for fear their marvellous skill, and magic, and beauty, should grow too strong for them outside in the world. The Quendi and Teleri are little moved, but the Noldoli, the wisest of the Elves, become affected. They begin at whiles to murmur against the Gods and their kindred; they are filled with vanity of their skill.

Most of all does Morgoth fan the flames of the heart of Fëanor, but all the while he lusts for the immortal Silmarils, although Fëanor has cursed for ever anyone, God or Elf or mortal that shall come hereafter, who touches them. Morgoth lying tells Fëanor that Fingolfin and his son Fingon are plotting to usurp the leadership of the Gnomes from Fëanor and his sons, and to gain the Silmarils. A quarrel breaks out between the sons of Finwë. Fëanor is summoned before the Gods, and the lies of Morgoth laid bare. Fëanor is banished from Tûn, and with him goes Finwë who loves Fëanor best of his sons, and many of the Gnomes. They build a Treasury northward in Valinor in the hills near Mandos' halls. Fingolfin rules the Gnomes that are left in Tûn. Thus Morgoth's words seem justified and the bitterness he sowed goes on after his words are disproved.

Tulkas is sent to put Morgoth in chains once more, but he escapes through the pass of Kôr into the dark region beneath the feet of Taniquetil called Arvalin, where the shadow is thickest in all the world. There he finds Ungoliant, Gloomweaver, who dwells in a cleft in the mountains, and sucks up light or shining things to spin them out again in webs of black and choking darkness, fog, and gloom. With Ungoliant he plots revenge. Only a terrible reward will bring her to dare the dangers of Valinor or the sight of the Gods. She weaves a dense gloom about her to protect her and swings on cords from pinnacle to pinnacle till she has scaled the highest peak of the mountains in the south of Valinor (little guarded because of their height and their distance from the old fortress of Morgoth). She makes a ladder that Morgoth can scale. They creep into Valinor. Morgoth stabs the Trees and Ungoliant sucks up their juices, belching forth clouds of blackness. The Trees succumb slowly to the poisoned sword, and to the venomous lips of Ungoliant.

The Gods are dismayed by a twilight at midday, and vapours of black float in about the ways of the city. They are too late. The Trees die while they wail about them. But Tulkas and Oromë and many others hunt on horseback in the gathering gloom for Morgoth. Wherever Morgoth goes there the confusing darkness is greatest owing to the webs of Ungoliant. Gnomes from the Treasury of Finwë come in and report that Morgoth is assisted by a spider of darkness. They had seen them making for the North. Morgoth had stayed his flight at the Treasury, slain Finwë and many of his men, and carried off the Silmarils and a vast hoard of the most splendid jewels of the Elves.

In the meanwhile Morgoth escapes by Ungoliant's aid northward and crosses the Grinding Ice. When he has re-gained the northern regions of the world Ungoliant summons him to pay the other half of her reward. The first half was the sap of the Trees of Light. Now she claims one half of the jewels. Morgoth yields them up and she devours them. She is now become monstrous, but he will not give her any share in the Silmarils. She enmeshes him in a black web, but he is rescued by the Balrogs with whips of flame, and the hosts of the Orcs; and Ungoliant goes away into the uttermost South.

Morgoth returns to Angband, and his power and the numbers of his demons and Orcs becomes countless. He forges an iron crown and sets therein the Silmarils, though his hands are burned black by them, and he is never again free from the pain of the burning. The crown he never leaves off for a moment, and he never leaves the deep dungeons of his fortress, governing his vast armies from his deep throne.

When it became clear that Morgoth had escaped the Gods assemble about the dead Trees and sit in the darkness stricken and dumb for a long while, caring about nothing. The day which Morgoth chose for his attack was a day of festival throughout Valinor. Upon this day it was the custom of the chief Valar and many of the Elves, especially the Quendi, to climb the long winding paths in endless procession to Manwë's halls upon Taniquetil. All the Quendi and some of the Noldoli (who under Fingolfin dwelt still in Tûn) had gone to Taniquetil, and were singing upon its topmost height when the watchers from afar descried the fading of the Trees. Most of the Noldoli were in the plain, and the Teleri upon the shore. The fogs and darkness drift in now off the seas through the pass of Kôr as the Trees die. Fëanor summons the Gnomes to Tûn (rebelling against his banishment).

There is a vast concourse on the square on the summit of Kôr about the tower of Ing, lit by torches. Fëanor makes a violent speech, and though his wrath is for Morgoth his words are in part the fruit of Morgoth's lies. He bids the Gnomes fly in the darkness while the Gods are wrapped in mourning, to seek freedom in the world and to seek out Morgoth, now Valinor is no more blissful than the world outside. Fingolfin and Fingon speak against him. The assembled Gnomes vote for flight, and Fingolfin and Fingon yield; they will not desert their people, but they retain command over a half of the Noldoli of Tûn.

The flight begins. The Teleri will not join. The Gnomes cannot escape without boats, and do not dare to cross the Grinding Ice. They attempt to seize the swan-ships in Swanhaven, and a fight ensues (the first between the races of the Earth) in which many Teleri are slain, and their ships carried off. A curse is pronounced upon the Gnomes, that they shall after suffer often from treachery and the fear of treachery among their own kindred in punishment for the blood spilled at Swanhaven. They sail North along the coast of Valinor. Mandos sends an emissary, who speaking from a high cliff hails them as they sail by, and warns them to return, and when they will not, speaks the 'Prophecy of Mandos' concerning the fate of after days.

The Gnomes come to the narrowing of the seas, and prepare to sail. While they are encamped upon the shore Fëanor and his sons and people sail off taking with them all the boats, and leave Fingolfin on the far shore treacherously, thus beginning the curse of Swanhaven. They burn the boats as soon as they land in the East of the world, and Fingolfin's people see the light in the sky. The same light also tells the Orcs of the landing.

Fingolfin's people wander miserably. Some under Fingolfin return to Valinor to seek the Gods' pardon. Fingon leads the main host North, and over the Grinding Ice. Many are lost.

Among the poems that my father embarked on during his years at the University of Leeds (most notably the *Lay of the Children of Húrin* in alliterative verse) was *The Flight of the Noldoli from Valinor*. This poem, also in alliterative verse, was abandoned after 150 lines. It is certain that it was written at Leeds, in (I think it extremely probable) 1925, the year in which he took up his appointment to the professorship of Anglo-Saxon at Oxford. From this poetic fragment I will cite a part, beginning at the 'vast concourse on the square on the summit of Kôr' where Fëanor 'made a violent speech', described in a passage of the *Sketch of the Mythology* p.32. The name *Finn* at lines 4 and 16 is the Gnomish form of Finwë, the father of Fëanor; *Bredhil* at line 49 the Gnomish name of Varda.

But the Gnomes were numbered   by name and kin,
marshalled and ordered   in the mighty square
upon the crown of Kôr.   There cried aloud
the fierce son of Finn.   Flaming torches
he held and whirled   in his hands aloft,   5
those hands whose craft   the hidden secret

knew, that none   Gnome or mortal
hath matched or mastered   in magic or in skill.
'Lo! slain is my sire   by the sword of fiends,
his death he has drunk   at the doors of his hall   10
and deep fastness,   where darkly hidden
the Three were guarded,   the things unmatched
that Gnome and Elf   and the Nine Valar
can never remake   or renew on earth,
recarve or rekindle   by craft or magic,   15
not Fëanor Finn's son   who fashioned them of yore –
the light is lost   whence he lit them first,
the fate of Faërie   hath found its hour.

Thus the witless wisdom   its reward hath earned
of the Gods' jealousy,   who guard us here   20
to serve them, sing to them   in our sweet cages,
to contrive them gems   and jewelled trinkets,
their leisure to please   with our loveliness,
while they waste and squander   work of ages,
nor can Morgoth master   in their mansions sitting   25
at countless councils.   Now come ye all,
who have courage and hope!   My call harken
to flight, to freedom   in far places!
The woods of the world   whose wide mansions
yet in darkness dream   drowned in slumber,   30
the pathless plains   and perilous shores
no moon yet shines on   nor mounting dawn
in dew and daylight   hath drenched for ever,
far better were these   for bold footsteps

than gardens of the Gods   gloom-encircled   35
with idleness filled   and empty days.
Yea! though the light lit them   and the loveliness
beyond heart's desire   that hath held us slaves
here long and long.   But that light is dead.
Our gems are gone,   our jewels ravished;   40
and the Three, my Three,   thrice-enchanted
globes of crystal   by gleam undying
illumined, lit   by living splendour
and all hues' essence,   their eager flame –
Morgoth has them   in his monstrous hold,   45
my Silmarils.   I swear here oaths
unbreakable bonds   to bind me ever,
by Timbrenting   and the timeless halls
of Bredhil the Blessed   that abides thereon –
may she hear and heed –   to hunt endlessly   50
unwearying unwavering   through world and sea,
through leaguered lands,   lonely mountains,
over fens and forest   and the fearful snows,
till I find those fair ones,   where the fate is hid
of the folk of Elfland   and their fortune locked,   55
where alone now lies   the light divine.'

Then his sons beside him,   the seven kinsmen,
crafty Curufin,   Celegorm the fair,
Damrod and Díriel   and dark Cranthir,
Maglor the mighty,   and Maidros tall   60
(the eldest, whose ardour   yet more eager burnt
than his father's flame,   than Fëanor's wrath;

him fate awaited   with fell purpose),
these leapt with laughter   their lord beside,
with linkéd hands   there lightly took   65
the oath unbreakable;   blood thereafter
it spilled like a sea   and spent the swords
of endless armies,   nor hath ended yet.

*

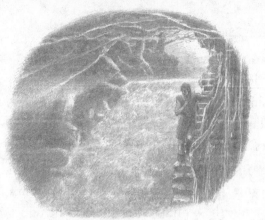

The Tale of
THE FALL OF GONDOLIN

Then said Littleheart son of Bronweg: 'Know then that Tuor was a man who dwelt in very ancient days in that land of the North called Dor-lómin or the Land of Shadows, and of the Eldar the Noldoli know it best.

Now the folk whence Tuor came wandered the forests and fells and knew not and sang not of the sea; but Tuor dwelt not with them, and lived alone about that lake called Mithrim, now hunting in its woods, now making music beside its shores on his rugged harp of wood and the sinews of bears. Now many hearing of the power of his rough songs came from near and far to hearken to his harping, but Tuor left his singing and departed to lonely places. Here he learnt many strange things and got knowledge of the wandering Noldoli, who taught him much of their speech and lore; but he was not fated to dwell for ever in those woods.

Thereafter it is said that magic and destiny led him on a day to a cavernous opening down which a hidden river flowed from Mithrim. And Tuor entered that cavern seeking to learn its secret, but the waters of Mithrim drove him forward into the heart of the rock and he might not win back into the light. And this, it is said, was the will of Ulmo Lord of Waters at whose prompting the Noldoli had made that hidden way.

Then came the Noldoli to Tuor and guided him along dark passages amid the mountains until he came out in the light once more, and saw that the river flowed swiftly in a ravine of great depth with sides unscalable. Now Tuor desired no more to return but went ever forward, and the river led him always toward the west.

The sun rose behind his back and set before his face, and where the water foamed among many boulders or fell over falls there were at times rainbows woven across the ravine, but at evening its smooth sides would glow in the setting sun, and for these reasons Tuor called it Golden Cleft or the Gully of the Rainbow Roof, which is in the speech of the Gnomes Glorfalc or Cris Ilbranteloth.

Now Tuor journeyed here for three days, drinking the waters of the secret river and feeding on its fish; and these were of gold and blue and silver and of many wondrous shapes. At length the ravine widened, and ever as it opened its sides became lower and more rough, and the bed of the river more impeded with boulders against which the waters foamed and spouted. Long times would Tuor sit and gaze at the splashing water and listen to its voice, and then he would rise and leap onward from stone to stone singing as he went; or as the stars came out in the narrow strip of heaven above the gully he would raise echoes to answer the fierce twanging of his harp.

One day after a great journey of weary going Tuor at deep evening heard a cry, and he might not decide of what creature it came. Now he said: 'It is a fay-creature', now, 'Nay, 'tis but some small beast that waileth among the rocks'; or again it seemed to him that an unknown bird piped with a voice new to his ears and strangely sad – and because he had not heard the voice of any bird in all his wandering down Golden Cleft he was glad of the sound although it was mournful. On the next day at an hour of the morning he heard the same cry above his head, and looking up beheld three great white birds beating back up the gully on strong wing, and uttering cries like to the ones he had heard amid the dusk. Now these were the gulls, the birds of Ossë.

In this part of that riverway there were islets of rock amid the currents, and fallen rocks fringed with white sand at the gullyside, so that it was ill-going, and seeking a while Tuor found a spot where he might with labour scale the cliffs at last. Then came a fresh wind against his face, and he said: 'This is very good and like the drinking of wine,' but he knew not that he was near the confines of the Great Sea.

As he went along above the waters that ravine again drew together and the walls towered up, so that he fared on a high cliff-top, and there came a narrow neck, and this was full of noise. Then Tuor looking downward saw the greatest of marvels, for it seemed that a flood of angry water would come up the narrows and flow back against the river to its source, but that water which had come down from distant

Mithrim would still press on, and a wall of water rose nigh to the cliff-top, and it was crowned with foam and twisted by the winds. Then the waters of Mithrim were overthrown and the incoming flood swept roaring up the channel and whelmed the rocky islets and churned the white sand – so that Tuor fled and was afraid, who did not know the ways of the Sea; but the Ainur put it into his heart to climb from the gully when he did, or had he been whelmed in the incoming tide, and that was a fierce one by reason of a wind from the west. Then Tuor found himself in a rugged country bare of trees, and swept by a wind coming from the set of the sun, and all the shrubs and bushes leaned to the dawn because of the prevalence of that wind. And here for a while he wandered till he came to the black cliffs by the sea and saw the ocean and its waves for the first time, and at that hour the sun sank beyond the rim of Earth far out to sea, and he stood on the cliff-top with outspread arms, and his heart was filled with a longing very great indeed. Now some say that he was the first of Men to reach the Sea and look upon it and know the desire it brings; but I know not if they say well.

In those regions he set up his abode, dwelling in a cove sheltered by great sable rocks, whose floor was of white sand, save when the high flood partly overspread it with blue water; nor did foam or froth come there save at times of the direst tempest. There long he sojourned alone and roamed about the shore or fared over the rocks at the ebb, marvelling at the pools and the great weeds, the dripping caverns and the strange sea-fowl that he saw and came to know; but the rise and fall of the water and the voice of the waves was ever to him the greatest wonder and ever did it seem a new and unimaginable thing.

Now on the quiet waters of Mithrim over which the voice of the duck or moorhen would carry far he had fared much in a small boat with a prow fashioned like to the neck of a swan, and this he had lost on the day of his finding the hidden river. On the sea he adventured not as yet, though his heart was ever egging him with a strange longing thereto, and on quiet evenings when the sun went down beyond the edge of the sea it grew to a fierce desire.

Timber he had that came down the hidden river; a goodly wood it was, for the Noldoli hewed it in the forests of Dor-lómin and floated it to him of a purpose. But he built not as yet aught save a dwelling in a sheltered place of his cove, which tales among the Eldar since name Falasquil. This by slow labour he adorned with fair carvings of the beasts and trees and flowers and birds that he knew about the waters of Mithrim, and ever among them was the Swan the chief, for Tuor loved this emblem and it became the sign of himself, his kindred and folk thereafter. There he passed a very great while until the loneliness of the empty sea got into his heart, and even Tuor the solitary longed for the voice of men. Herewith the Ainur had something to do: for Ulmo loved Tuor.

One morning while casting his eye along the shore – and it was then the latest days of summer – Tuor saw three swans flying high and strong from the northward. Now these birds he had not before seen in these regions, and he took them for a sign, and said; 'Long has my heart been set on a journey far from here; lo! now at length I will follow these swans.' Behold, the swans dropped into the water of his cove and there swimming thrice about rose again and winged slowly south along the coast, and Tuor bearing his harp and spear followed them.

It was a great day's journey that Tuor put behind him that day; and he came ere evening to a region where trees again appeared, and the manner of the land through which he now fared differed greatly from those shores about Falasquil. There had Tuor known mighty cliffs beset with caverns and great spoutholes, and deep-walled coves, but from the cliff-tops a rugged land and flat ran bleakly back to where a blue rim far to the east spoke of distant hills. Now however did he see a long and sloping shore and stretches of sand, while the distant hills marched ever nearer to the margin of the sea, and their dark slopes were clad with pine or fir and about their feet sprang birches and ancient oaks. From the feet of the hills fresh torrents rushed down narrow chasms and so found the shores and the salt waves. Now some of these clefts Tuor might not overleap, and often was it ill-going in these places, but still he laboured on, for the swans fared ever before him, now circling suddenly, now speeding forward, but never coming to earth, and the rush of their strong-beating wings encouraged him.

It is told that in this manner Tuor fared onward for a great number of days, and that winter marched from the North somewhat speedier than he for all his tirelessness. Nevertheless came he without scathe of beast or weather at a time of first spring to a river mouth. Now here was the land less northerly and more kindly than about the issuing of Golden Cleft, and moreover by a trend of the coast was the sea now rather to the south of him than to the west, as he could mark by the sun and stars; but he had kept his right hand always to the sea.

The river flowed down a goodly channel and on its banks were rich lands: grasses and moist meadow to the one side and tree-grown slopes of the other; its waters met the sea sluggishly and fought not as the waters of Mithrim in the north. Long tongues of land lay islanded in its course covered with reeds and bushy thicket, until further to seaward sandy spits ran out; and these were places beloved by such a multitude of birds as Tuor had nowhere yet encountered. Their piping and wailing and whistling filled the air; and here amid their white wings Tuor lost sight of the three swans, nor saw he them again.

Then did Tuor grow for a season weary of the sea, for the buffeting of his travel had been sore. Nor was this without Ulmo's devising, and that night the Noldoli came to him and he arose from sleep. Guided by their blue lanterns he found a way beside the river border, and strode so mightily inland that when dawn filled the sky to his right hand lo! the sea and its voice were far behind him, and the wind came from before him so that its odour was not even in the air. Thus came he soon to that region that has been called Arlisgion 'the place of reeds', and this is in those lands that are to the south of Dor-lómin and separated therefrom by the Shadowy Mountains whose spurs run even to the sea.

From these mountains came this river, and of a great clearness and marvellous chill were its waters even at this place. Now this is a river most famous in the histories of Eldar and Noldoli and in all tongues is it named Sirion. Here Tuor rested a while until driven by desire he arose once more to journey further and further by many days' marches along the river borders. Full spring had not yet brought summer when he came to a region yet more lovely. Here the song of small birds shrilled about him with a music of loveliness, for there are no birds that sing like the songbirds of the Land of Willows; and to this region of wonder he had now come. Here the river wound in wide curves with low banks through a great plain of the sweetest grass and very long and green; willows of untold age were about its borders, and its wide bosom was strewn with water-lily leaves, whose flowers were not yet in the earliness of the year, but beneath the willows the green swords of the flaglilies were drawn, and sedges stood, and reeds in embattled array. Now there dwelt in these dark places a spirit of whispers, and it whispered to Tuor at dusk and he was loath to depart; and at morn for the glory of the unnumbered buttercups he was yet more loath, and he tarried.

Here saw he the first butterflies and was glad at the sight; and it is said that all butterflies and their kindred were born in the valley of the Land of Willows. Then came the summer and the time of moths and the warm evenings, and Tuor wondered at the multitude of flies, at their buzzing and the droning of the beetles and the hum of bees; and to all these things he gave names of his own, and wove the names into new songs on his old harp; and these songs were softer than his singing of old.

Then Ulmo grew in dread lest Tuor dwell for ever here and the great things of his design come not to fulfilment. Therefore he feared longer to trust Tuor's guidance to the Noldoli alone, who did service to him in secret, and out of fear of Melko wavered much. Nor were they strong against the magic of that place of willows, for very great was its enchantment.

Behold now Ulmo leapt upon his car before the doorway of his palace below the still waters of the Outer Sea; and his car was drawn by narwhal and sealion and was in fashion like a whale; and amidst the sounding of great conches he sped from Ulmonan. So great was the speed of his going that in days, and not in years without count as might be thought, he reached the mouth of the river. Up this his car might not fare without hurt to its water and its banks; therefore Ulmo, loving all rivers and this one more than most, went thence on foot, robed to the middle in mail like the scales of blue and silver fishes; but his hair was a bluish silver and his beard to his feet was of the same hue, and he bore neither helm nor crown. Beneath his mail fell the skirts of his kirtle of shimmering greens, and of what substance these were woven is not known, but whoso looked into the depths of their subtle colours seemed to behold the faint movements of deep waters shot with the stealthy lights of phosphorescent fish that live in the abyss. Girt was he with a rope of mighty pearls, and he was shod with mighty shoes of stone.

Thither he bore too his great instrument of music; and

this was of strange design, for it was made of many long twisted shells pierced with holes. Blowing therein and playing with his long fingers he made deep melodies of a magic greater than any other among musicians hath ever compassed on harp or lute, on lyre or pipe, or instruments of the bow. Then coming along the river he sat among the reeds at twilight and played upon his thing of shells; and it was nigh to those places where Tuor tarried. And Tuor hearkened and was stricken dumb. There he stood knee-deep in the grass and heard no more the hum of insects, nor the murmur of the river borders, and the odour of flowers entered not into his nostrils; but he heard the sound of waves and the wail of sea-birds, and his soul leapt for rocky places and the ledges that reek of fish, for the splash of the diving cormorant and those places where the sea bores into the black cliffs and yells aloud.

Then Ulmo arose and spoke to him and for dread he came near to death, for the depth of the voice of Ulmo is of the uttermost depth: even as deep as his eyes which are the deepest of all things. And Ulmo said: 'O Tuor of the lonely heart, I will not that thou dwell for ever in fair places of birds and flowers; nor would I lead thee through this pleasant land, but that so it must be. But fare now on thy destined journey and tarry not, for far from hence is thy weird set. Now must thou seek through the lands for the city of the folk called Gondothlim or the dwellers in stone, and the Noldoli shall escort thee thither in secret for fear of the spies of Melko. Words I will set to your mouth there, and there you shall abide awhile. Yet maybe thy life shall turn again to the mighty waters; and of a surety a child shall come of thee than whom no man shall know more of the uttermost deeps, be it of the sea or of the firmament of heaven.'

Then spoke Ulmo also to Tuor some of his design and desire, but thereof Tuor understood little at that time and feared greatly. Then Ulmo was wrapped in a mist as it were of sea-air in those inland places, and Tuor, with that music in his ears, would fain return to the regions of the Great Sea; yet remembering his bidding turned and went inland along the river, and so fared till day. Yet he that has heard the conches of Ulmo hears them call him till death, and so did Tuor find.

When day came he was weary and slept till it was nigh dusk again, and the Noldoli came to him and guided him. So fared he many days by dusk and dark and slept by day, and because of this it came afterwards that he remembered not over well the paths that he traversed in those times. Now Tuor and his guides held on untiring, and the land became one of rolling hills and the river wound about their feet, and there were many dales of exceeding pleasantness; but here the Noldoli became ill at ease. 'These,' said they, 'are the confines of those regions which Melko infesteth with his Goblins, the people of hate. Far to the north – yet alas not far enough, would they were ten thousand leagues – lie the Mountains of Iron where sits the power and terror of Melko, whose thralls we are. Indeed in this guiding of thee we do in secret from him, and did he know all our purposes the torment of the Balrogs would be ours.'

Falling then into such fear the Noldoli soon after left him and he fared alone amid the hills, and their going proved ill afterwards, for 'Melko has many eyes', it is said, and while Tuor fared with the Gnomes they took him twilight ways and by many secret tunnels through the hills. But now he became lost, and climbed often to the tops of knolls and hills scanning the lands about. Yet he might not see signs of any dwelling of folk, and indeed the city of the Gondothlim was not found with ease, seeing that Melko and his spies had not even yet discovered it. It is said nonetheless that at this time those spies got wind thus that the strange foot of Man had been set in those lands, and that for that Melko doubled his craft and watchfulness.

Now when the Gnomes out of fear deserted Tuor, one Voronwë or Bronweg followed afar off despite his fear, when chiding availed not to enhearten the others. Now Tuor had fallen into a great weariness and was sitting beside the rushing stream, and the sea-longing was about his heart, and he was minded once more to follow this river back to the wide waters and the roaring waves. But this Voronwë the faithful came up with him again, and standing by his ear said: 'O Tuor, think not that but thou shalt again one day see thy desire; arise now, and behold, I will not leave thee. I am not of the road-learned of the Noldoli, being a craftsman and maker of things made by hand of wood and of metal, and I joined not the band of escort till late. Yet of old have I heard whispers and sayings said in secret amid the weariness of thraldom, concerning a city where Noldoli might be free could they find the hidden way thereto; and we twain may without a doubt find a road to the City of Stone, where is that freedom of the Gondothlim.'

Know then that the Gondothlim were that kin of the Noldoli who alone escaped Melko's power when at the Battle of Unnumbered Tears he slew and enslaved their folk and wove spells about them and caused them to dwell in the Hells of Iron, faring thence at his will and bidding only.

Long time did Tuor and Voronwë seek for the city of that folk, until after many days they came upon a deep dale amid the hills. Here went the river over a very stony bed with much rush and noise, and it was curtained with a heavy growth of alders; but the walls of the dale were sheer, for they were nigh to some mountains which Voronwë knew not. There in the green wall that Gnome found an opening like a great door with sloping sides, and this was cloaked with thick bushes and long-tangled undergrowth; yet Voronwë's piercing sight might not be deceived. Nonetheless it is said that such a magic had its builders set about it (by aid of Ulmo whose power ran in that river even if the dread of Melko fared upon its banks) that none save of the blood of the Noldoli might light on it thus by chance; nor would Tuor have found it ever but for the steadfastness of that Gnome Voronwë. Now the Gondothlim made their abode thus secret out of dread of Melko; yet even so no few of the braver Noldoli would slip down the river Sirion from those mountains, and if many perished so by Melko's evil, many finding this magic passage came at last to the City of Stone and swelled its people.

Greatly did Tuor and Voronwë rejoice to find this gate,

yet entering they found there a way dark, rough-going, and circuitous; and long time they travelled faltering within its tunnels. It was full of fearsome echoes, and there a countless stepping of feet would come behind them, so that Voronwë became adread, and said: 'It is Melko's goblins, the Orcs of the hills.' Then would they run, falling over stones in the blackness, till they perceived it was but the deceit of the place. Thus did they come, after it seemed a measureless time of fearful groping, to a place where a far light glimmered, and making for this gleam they came to a gate like that by which they had entered, but in no way overgrown. Then they passed into the sunlight and could for a while see nought, but instantly a great gong sounded and there was a clash of armour, and behold, they were surrounded by warriors in steel. Then they looked up and could see, and lo! they were at the foot of steep hills, and these hills made a great circle wherein lay a wide plain, and set therein, not rightly at the midmost but rather nearer to that place where they stood, was a great hill with a level top, and upon that summit rose a city in the new light of the morning.

Then Voronwë spoke to the guard of the Gondothlim, and his speech they comprehended, for it was the sweet tongue of the Gnomes. Then spoke Tuor also and questioned where they might be, and who might be the folk in arms who stood about, for he was in amaze and wondered much at the goodly fashion of their weapons. Then it was said to him by one of that company: 'We are the guardians of the issue of the Way of Escape. Rejoice that ye have found it, for behold before you the City of Seven Names where all who war with Melko may find hope.'

Then said Tuor: 'What be those names?' And the chief of the guard made answer: 'It is said and it is sung: "Gondobar am I called and Gondothlimbar, City of Stone and City of the Dwellers in Stone; Gondolin the Stone of Song and Gwarestrin am I named, the Tower of Guard, Gar Thurion or the Secret Place, for I am hidden from the eyes of Melko; but they who love me most greatly call me Loth, for like a flower am I, even Lothengriol the flower that blooms on the plain." Yet,' said he, 'in our daily speech we speak and we name it mostly Gondolin.' Then said Voronwë: 'Bring us thither, for we fain would enter,' and Tuor said that his heart desired much to tread the ways of that fair city.

Then said the chief of the guard that they themselves must abide here, for there were yet many days of their moon of watch to pass, but that Voronwë and Tuor might pass on to Gondolin; and moreover that they would need thereto no guide, for 'Lo, it stands fair to see and very clear, and its towers prick the heavens above the Hill of Watch in the midmost plain.' Then Tuor and his companion fared over the plain that was of a marvellous level, broken but here and there by boulders round and smooth which lay amid a sward, and by pools in rocky beds. Many fair pathways lay across that plain, and they came after a day's light march to the foot of the Hill of Watch (which is in the tongue of the Noldoli Amon Gwareth). Then did they begin to ascend the winding stairways which climbed up to the city gate; nor might any one reach that city save on foot and espied from the walls. As the westward gate was golden in the last sun-light did they come to the long stair's head, and many eyes gazed upon them from the battlements and towers.

But Tuor looked upon the walls of stone, and the uplifted towers, upon the glistering pinnacles of the town, and he looked upon the stairs of stone and marble, bordered by slender balustrades and cooled by the leap of threadlike waterfalls seeking the plain from the fountains of Amon Gwareth, and he fared as one in some dream of the Gods, for he deemed not such things were seen by men in the visions of their sleep, so great was his amaze at the glory of Gondolin.

Even so came they to the gates, Tuor in wonder and Voronwë in great joy that daring much he had both brought Tuor hither in the will of Ulmo and had himself thrown off the yoke of Melko for ever. Though he hated him no wise less, no longer did he dread that Evil One with a binding terror (and of a sooth that spell which Melko held over the Noldoli was one of bottomless dread, so that he seemed ever nigh them even were they far from the Hells of Iron, and their hearts quaked and they fled not even when they could; and to this Melko trusted often).

Now is there a sally from the gates of Gondolin and a throng comes about these twain in wonder, rejoicing that yet another of the Noldoli has fled hither from Melko, and marvelling at the stature and the great limbs of Tuor, his heavy spear barbed with fish bone and his great harp. Rugged was his aspect, and his locks were unkempt, and he was clad in the skins of bears. It is written that in those days the fathers of the fathers of men were of less stature than men now are, and the children of Elfinesse of greater growth, yet was Tuor taller than any that stood there. Indeed the Gondothlim were not bent of back as some of their unhappy kin became, labouring without rest at delving and hammering for Melko, but small were they and slender and very lithe. They were swift of foot and surpassing fair; sweet and sad were their mouths, and their eyes had ever a joy within quivering to tears; for in those times the Gnomes were exiles at heart, haunted with a desire for their ancient homes that faded not. But fate and unconquerable eagerness after knowledge had driven them into far places, and now were they hemmed by Melko and must make their abiding as fair as they might by labour and by love.

How it came ever that among men the Noldoli have been confused with the Orcs who are Melko's goblins, I know not, unless it be that certain of the Noldoli were twisted to the evil of Melko and mingled among these Orcs, for all that race were bred by Melko of the subterranean heats and slime. Their hearts were of granite and their bodies deformed; foul their faces which smiled not, but their laugh that of the clash of metal, and to nothing were they more fain than to aid in the basest of the purposes of Melko. The greatest hatred was between them and the Noldoli, who named them *Glamhoth*, or folk of dreadful hate.

Behold, the armed guardians of the gate pressed back the thronging folk that gathered about the wanderers, and one among them spoke saying: 'This is a city of watch and ward, Gondolin on Amon Gwareth, where all may be free who are of true heart, but none may be free to enter unknown. Tell me then your names.' But Voronwë named himself Bronweg of the Gnomes, come hither by the will of Ulmo as guide to this son of Men; and Tuor said: 'I am Tuor son of Peleg son of Indor of the house of the Swan of the sons of the Men of the North who live far hence, and I fare hither by the will of Ulmo of the Outer Oceans.'

Then all who listened grew silent, and his deep and rolling voice held them in amaze, for their own voices were fair as the plash of fountains. Then a saying arose among them: 'Lead him before the king.'

Then did the throng return within the gates and the wanderers with them, and Tuor saw they were of iron and of great height and strength. Now the streets of Gondolin were paved with stone and wide, kerbed with marble, and fair houses and courts amid gardens of bright flowers were set about the ways, and many towers of great slenderness and beauty builded of white marble and carved most marvellously rose to the heaven. Squares there were lit with fountains and the home of birds that sang amid the branches of their aged trees, but of all these the greatest was that place where stood the king's palace, and the tower thereof was the loftiest in the city, and the fountains that played before the doors shot twenty fathoms and seven in the air and fell in a singing rain of crystal: therein did the sun glitter splendidly by day, and the moon most magically shimmered by night. The birds that dwelt there were of the whiteness of snow and their voices sweeter than a lullaby of music.

On either side of the doors of the palace were two trees,

one that bore blossom of gold and the other of silver, nor did they ever fade, for they were shoots of old from the glorious trees of Valinor that lit those places before Melko and Gloomweaver withered them: and those trees the Gondothlim named Glingol and Bansil.

Then Turgon king of Gondolin robed in white with a belt of gold, and a coronet of garnets was upon his head, stood before his doors and spoke from the head of the white stairs that led thereto. 'Welcome, O Man of the Land of Shadows. Lo! thy coming was set in our books of wisdom, and it has been written that there would come to pass many great things in the homes of the Gondothlim whenso thou faredst hither.'

Then spoke Tuor, and Ulmo set power in his heart and majesty in his voice. 'Behold, O father of the City of Stone, I am bidden by him who maketh deep music in the Abyss, and who knoweth the mind of Elves and Men, to say unto thee that the days of Release draw nigh. There have come to the ears of Ulmo whispers of your dwelling and your hill of vigilance against the evil of Melko, and he is glad: but his heart is wroth and the hearts of the Valar are angered who sit in the mountains of Valinor and look upon the world from the peak of Taniquetil, seeing the sorrow of the thraldom of the Noldoli and the wanderings of Men; for Melko ringeth them in the Land of Shadows beyond the hills of iron. Therefore have I been brought by a secret way to bid you number your hosts and prepare for battle, for the time is ripe.'

Then spoke Turgon: 'That will I not do, though it be the words of Ulmo and all the Valar. I will not adventure this my people against the terror of the Orcs, nor emperil my city against the fire of Melko.'

Then spoke Tuor: 'Nay, if thou dost not now dare greatly then will the Orcs dwell for ever and possess in the end most of the mountains of the Earth, and cease not to trouble both Elves and Men, even though by other means the Valar contrive hereafter to release the Noldoli; but if thou trust now to the Valar, though terrible the encounter, then shall the Orcs fall, and Melko's power be minished to a little thing.'

But Turgon said that he was king of Gondolin and no will should force him against his counsel to emperil the dear labour of long ages gone; but Tuor said, for thus was he bidden by Ulmo who had feared the reluctance of Turgon: 'Then am I bidden to say that men of the Gondothlim repair swiftly and secretly down the river Sirion to the sea, and there build them boats and go seek back to Valinor: lo! the paths thereto are forgotten and the highways faded from the world, and the seas and mountains are about it, yet still dwell there the Elves on the hill of Kôr and the Gods sit in Valinor, though their mirth is minished for sorrow and fear of Melko, and they hide their land and weave about it inaccessible magic that no evil come to its shores. Yet still might thy messengers win there and turn their hearts that they rise in wrath and smite Melko, and destroy the Hells of Iron that he has wrought beneath the Mountains of Darkness.'

Then said Turgon: 'Every year at the lifting of winter have messengers repaired swiftly and by stealth down the river that is called Sirion to the coasts of the Great Sea, and there builded them boats whereto have swans and gulls been harnessed or the strong wings of the wind, and these have sought back beyond the moon and sun to Valinor; but the paths thereto are forgotten and the highways faded from the world, and the seas and mountains are about it, and they that sit within in mirth reck little of the dread of Melko or the sorrow of the world, but hide their land and weave about it inaccessible magic, that no tidings of evil come ever to their ears. Nay, enough of my people have for years untold gone out to the wide waters never to return, but have perished in the deep places or wander now lost in the shadows that have no paths; and at the coming of next year no more shall fare to the sea, but rather will we trust to ourselves and our city for the warding off of Melko; and thereto have the Valar been of scant help aforetime.'

Then Tuor's heart was heavy, and Voronwë wept; and Tuor sat by the great fountain of the king and its splashing recalled the music of the waves, and his soul was troubled by the conches of Ulmo and he would return down the waters of Sirion to the sea. But Turgon, who knew that Tuor, mortal as he was, had the favour of the Valar, marking his stout glance and the power of his voice sent to him and bade him dwell in Gondolin and be in his favour, and abide even in the royal halls if he would.

Then Tuor, for he was weary, and that place was fair, said yea; and hence cometh the abiding of Tuor in Gondolin. Of all Tuor's deeds among the Gondothlim the tales tell not, but it is said that many a time would he have stolen thence, growing weary of the concourses of folk, and thinking of empty forest and fell or hearing afar the sea-music of Ulmo, had not his heart been filled with love for a woman of the Gondothlim, and she was a daughter of the king.

Now Tuor learnt many things in those realms taught by Voronwë whom he loved, and who loved him exceeding greatly in return; or else was he instructed by the skilled men of the city and the wise men of the king. Wherefore he became a man far mightier than aforetime and wisdom was in his counsel; and many things became clear to him that were unclear before, and many things known that are still unknown to mortal men. There he heard concerning that city of Gondolin and how unstaying labour through ages of years had not sufficed to its building and adornment whereat folk travailed yet; of the delving of that hidden tunnel he heard, which the folk named the Way of Escape, and how there had been divided counsels in that matter, yet pity for the enthralled Noldoli had prevailed in the end to its making; of the guard without ceasing he was told, that was held there in arms and likewise at certain low places in the encircling mountains, and how watchers dwelt ever vigilant on the highest peaks of that range beside builded beacons ready for the fire; for never did that folk cease to look for an onslaught of the Orcs did their stronghold become known.

Now however was the guard of the hills maintained rather by custom than necessity, for the Gondothlim had long ago with unimagined toil levelled and cleared and delved all that plain about Amon Gwareth, so that scarce Gnome or bird or beast or snake could approach but was espied from many leagues off, for among the Gondothlim were many whose eyes were keener than the very hawks of Manwë Súlimo

Lord of Gods and Elves who dwells upon Taniquetil; and for this reason did they call that vale Tumladen or the valley of smoothness. Now this great work was finished to their mind, and folk were the busier about the quarrying of metals and the forging of all manner of swords and axes, spears and bills, and the fashioning of coats of mail, byrnies and hauberks, greaves and vambraces, helms and shields. Now it was said to Tuor that already the whole folk of Gondolin shooting with bows without stay day or night might not expend their hoarded arrows in many years, and that yearly their fear of the Orcs grew the less for this.

There learnt Tuor of building with stone, of masonry and the hewing of rock and marble; crafts of weaving and spinning, broidure and painting, did he fathom, and cunning in metals. Musics most delicate he there heard; and in these were they who dwelt in the southern city the most deeply skilled, for there played a profusion of murmuring founts and springs. Many of these subtleties Tuor mastered and learned to entwine with his songs to the wonder and heart's joy of all who heard. Strange stories of the Sun and Moon and Stars, of the manner of the Earth and its elements, and of the depths of heaven, were told to him; and the secret characters of the Elves he learnt, and their speeches and old tongues, and heard tell of Ilúvatar, the Lord for Always, who dwelleth beyond the world, of the great music of the Ainur about Ilúvatar's feet in the uttermost deeps of time, whence came the making of the world and the manner of it, and all therein and their governance.

Now for his skill and his great mastery over all lore and

craft whatsoever, and his great courage of heart and body, did Tuor become a comfort and stay to the king who had no son; and he was beloved by the folk of Gondolin. Upon a time the king caused his most cunning artficers to fashion a suit of armour for Tuor as a great gift, and it was made of Gnome-steel overlaid with silver; but his helm was adorned with a device of metals and jewels like to two swan-wings, one on either side, and a swan's wing was wrought on his shield; but he carried an axe rather than a sword, and this in the speech of the Gondothlim he named Dramborleg, for its buffet stunned and its edge clove all armour.

A house was built for him upon the southern walls, for he loved the free airs and liked not the close neighbourhood of other dwellings. There it was his delight often to stand on the battlements at dawn, and folk rejoiced to see the new light catch the wings of his helm – and many murmured and would fain have backed him into battle with the Orcs, seeing that the speeches of those two, Tuor and Turgon, before the palace were known to many; but the matter went not further for reverence of Turgon, and because at this time in Tuor's heart the thought of the words of Ulmo seemed to have grown dim and far off.

Now came days when Tuor had dwelt among the Gon-dothlim many years. Long had he known and cherished a love for the king's daughter, and now was his heart full of that love. Great love too had Idril for Tuor, and the strands of her fate were woven with his even from that day when first she gazed upon him from a high window as he stood a way-worn suppliant before the palace of the king. Little cause had Turgon to withstand their love, for he saw in Tuor a kinsman of comfort and great hope. Thus was first wed a child of Men with a daughter of Elfinesse, nor was Tuor the last. Less bliss have many had than they, and their sorrow in the end was great. Yet great was the mirth of those days when Idril and Tuor were wed before the folk in Gar Ainion, the Place of the Gods, nigh to the king's halls. A day of merriment was that wedding to the city of Gondolin, and of the greatest happiness to Tuor and Idril. Thereafter dwelt they in joy in that house upon the walls that looked out south over Tumladen, and this was good to the hearts of all in the city save Meglin alone. Now that Gnome was come of an ancient house, though now were its numbers less than others, but he himself was nephew to the king by his mother the king's sister Isfin; and that tale may not here be told.

Now the sign of Meglin was a sable Mole, and he was great among quarrymen and a chief of the delvers after ore; and many of these belonged to his house. Less fair was he than most of this goodly folk, swart and of none too kindly mood, so that he won small love, and whispers there were that he had Orc's blood in his veins, but I know not how this could be true. Now he had bid often with the king for the hand of Idril, yet Turgon finding her very loath had as often said nay, for him seemed Meglin's suit was caused as much by the desire of standing in high power beside the royal throne as by love of that fair maid. Fair indeed was she and brave thereto; and the people called her Idril of the Silver Feet in that she went ever barefoot and bareheaded, king's daughter as she was, save only at pomps of the Ainur; and Meglin gnawed his anger seeing Tuor thrust him out.

In these days came to pass the fulfilment of the time of the desire of the Valar and the hope of the Eldalië, for in great love Idril bore to Tuor a son and he was called Eärendel. Now thereto there are many interpretations both among Elves and Men, but belike it was a name wrought of some secret tongue among the Gondothlim and that has perished with them from the dwellings of the Earth.

Now this babe was of greatest beauty; his skin of a shining white and his eyes of a blue surpassing that of the sky in southern lands – bluer than the sapphires of the raiment of Manwë; and the envy of Meglin was deep at his birth, but the joy of Turgon and all the people very great indeed.

Behold now many years have gone since Tuor was lost amid the foothills and deserted by those Noldoli; yet many years too have gone since to Melko's ears came first those strange tidings – faint were they and various in form – of a man wandering amid the dales of the waters of Sirion. Now Melko was not much afraid of the race of Men in those days of his great power, and for this reason did Ulmo work through one of this kindred for the better deceiving of Melko, seeing that no Valar and scarce any of the Eldar or Noldoli might stir unmarked of his vigilance. Yet nonetheless foreboding smote that ill heart at the tidings, and he got together a mighty army of spies: sons of the Orcs were there with eyes of yellow and green like cats that could pierce all glooms and see through mist or fog or night; snakes that could go everywhither and search all crannies or the deepest pits or the highest peaks, listen to every whisper that ran in the grass or echoed in the hills; wolves there were and ravening dogs and great weasels full of the thirst of blood whose nostrils could take scent moons old through running water, or whose eyes find among shingle footsteps that had passed a lifetime since; owls came and falcons whose keen glances might descry by day or night the fluttering of small birds in all the woods of the world, and the movement of every mouse or vole or rat that crept or dwelt throughout the Earth. All these he summoned to his Hall of Iron, and they came in multitudes. Thence he sent them over the Earth to seek this man who had escaped from the Land of Shadows, but yet far more curiously and more intently to search out the dwelling of the Noldoli that had escaped his thraldom; for these his heart burnt to destroy or to enslave.

Now while Tuor dwelt in happiness and in great increase of knowledge and might in Gondolin, these creatures through the years untiring nosed among the stones and rocks, hunted the forests and the heaths, espied the airs and lofty places, tracked all the paths about the dales and plains, and neither let nor stayed. From this hunt they brought a wealth of tidings to Melko – indeed among many hidden things that they dragged to light they discovered that 'Way of Escape' whereby Tuor and Voronwë entered aforetime. Nor had they done so save by constraining some of the less stout of the Noldoli with dire threats of torment to join in that great ransacking; for because of the magic about that gate no folk of Melko unaided by the Gnomes could come to it. Yet now they had pried of late far into its tunnels and captured within many of the Noldoli creeping there to flee from thraldom. They had scaled too the Encircling Hills at certain places and gazed upon the beauty of the city of Gondolin and the strength of Amon Gwareth from afar; but into the plain they could not win for the vigilance of its guardians and the difficulty of those mountains. Indeed the Gondothlim were mighty archers, and bows they made of a marvel of power. Therewith they might shoot an arrow into heaven seven times as far as could the best bowman among Men shoot at a mark upon the ground; and they would have suffered no falcon to hover long over their plain or snake to crawl therein; for they liked not creatures of blood, broodlings of Melko.

Now in those days was Eärendel one year old when these ill tidings came to that city of the spies of Melko and how they encompassed the vale of Tumladen around. Then Turgon's heart was saddened, remembering the words of Tuor in past years before the palace doors; and he caused the watch and ward to be thrice strengthened at all points, and engines of war to be devised by his artificers and set upon the hill. Poisonous fires and hot liquids, arrows and great rocks, was he prepared to shoot down on any who would assail those gleaming walls; and then he abode as well content as might be, but Tuor's heart was heavier than the king's, for now the words of Ulmo came ever to his mind, and their purport and gravity he understood more deeply than of old; nor did he find any great comfort in Idril, for her heart boded more darkly even than his own.

Know then that Idril had a great power of piercing with her thought the darkness of the hearts of Elves and Men, and the glooms of the future thereto – further even than is the common power of the kindreds of the Eldalië; therefore she spoke thus on a day to Tuor: 'Know, my husband, that my heart misgives me for doubt of Meglin, and I fear that he will bring an ill on this fair realm, though by no means may I see how or when – yet I dread lest all that he knows of our doings and preparations become in some manner known to the Foe, so that he devise a new means of whelming us, against which we have thought of no defence. Lo! I dreamed on a night that Meglin builded a furnace, and coming at us unawares flung therein Eärendel our babe, and would after thrust in thee and me; but that for sorrow at the death of our fair child I would not resist.'

And Tuor answered: 'There is reason in thy fear, for neither is my heart good towards Meglin; yet is he the nephew of the king and thine own cousin, nor is there charge against him, and I see nought to do but to abide and watch.'

But Idril said: 'This is my rede thereto: gather thou in deep secret those delvers and quarrymen who by careful trial are found to hold least love for Meglin by reason of the pride and arrogance of his dealings among them. From these thou must choose trusty men to keep watch upon Meglin whenso he fares to the outer hills, yet I counsel thee to set the greater part of those in whose secrecy thou canst confide at a hidden delving, and to devise with their aid – howsoever cautious and slow that labour be – a secret way from thy house here beneath the rocks of this hill unto the vale below. Now this way must not lead toward the Way of Escape, for my heart bids me trust it not, but even to that far distant pass, the Cleft of the Eagles in the southern mountains; and the further this delving reach thitherward beneath the plain so much the better would I esteem it – yet let all this labour be kept dark save from a few.'

Now there are none such delvers of earth or rock as the Noldoli (and this Melko knows), but in those places is the earth of a great hardness; and Tuor said: 'The rocks of the hill of Amon Gwareth are as iron, and only with much travail may they be cloven; yet if this be done in secret then must great time and patience be added; but the stone of the floor of the Vale of Tumladen is as forgéd steel, nor may it be hewn without the knowledge of the Gondothlim save in moons and years.'

Idril said then: 'Sooth this may be, but such is my rede, and there is yet time to spare.' Then Tuor said that he might not see all its purport, 'but "better is any plan than a lack of counsel", and I will do even as thou sayest.'

Now it so chanced that not long after Meglin went to the hills for the getting of ore, and straying in the mountains alone was taken by some of the Orcs prowling there, and they would do him evil and terrible hurt, knowing him to be a man of the Gondothlim. This was however unknown of Tuor's watchers. But evil came into the heart of Meglin, and he said to his captors: 'Know then that I am Meglin son of Eöl, who had to wife Isfin sister of Turgon king of the Gondothlim.' But they said: 'What is that to us?' And Meglin answered: 'Much is that to you; for if you slay me, be it speedy or slow, ye will lose great tidings concerning the city of Gondolin that your master would rejoice to hear.'

Then the Orcs stayed their hands, and said they would give him life if the matters he opened to them seemed to merit that; and Meglin told them of all the fashion of that plain and city, of its walls and their height and thickness, and the valour of its gates; of the host of men at arms who now obeyed Turgon he spoke, and the countless hoard of weapons gathered for their equipment, of the engines of war and the venomous fires.

Then the Orcs were wroth, and having heard these matters were yet for slaying him there and then as one who impudently enlarged the power of his miserable folk to the mockery of the great might and puissance of Melko; but Meglin catching at a straw said: 'Think ye not that ye would rather pleasure your master if ye bore to his feet so noble a captive, that he might hear my tidings of himself and judge of their verity?'

Now this seemed good to the Orcs, and they returned from the mountains about Gondolin to the Hills of Iron and the dark halls of Melko; thither they haled Meglin with them, and now was he in a sore dread. But when he knelt before the black throne of Melko in terror of the grimness of the shapes about him, of the wolves that sat beneath that chair and of the adders that twined about its legs, Melko bade him speak. Then told he those tidings, and Melko hearkening spoke very fair to him, that the insolence of his heart in great measure returned.

Now the end of this was that Melko aided by the cunning of Meglin devised a plan for the overthrow of Gondolin. For this Meglin's reward was to be a great captaincy among the

Orcs – yet Melko purposed not in his heart to fulfil such a promise – but Tuor and Eärendel should Melko burn, and Idril be given to Meglin's arms – and such promises was that evil one fain to redeem. Yet as meed of treachery did Melko threaten Meglin with the torment of the Balrogs. Now these were demons with whips of flame and claws of steel by whom he tormented those of the Noldoli who durst withstand him in anything – and the Eldar have called them Malkarauki. But the rede that Meglin gave to Melko was that not all the host of the Orcs nor the Balrogs in their fierceness might by assault or siege hope ever to overthrow the walls and gates of Gondolin even if they availed to win unto the plain without. Therefore he counselled Melko to devise out of his sorceries a succour for his warriors in their endeavour. From the greatness of his wealth of metals and his powers of fire he bid him make beasts like snakes and dragons of irresistible might that should overcreep the Encircling Hills and lap that plain and its fair city in flame and death.

Then Meglin was bidden fare home lest at his absence men suspect somewhat; but Melko wove about him the spell of bottomless dread, and he had thereafter neither joy nor quiet in his heart. Nonetheless he wore a fair mask of good liking and gaiety, so that men said: 'Meglin is softened', and he was held in less disfavour; yet Idril feared him the more. Now Meglin said: 'I have laboured much and am minded to rest, and to join in the dance and the song and the merrymakings of the folk', and he went no more quarrying stone or ore in the hills: yet in sooth he sought herein to drown his fear and disquiet. A dread possessed him that Melko was ever at hand,

and this came of the spell; and he durst never again wander amid the mines lest he again fall in with the Orcs and be bidden once more to the terrors of the halls of darkness.

Now the years fare by, and egged by Idril Tuor keepeth ever at his secret delving; but seeing that the leaguer of spies hath grown thinner Turgon dwelleth more at ease and in less fear. Yet these years are filled by Melko in the utmost ferment of labour, and all the thrall-folk of the Noldoli must dig unceasingly for metals while Melko sitteth and deviseth fires and calleth flames and smokes to come from the lower heats, nor doth he suffer any of the Noldoli to stray ever a foot from their places of bondage. Then on a time Melko assembled all his most cunning smiths and sorcerers, and of iron and flame they wrought a host of monsters such as have only at that time been seen and shall not again be till the Great End. Some were all of iron so cunningly linked that they might flow like slow rivers of metal or coil themselves around and above all obstacles before them, and these were filled in their innermost depths with the grimmest of the Orcs with scimitars and spears; others of bronze and copper were given hearts and spirits of blazing fire, and they blasted all that stood before them with the terror of their snorting or trampled whatso escaped the ardour of their breath; yet others were creatures of pure flame that writhed like ropes of molten metal, and they brought to ruin whatever fabric they came nigh, and iron and stone melted before them and became as water, and upon them rode the Balrogs in hundreds; and these were the most dire of all those monsters which Melko devised against Gondolin.

Now when the seventh summer had gone since the treason of Meglin, and Eärendel was yet of very tender years though a valorous child, Melko withdrew all his spies, for every path and corner of the mountains was now known to him; yet the Gondothlim thought in their unwariness that Melko would no longer seek against them, perceiving their might and the impregnable strength of their dwelling.

But Idril fell into a dark mood and the light of her face was clouded, and many wondered thereat; yet Turgon reduced the watch and ward to its ancient numbers, and to somewhat less, and as autumn came and the gathering of fruits was over folk turned with glad hearts to the feasts of winter: but Tuor stood upon the battlements and gazed upon the Encircling Hills.

Now behold, Idril stood beside him, and the wind was in her hair, and Tuor thought that she was exceeding beautiful, and stooped to kiss her; but her face was sad, and she said: 'Now come the days when thou must make choice,' and Tuor knew not what she said. Then drawing him within their halls she said to him how her heart misgave her for fear concerning Eärendel their son, and for boding that some great evil was nigh, and that Melko would be at the bottom of it. Then Tuor would comfort her, but might not, and she questioned him concerning the secret delving, and he said how it now led a league into the plain, and at that was her heart somewhat lightened. But still she counselled that the delving be pressed on, and that henceforth should speed weigh more than secrecy, 'because now is the time very near.' And another rede she gave him, and this he took also, that certain of the bravest and most true among the lords and warriors of the Gondothlim be chosen with care and told of that secret way and its issue. These she counselled him to make into a stout guard and to give them his emblem to wear that they become his folk, and to do this under pretext of the right and dignity of a great lord, kinsman to the king. 'Moreover,' said she, 'I will get my father's favour to that.' In secret too she whispered to folk that if the city came to its last stand or Turgon be slain that they rally about Tuor and her son, and to this they laughed a yea, saying however that Gondolin would stand as long as Taniquetil or the Mountains of Valinor.

Yet to Turgon she spoke not openly, nor suffered Tuor to do so, as he desired, despite their love and reverence for him – a great and a noble and a glorious king he was – seeing that he trusted in Meglin and held with blind obstinacy his belief in the impregnable might of the city and that Melko sought no more against it, perceiving no hope therein. Now in this he was ever strengthened by the cunning sayings of Meglin. Behold, the guile of that Gnome was very great, for he wrought much in the dark, so that folk said: 'He doth well to bear the sign of a sable mole'; and by reason of the folly of certain of the quarrymen, and yet more by reason of the loose words of certain among his kin to whom word was somewhat unwarily spoken by Tuor, he gathered a knowledge of the secret work and laid against that a plan of his own.

So winter deepened, and it was very cold for those regions, so that frost fared about the plain of Tumladen and ice lay on its pools; yet the fountains played ever on Amon Gwareth and the two trees blossomed, and folk made merry till the day of terror that was hidden in the heart of Melko.

In these ways that bitter winter passed, and the snows lay deeper than ever before on the Encircling Hills; yet in its time a spring of wondrous glory melted the skirts of those white mantles and the valley drank the waters and burst into flowers. So came and passed with revelry of children the festival of Nost-na-Lothion or the Birth of Flowers, and the hearts of the Gondothlim were uplifted for the good promise of the year, and now at length is that great feast Tarnin Austa or the Gates of Summer near at hand. For know that on a night it was their custom to begin a solemn ceremony at midnight, continuing it even till the dawn of Tarnin Austa broke, and no voice was uttered in the city from midnight till the break of day, but the dawn they hailed with ancient songs. For years uncounted had the coming of summer thus been greeted with music of choirs, standing upon their gleaming eastern wall; and now comes even the night of vigil and the city is filled with silver lamps, while in the groves upon the new-leaved trees lights of jewelled colours swing, and low musics go along the ways, but no voice sings until the dawn.

The sun has sunk beyond the hills and folk array them for the festival very gladly and eagerly – glancing in expectation to the East. Lo! even when she had gone and all was dark, a new light suddenly began, and a glow there was, but it was beyond the northward heights, and men marvelled, and there was a thronging of the walls and battlements. Then

wonder grew to doubt as the light waxed and became yet
redder, and doubt to dread as men saw the snow upon the
mountains dyed as it were with blood. And thus it was that
the fire-serpents of Melko came upon Gondolin.

Then came over the plain riders who bore breathless
tidings from those who kept vigil on the peaks; and they
told of the fiery hosts and the shapes like dragons, and said:
'Melko is upon us.' Great was the fear and anguish within
that beauteous city, and the streets and byways were filled
with the weeping of women and the wailing of children,
and the squares with the mustering of soldiers and the ring
of arms. There were the gleaming banners of all the great
houses and kindreds of the Gondothlim. Mighty was the
array of the house of the king and their colours were white
and gold and red, and their emblems the moon and the sun
and the scarlet heart. Now in the midmost of these stood
Tuor above all heads, and his mail of silver gleamed; and
about him was a press of the stoutest of the folk. Lo! all these
wore wings as it were of swans or gulls upon their helms,
and the emblem of the White Wing was upon their shields.
But the folk of Meglin were drawn up in the same place, and
sable was their harness, and they bore no sign or emblem,
but their round caps of steel were covered with moleskin,
and they fought with axes two-headed like mattocks. There
Meglin prince of Gondobar gathered many warriors of dark
countenance and lowering gaze about him, and a ruddy glow
shone upon their faces and gleamed about the polished sur-
faces of their accoutrement. Behold, all the hills to the north
were ablaze, and it was as if rivers of fire ran down the slopes

that led to the plain of Tumladen, and folk might already feel the heat thereof.

And many other kindreds were there, the folk of the Swallow and the Heavenly Arch, and from these folk came the greatest number and the best of the bowmen, and they were arrayed upon the broad places of the walls. Now the folk of the Swallow bore a fan of feathers on their helms, and they were arrayed in white and dark blue and in purple and black and showed an arrowhead on their shields. Their lord was Duilin, swiftest of all men to run and leap and surest of archers at a mark. But they of the Heavenly Arch being a folk of uncounted wealth were arrayed in a glory of colours, and their arms were set with jewels that flamed in the light now over the sky. Every shield of that battalion was of the blue of the heavens and its boss a jewel built of seven gems, rubies and amethysts and sapphires, emeralds, chrysoprase, topaz, and amber, but an opal of great size was set in their helms. Egalmoth was their chieftain, and wore a blue mantle upon which the stars were broidered in crystal, and his sword was bent – now none else of the Noldoli bore curved swords – yet he trusted rather to the bow, and shot therewith further than any among that host.

There too were the folk of the Pillar and of the Tower of Snow, and both these kindreds were marshalled by Penlod, tallest of Gnomes. There were those of the Tree, and they were a great house, and their raiment was green. They fought with iron-studded clubs or with slings, and their lord Galdor was held the most valiant of all the Gondothlim save Turgon alone. There stood the house of the Golden Flower who bore a rayed sun upon their shield, and their chief Glorfindel bore a mantle so broidered in threads of gold that it was diapered with celandine as a field in spring; and his arms were damascened with cunning gold.

Then came there from the south of the city the people of the Fountain, and Ecthelion was their lord, and silver and diamonds were their delight; and swords very long and bright and pale did they wield, and they went into battle to the music of flutes. Behind them came the host of the Harp, and this was a battalion of brave warriors; but their leader Salgant was a craven, and he fawned upon Meglin. They were dight with tassels of silver and tassels of gold, and a harp of silver shone in their blazonry upon a field of black; but Salgant bore one of gold, and he alone rode into battle of all the sons of the Gondothlim, and he was heavy and squat.

Now the last of the battalions was furnished by the folk of the Hammer of Wrath, and of these came many of the best smiths and craftsmen, and all that kindred reverenced Aulë the Smith more than all other Ainur. They fought with great maces like hammers, and their shields were heavy, for their arms were very strong. In older days they had been much recruited by Noldoli who escaped from the mines of Melko, and the hatred of this house for the works of that evil one and the Balrogs his demons was exceeding great. Now their leader was Rog, strongest of the Gnomes, scarce second in valour to that Galdor of the Tree. The sign of this people was the Stricken Anvil, and a hammer that smiteth sparks about it was set on their shields, and red gold and black iron was their delight. Very numerous was that battalion, nor had any amongst them a faint heart, and they won the greatest glory of all those fair houses in that struggle against doom; yet were they ill-fated, and none ever fared away from that field, but fell about Rog and vanished from the Earth; and with them much craftsmanship and skill has vanished for ever.

This was the fashion and the array of the eleven houses of the Gondothlim with their signs and emblems, and the bodyguard of Tuor, the folk of the Wing, was accounted the twelfth. Now is the face of that chieftain grim and he looks not to live long – and there in his house upon the walls Idril arrays herself in mail, and seeks Eärendel. And that child was in tears for the strange lights of red that played about the walls of the chamber where he slept; and tales that his nurse Meleth had woven him concerning fiery Melko at times of his waywardness came to him and troubled him. But his mother coming set about him a tiny coat of mail that she had let fashion in secret, and at that he was glad and exceeding proud, and he shouted for pleasure. Yet Idril wept, for much had she cherished in her heart the fair city and her goodly house, and the love of Tuor and herself that had dwelt therein; but now she saw its destroying nigh at hand, and feared that her contriving would fail against this overwhelming might of the terror of the serpents.

It was now four hours still from the middle night, and the sky was red in the north and in the east and west; and those serpents of iron had reached the levels of Tumladen, and those fiery ones were among the lowest slopes of the hills, so that the guards were taken and set in evil torment by the

Balrogs that scoured all about, saving only to the furthest south where was Cristhorn the Cleft of Eagles.

Then did King Turgon call a council, and thither fared Tuor and Meglin, as royal princes; and Duilin came with Egalmoth and Penlod the tall, and Rog strode thither with Galdor of the Tree and golden Glorfindel and Ecthelion of the voice of music. Thither too fared Salgant atremble at the tidings, and other nobles beside of less blood but better heart.

Then spoke Tuor and this was his rede, that a mighty sally be made forthwith, ere the light and heat grew too great in the plain; and many backed him, being but of different minds as to whether the sally should be made by the entire host with the maids and wives and children amidmost, or by diverse bands seeking out in many directions; and to this last Tuor leaned.

But Meglin and Salgant alone held other counsel and were for holding to the city and seeking to guard those treasures that lay within. Out of guile did Meglin speak thus, fearing lest any of the Noldoli escape the doom that he had brought upon them, and he dreaded lest his treason become known and somehow vengeance find him in after days. But Salgant spoke both echoing Meglin and being grievously afraid of issuing from the city, for he was fain rather to do battle from an impregnable fortress than to risk hard blows upon the field.

Then the lord of the house of the Mole played upon the one weakness of Turgon, saying: 'Lo! O King, the city of Gondolin contains a wealth of jewels and metals and stuffs

and of things wrought by the hands of the Gnomes to surpassing beauty, and all these thy lords – more brave meseems
than wise – would abandon to the Foe. Even should victory
be thine upon the plain thy city will be sacked and the
Balrogs get hence with a measureless booty'; and Turgon
groaned, for Meglin had known his great love for the wealth
and loveliness of that burg upon Amon Gwareth. Again said
Meglin, putting fire in his voice: 'Lo! Hast thou for nought
laboured through years uncounted at the building of walls of
impregnable thickness and in the making of gates whose
valour may not be overthrown; is the power of the hill Amon
Gwareth become as lowly as the deep vale, or the hoard of
weapons that lie upon it and its unnumbered arrows of so
little worth that in the hour of peril thou wouldst cast all
aside and go naked into the open against enemies of steel and
fire, whose trampling shakes the earth and the Encircling
Mountains ring with the clamour of their footsteps?'

And Salgant quailed to think of it and spoke noisily,
saying: 'Meglin speaks well, O King, hear thou him.' Then
the king took the counsel of those twain though all the lords
said otherwise, nay rather the more for that: therefore at his
bidding does all that folk abide now the assault upon their
walls. But Tuor wept and left the king's hall, and gathering
the men of the Wing went through the streets seeking his
home; and by that hour was the light great and lurid and
there was stifling heat and a black smoke and stench arose
about the pathways to the city.

And now came the Monsters across the valley and the
white towers of Gondolin reddened before them; but the

stoutest were in dread seeing those dragons of fire and those serpents of bronze and iron that fare already about the hill of the city; and they shot unavailing arrows at them. Then is there a cry of hope, for behold, the snakes of fire may not climb the hill for its steepness and for its glassiness, and by reason of the quenching waters that fall upon its sides; yet they lie about its feet and a vast steam arises where the streams of Amon Gwareth and the flames of the serpents drive together. Then grew there such a heat that women became faint and men sweated to weariness beneath their mail, and all the springs of the city, save only the fountain of the king, grew hot and smoked.

But now Gothmog lord of Balrogs, captain of the hosts of Melko, took counsel and gathered all his things of iron that could coil themselves around and above all obstacles before them. These he bade pile themselves before the northern gate; and behold, their great spires reached even to its threshold and thrust at the towers and bastions about it, and by reason of the exceeding heaviness of their bodies those gates fell, and great was the noise thereof: yet the most of the walls around them still stood firm. Then the engines and the catapults of the king poured darts and boulders and molten metals on those ruthless beasts, and their hollow bellies clanged beneath the buffeting, yet it availed not for they might not be broken, and the fires rolled off them. Then were the topmost opened about their middles, and an innumerable host of the Orcs, the goblins of hatred, poured therefrom into the breach; and who shall tell of their scimitars or the flash of their broad-bladed spears with which they stabbed?

Then did Rog shout in a mighty voice, and all the people of the Hammer of Wrath and the kindred of the Tree with Galdor the valiant leapt at the foe. There the blows of their great hammers and the dint of their clubs rang to the Encircling Mountains and the Orcs fell like leaves; and those of the Swallow and the Arch poured arrows like the dark rains of autumn upon them, and both Orcs and Gondothlim fell thereunder for the smoke and the confusion. Great was that battle, yet for all their valour the Gondothlim by reason of the might of ever increasing numbers were borne slowly backwards till the goblins held part of the northernmost city.

At this time is Tuor at the head of the folk of the Wing struggling in the turmoil of the streets, and now he wins through to his house and finds that Meglin is before him. Trusting in the battle now begun about the northern gate and in the uproar in the city, Meglin had looked to this hour for the consummation of his designs. Learning much of the secret delving of Tuor (yet only at the last moment had he got this knowledge and he could not discover all) he said nought to the king or any other, for it was his thought that of a surety that tunnel would go in the end toward the Way of Escape, this being the most nigh to the city, and he had a mind to use this to his good, and to the ill of the Noldoli. Messengers by great stealth he despatched to Melko to set a guard about the outer issue of that Way when the assault was made; but he himself thought now to take Eärendel and cast him into the fire beneath the walls, and seizing Idril he would constrain her to guide him to the secrets of the passage, that he might win out of this terror of fire and slaughter and drag her withal along with him to the lands of Melko. Now Meglin was afeared that even the secret token which Melko had given him would fail in that direful sack, and was minded to help that Ainu to the fulfilment of his promises of safety. No doubt had he however of the death of Tuor in that great burning, for to Salgant he had confided the task of delaying him in the king's halls and egging him straight thence into the deadliest of the fight – but lo! Salgant fell into a terror unto death, and he rode home and lay there now aquake on his bed; but Tuor fared home with the folk of the Wing.

Now Tuor did this, though his valour leapt to the noise of war, that he might take farewell of Idril and Eärendel, and speed them with a bodyguard down the secret way ere he returned himself to the battle throng to die if must be: but he found a press of the Mole-folk about his door, and these were the grimmest and least good-hearted of folk that Meglin might get in that city. Yet were they free Noldoli and under no spell of Melko's like their master, wherefore though for the lordship of Meglin they aided not Idril, no more would they touch of his purpose despite all his curses.

Now then Meglin had Idril by the hair and sought to drag her to the battlements out of cruelty of heart, that she might see the fall of Eärendel to the flames; but he was cumbered by that child, and she fought, alone as she was, like a tigress for all her beauty and slenderness. There he now struggles and delays amid oaths while that folk of the Wing draws nigh – and lo! Tuor gives a shout so great that the Orcs hear it afar and waver at the sound of it. Like a crash of tempest the guard of the Wing were amid the men of the Mole, and these were stricken asunder. When Meglin saw this he would stab Eärendel with a short knife he had; but that child bit his left hand, that his teeth sank in, and he staggered, and stabbed weakly, and the mail of the small coat turned the blade aside; and thereupon Tuor was upon him and his wrath was terrible to see. He seized Meglin by that hand that held the knife and broke the arm with the wrench, and then taking him by the middle leapt with him upon the walls, and flung him far out. Great was the fall of his body, and it smote Amon Gwareth three times ere it pitched in the midmost of the flames; and the name of Meglin has gone out in shame from among Eldar and Noldoli.

Then the warriors of the Mole being more numerous than those few of the Wing, and loyal to their lord, came at Tuor, and there were great blows, but no man might stand before the wrath of Tuor, and they were smitten and driven to fly into what dark holes they might, or flung from the walls. Then Tuor and his men must get them to the battle of the Gate, for the noise of it has grown very great, and Tuor has it still in his heart that the city may stand; yet with Idril he left there Voronwë against his will and some other swordsmen to be guard for her till he returned or might send tidings from the fray.

Now was the battle at that gate very evil indeed, and Duilin of the Swallow as he shot from the walls was smitten by a fiery bolt of the Balrogs who leapt about the base of Amon Gwareth; and he fell from the battlements and perished. Then the Balrogs continued to shoot darts of fire and flaming arrows like small snakes into the sky, and these fell upon the roofs and gardens of Gondolin till all the trees were scorched, and the flowers and grass burned up, and the whiteness of those walls and colonnades was blackened and seared: yet a worse matter was it that a company of those demons climbed upon the coils of the serpents of iron and thence loosed unceasingly from their bows and slings till a fire began to burn in the city to the back of the main army of the defenders.

Then said Rog in a great voice: 'Who now shall fear the Balrogs for all their terror? See before us the accursed ones who for ages have tormented the children of the Noldoli, and who now set a fire at our backs with their shooting. Come ye of the Hammer of Wrath and we will smite them for their evil.' Thereupon he lifted his mace, and its handle was long; and he made a way before him by the wrath of his onset even unto the fallen gate: but all the people of the Stricken Anvil ran behind like a wedge, and sparks came from their eyes for the fury of their rage. A great deed was that sally, as the Noldoli sing yet, and many of the Orcs were borne backward into the fires below; but the men of Rog leapt even upon the coils of the serpents and came at those Balrogs and smote them grievously, for all they had whips of flame and claws of steel, and were in stature very great. They battered them into nought, or catching at their whips wielded these against them, that they tore them even as they had aforetime torn the Gnomes; and the number of Balrogs that perished was a marvel and dread to the hosts of Melko, for ere that day never had any of the Balrogs been slain by the hand of Elves or Men.

Then Gothmog Lord of Balrogs gathered all his demons that were about the city and ordered them thus: a number made for the folk of the Hammer and gave before them, but the greater company rushing upon the flank contrived to get to their backs, higher upon the coils of the drakes and nearer to the gates, so that Rog might not win back save with great slaughter among his folk. But Rog seeing this essayed not to win back, as was hoped, but with all his folk fell on those whose part was to give before him; and they fled before him now of dire need rather than of craft. Down into the plain were they harried, and their shrieks rent the airs of Tumladen. Then that house of the Hammer fared about smiting and hewing the astonied bands of Melko till they were hemmed at the last by an overwhelming force of the Orcs and the Balrogs, and a fire-drake was loosed upon them. There did they perish about Rog hewing to the last till iron and flame overcame them, and it is yet sung that each man of the Hammer of Wrath took the lives of seven foemen to pay for his own. Then did dread fall more heavily still upon the Gondothlim at the death of Rog and the loss of his battalion, and they gave back further yet into the city, and Penlod perished there in a lane with his back to the wall, and about him many of the men of the Pillar and many of the Tower of Snow.

Now therefore Melko's goblins held all the gate and a great part of the walls on either side, whence numbers of the Swallow and those of the Rainbow were thrust to doom; but within the city they had won a great space reaching nigh to the centre, even to the Place of the Well that adjoined the

Square of the Palace. Yet about those ways and around the gate their dead were piled in uncounted heaps, and they halted therefore and took counsel, seeing that for the valour of the Gondothlim they had lost many more than they had hoped and far more than those defenders. Fearful too they were for that slaughter Rog had done amid the Balrogs, because of those demons they had great courage and confidence of heart.

Now then the plan that they made was to hold what they had won, while those serpents of bronze and with great feet for trampling climbed slowly over those of iron, and reaching the walls there opened a breach wherethrough the Balrogs might ride upon the dragons of flame: yet they knew this must be done with speed, for the heats of those drakes lasted not for ever, and might only be plenished from the wells of fire that Melko had made in the fastness of his own land.

But even as their messengers were sped they heard a sweet music that was played amid the host of the Gondothlim and they feared what it might mean: and lo! there came Ecthelion and the people of the Fountain whom Turgon till now had held in reserve, for he watched the most of that affray from the heights of his tower. Now marched these folk to a great playing of their flutes, and the crystal and silver of their array was most lovely to see amid the red light of the fires and the blackness of the ruins.

Then on a sudden their music ceased and Ecthelion of the fair voice shouted for the drawing of swords, and before the Orcs might foresee his onslaught the flashing of those pale blades was amongst them. It is said that Ecthelion's folk there slew more of the goblins than fell ever in all the battles of the Eldalië with that race, and that his name is a terror among them to this latest day, and a warcry to the Eldar.

Now it is that Tuor and the men of the Wing fare into the fight and range themselves beside Ecthelion and those of the Fountain, and the twain strike mighty blows and ward each many a thrust from the other, and harry the Orcs so that they win back almost to the gate. But there behold a quaking and a trampling, for the dragons labour mightily at beating a path up Amon Gwareth and at casting down the walls of the city; and already there is a gap therein and a confusion of masonry where the ward-towers have fallen in ruin. Bands of the Swallow and of the Arch of Heaven there fight bitterly amid the wreck or contest the walls to east and west with the foe; but even as Tuor comes nigh driving the Orcs, one of those brazen snakes heaves against the western wall and a great mass of it shakes and falls, and behind comes a creature of fire and Balrogs upon it. Flames gust from the jaws of that worm and folk wither before it, and the wings of the helm of Tuor are blackened, but he stands and gathers about him his guard and all of the Arch and Swallow he can find, whereas on his right Ecthelion rallies the men of the Fountain of the South.

Now the Orcs again take heart from the coming of the drakes, and they mingle with the Balrogs that pour about the breach, and they assail the Gondothlim grievously. There Tuor slew Othrod a lord of the Orcs cleaving his helm, and Balcmeg he hewed asunder, and Lug he smote with his axe that his limbs were cut from beneath him at the knee, but Ecthelion shore through two captains of the goblins at a sweep and cleft the head of Orcobal their chiefest champion to his teeth; and by reason of the great doughtiness of those two lords they came even unto the Balrogs. Of those demons of power Ecthelion slew three, for the brightness of his sword cleft the iron of them and did hurt to their fire, and they writhed; yet of the leap of that axe Dramborleg that was swung by the hand of Tuor were they still more afraid, for it sang like the rush of eagle's wings in the air and took death as it fell, and five of them went down before it.

But so it is that few cannot fight always against the many, and Ecthelion's left arm got a sore rent from a whip of the Balrog's and his shield fell to earth even as that dragon of fire drew nigh amid the ruin of the walls. Then Ecthelion must lean on Tuor, and Tuor might not leave him, though the very feet of the trampling beast were upon them, and they were like to be overborne: but Tuor hewed at a foot of the creature so that flame spouted forth, and that serpent screamed, lashing with its tail; and many of both Orcs and Noldoli got their death therefrom. Now Tuor gathered his might and lifted Ecthelion, and amid a remnant of the folk got thereunder and escaped the drake; yet dire was the killing of men that beast had wrought, and the Gondothlim were sorely shaken.

Thus it was that Tuor son of Peleg gave before the foe, fighting as he yielded ground, and bore from that battle Ecthelion of the Fountain, but the drakes and the foemen held half the city and all the north of it. Thence marauding bands fared about the streets and did much ransacking, or slew in the dark men and women and children, and many, if occasion let, they bound and led back and flung in the iron chambers amid the dragons of iron, that they might drag them afterward to be thralls of Melko.

Now Tuor reached the Square of the Folkwell by a way entering from the north, and found there Galdor denying the western entry by the Arch of Inwë to a horde of the goblins, but about him was now but a few of those men of the Tree. There did Galdor become the salvation of Tuor, for he fell behind his men stumbling beneath Ecthelion over a body that lay in the dark, and the Orcs had taken them both but for the sudden rush of that champion and the dint of his club.

There were the scatterlings of the guard of the Wing and of the houses of the Tree and the Fountain, and of the Swallow and the Arch, welded to a good battalion, and by the counsel of Tuor they gave way out of that Place of the Well, seeing that the Square of the King that lay next was the more defensible. Now that place had aforetime contained many beautiful trees, both oak and poplar, around a great well of vast depth and great purity of water; yet at that hour it was full of the riot and ugliness of those hideous people of Melko, and those waters were polluted with their carcases.

Thus comes the last stout gathering of those defenders in the Square of the Palace of Turgon. Among them are many wounded and fainting, and Tuor is weary for the labours of the night and the weight of Ecthelion who is in a deadly swoon. Even as he led that battalion in by the Road of

Arches from the north-west (and they had much ado to prevent any foe getting behind their backs) a noise arose at the eastward of the square, and lo! Glorfindel is driven in with the last of the men of the Golden Flower.

Now these had sustained a terrible conflict in the Great Market to the east of the city, where a force of Orcs led by Balrogs came on them at unawares as they marched by a circuitous way to the fight about the gate. This they did to surprise the foe upon his left flank, but were themselves ambuscaded; there fought they bitterly for hours till a fire-drake new-come from the breach overwhelmed them, and Glorfindel cut his way out very hardly and with few men; but that place with its stores and its goodly things of fine workmanship was a waste of flames.

The story tells that Turgon had sent the men of the Harp to their aid because of the urgency of messengers from Glorfindel, but Salgant concealed this bidding from them, saying they were to garrison the square of the Lesser Market to the south where he dwelt, and they fretted thereat. Now however they brake from Salgant and were come before the king's hall; and that was very timely, for a triumphant press of foemen was at Glorfindel's heels. On these the men of the Harp unbidden fell with great eagerness and utterly redeemed the cravenhood of their lord, driving the enemy back into the market, and being leaderless fared even over wrathfully, so that many of them were trapped in the flames or sank before the breath of the serpent that revelled there.

Tuor now drank of the great fountain and was refreshed, and loosening Ecthelion's helm gave him to drink, splashing his face that his swoon left him. Now those lords Tuor and Glorfindel clear the square and withdraw all the men they may from the entrances and bar them with barriers, save as yet on the south. Even from that region comes now Egalmoth. He had had charge of the engines on the wall; but long since deeming matters to call rather for handstrokes about the streets than shooting upon the battlements he gathered some of the Arch and of the Swallow about him and cast away his bow. Then did they fare about the city dealing good blows whenever they fell in with bands of the enemy. Thereby he rescued many bands of captives and gathered no few wandering and driven men, and so got to the King's Square with hard fighting; and men were fain to greet him for they had feared him dead. Now are all the women and children that had gathered there or been brought in by Egalmoth stowed in the king's halls, and the ranks of the houses made ready for the last. In that host of survivors are some, be it however few, of all the kindreds save of the Hammer of Wrath alone; and the king's house is as yet untouched. Nor is this any shame, for their part was ever to bide fresh to the last and defend the king.

But now the men of Melko have assembled their forces, and seven dragons of fire have come with Orcs about them, and Balrogs upon them down all the ways from north, east, and west seeking the Square of the King. Then there was carnage at the barriers, and Egalmoth and Tuor went from place to place of the defence, but Ecthelion lay by the fountain; and that stand was the most stubborn-valiant that is remembered in all the songs or in any tale. Yet at long last a drake bursts the barrier to the north – and there had once been the issue of the Alley of Roses and a fair place to see or to walk in, but now there is but a lane of blackness and it is filled with noise.

Tuor stood then in the way of that beast, but was sundered from Egalmoth, and they pressed him backward even to the centre of the square nigh the fountain. There he became weary from the strangling heat and was beaten down by a great demon, even Gothmog lord of Balrogs, son of Melko. But lo! Ecthelion, whose face was of the pallor of grey steel and whose shield-arm hung limp at his side, strode above him as he fell, and that Gnome drove at the demon, yet did not give him his death, getting rather a wound to his sword-arm that his weapon left his grasp. Then leapt Ecthelion lord of the Fountain, fairest of the Noldoli, full at Gothmog even as he raised his whip, and his helm that had a spike upon it he drove into that evil breast, and he twined his legs about his foeman's thighs; and the Balrog yelled and fell forward; but those two dropped into the basin of the king's fountain which was very deep. There found that creature his bane; and Ecthelion sank steel-laden into the depths, and so perished the lord of the Fountain after fiery battle in cool waters.

Now Tuor had arisen when the assault of Ecthelion gave him space, and seeing that great deed he wept for his love of that fair Gnome of the Fountain, but being wrapped in battle he scarce cut his way to the folk about the palace. There seeing the wavering of the enemy by reason of the dread of the fall of Gothmog the marshal of the hosts, the royal house laid on and the king came down in splendour among them and hewed with them, that they swept again much of the square, and of the Balrogs slew even two score, which is a very great prowess indeed: but greater still did they do, for they hemmed in one of the fire-drakes for all his flaming, and forced him into the very waters of the fountain that he perished therein. Now this was the end of that fair water; and its pools turned to steam and its spring was dried up, and it shot no more into the heaven, but rather a vast column of vapour arose to the sky and the cloud therefrom floated over all the land.

Then dread fell on all for the doom of the fountain, and the square was filled with mists of scalding heat and blinding fogs, and the people of the royal house were killed therein by heat and by the foe and by the serpents and by one another; but a body of them saved the king, and there was a rally of men beneath Glingol and Bansil.

Then said the king: 'Great is the fall of Gondolin', and men shuddered, for such were the words of Amnon the prophet of old; but Tuor speaking wildly for ruth and love of the king cried: 'Gondolin stands yet, and Ulmo will not suffer it to perish!' Now they were at that time standing, Tuor by the Trees and the King upon the Stairs, as they had stood aforetime when Tuor spoke the embassy of Ulmo. But Turgon said: 'Evil have I brought upon the Flower of the Plain in despite of Ulmo, and now he leaveth it to wither in the fire. Lo! hope is no more in my heart for my city of loveliness, but the children of the Noldoli shall not be worsted for ever.'

Then did the Gondothlim clash their weapons, for many stood nigh, but Turgon said: 'Fight not against doom, O my children! Seek ye who may safety in flight, if perhaps there be time yet: but let Tuor have your lealty.' But Tuor said: 'Thou art king', and Turgon made answer: 'Yet no blow will I strike more', and he cast his crown at the roots of Glingol. Then did Galdor who stood there pick it up, but Turgon accepted it not, and bare of head climbed to the topmost pinnacle of that white tower that stood nigh his palace. There he shouted in a voice like a horn blown among the mountains, and all that were gathered beneath the Trees and the foemen in the mists of the square heard him: 'Great is the victory of the Noldoli!' And it is said that it was then middle night, and that the Orcs yelled in derision.

Then did men speak of a sally, and were of two minds. Many held that it were impossible to burst through, nor might they even so get over the plain or through the hills, and that it were better therefore to die about the king. But Tuor might not think well of the death of so many fair women and children, were it at the hands of their own folk in the last resort, or by the weapons of the enemy, and he spoke of the delving and of the secret way. Therefore did he counsel that they beg Turgon to have other mind, and coming among them lead that remnant southward to the walls and the entry of that passage; but he himself burnt with desire to fare thither and know how Idril and Eärendel might be, or to get tidings hence to them and bid them be gone speedily, for Gondolin was taken. Now Tuor's plan seemed to the lords desperate indeed – seeing the narrowness of the tunnel and the greatness of the company that must pass it – yet would they fain take this rede in their straits. But Turgon hearkened not, and bid them fare now ere it was too late, and 'Let Tuor,' said he, 'be your guide and your chieftain. But I Turgon will not leave my city, and will burn with it.' Then sped they messengers again to the tower, saying: 'Sire, who are the Gondothlim if thou perish? Lead us!' But he said: 'Lo! I abide here'; and a third time, and he said: 'If I am king, obey my behests, and dare not to parley further with my commands.' After that they sent no more and made ready for the forlorn attempt. But the folk of the royal house that yet lived would not budge a foot, but gathered thickly about the base of the king's tower. 'Here,' said they, 'we will stay if Turgon goes not forth'; and they might not be persuaded.

Now was Tuor torn sorely between his reverence for the king and the love for Idril and his child, wherewith his heart was sick; yet already serpents fare about the square trampling upon dead and dying, and the foe gathers in the mists for the last onslaught; and the choice must be made. Then because of the wailing of the women in the halls of the palace and the greatness of his pity for that sad remainder of the peoples of Gondolin, he gathered all that rueful company, maids, children, and mothers, and setting them amidmost marshalled as well as he might his men around them. Deepest he set them at flank and at rear, for he purposed falling back southward fighting as best he might with the rearguard as he went; and thus if it might so be to win down the Road of Pomps to the Place of the Gods ere any great force be sent to circumvent him. Thence was it his thought to go by the Way of Running Waters past the Fountains of the South to the walls and to his home; but the passage of the secret tunnel he doubted much. Thereupon espying his movement the foe made forthwith a great onslaught upon his left flank and his rear – from east and north – even as he began to withdraw; but his right was covered by the king's hall and the head of that column drew already into the Road of Pomps.

Then some hugest of the drakes came on and glared in the fog, and he must perforce bid the company to go at a run, fighting on the left at haphazard; but Glorfindel held the rear manfully and many more of the Golden Flower fell there. So it was that they passed the Road of Pomps and reached Gar Ainion, the Place of the Gods; and this was very open and at its middle the highest ground of all the city. Here Tuor looks for an evil stand and it is scarce in his hope to get much further; but behold, the foe seems already to slacken and scarce any follow them, and this is a wonder. Now comes Tuor at their head to the Place of Wedding, and lo! there stands Idril before him with her hair unbraided as on that day of their marriage before; and great is his amaze. By her stood Voronwë and none other, but Idril saw not even Tuor, for her gaze was set back upon the Place of the King that now lay somewhat below them. Then all that host halted and looked back whither her eyes gazed and their hearts stood still; for now they saw why the foe pressed them so little and the reason of their salvation. Lo! a drake was coiled even on the very steps of the palace and defiled their whiteness; but swarms of the Orcs ransacked therein and dragged forth forgotten women and children or slew men that fought alone. Glingol was withered to the stock and Bansil was blackened utterly, and the king's tower was beset. High up they could descry the form of the king, but about the base a serpent of iron spouting flame lashed and rowed with his tail, and Balrogs were round him; and there was the king's house in great anguish, and dread cries carried up to the watchers. So was it that the sack of the halls of Turgon and that most valiant stand of the royal house held the mind of the foe, so that Tuor got thence with his company, and stood now in tears upon the Place of the Gods.

Then said Idril: 'Woe is me whose father awaiteth doom even upon his topmost pinnacle; but seven times woe whose lord hath gone down before Melko and will stride home no more' – for she was distraught with the agony of that night.

Then said Tuor: 'Lo! Idril, it is I, and I live; yet now will I get thy father hence, be it from the Hells of Melko!' With that he would make down the hill alone, maddened by the grief of his wife; but she coming to her wits in a storm of weeping clasped his knees saying: 'My lord! My lord!' and delayed him. Yet even as they spoke a great noise and a yelling rose from that place of anguish. Behold, the tower leapt into a flame and in a stab of fire it fell, for the dragons crushed the base of it and all who stood there. Great was the clangour of that terrible fall, and therein passed Turgon King of the Gondothlim, and for that hour the victory was to Melko.

Then said Idril heavily: 'Sad is the blindness of the wise'; but Tuor said: 'Sad too is the stubbornness of those we love – yet it was a valiant fault,' then stooping he lifted and kissed her, for she was more to him than all the Gondothlim; but she wept bitterly for her father. Then turned Tuor to the captains, saying: 'Lo, we must get hence with all speed, lest we be surrounded'; and forthwith they moved onward as swiftly as they might and got them far from thence ere the Orcs tired of sacking the palace and rejoicing at the fall of the tower of Turgon.

Now are they in the southward city and meet but scattered bands of plunderers who fly before them; yet do they find fire and burning everywhere for the ruthlessness of that enemy. Women do they meet, some with babes and some laden with chattels, but Tuor would not let them bear away aught save a little food. Coming now at length to a greater quiet Tuor asked Voronwë for tidings, in that Idril spoke not and was well-nigh in a swoon; and Voronwë told him of how she and he had waited before the doors of the house while the noise of those battles grew and shook their hearts; and Idril wept for lack of tidings from Tuor. At length she had sped the most part of her guard down the secret way with Eärendel, constraining them to depart with imperious words, yet was her grief great at that sundering. She herself would bide, said she, nor seek to live after her lord; and then she fared about gathering womenfolk and wanderers and speeding them down the tunnel, and smiting marauders with her small band; nor might they dissuade her from bearing a sword.

At length they had fallen in with a band somewhat too numerous, and Voronwë had dragged her thence but by the luck of the Gods, for all else with them perished, and their foe burned Tuor's house; yet found not the secret way. 'Therewith,' said Voronwë, 'thy lady became distraught of weariness and grief, and fared into the city wildly to my great fear – nor might I get her to sally from the burning.'

About the saying of these words were they come to the southern walls and nigh to Tuor's house, and lo! it was cast down and the wreckage was asmoke; and thereat was Tuor bitterly wroth. But there was a noise that boded the approach of Orcs, and Tuor despatched that company as swiftly as might be down that secret way.

Now is there great sorrow upon that staircase as those exiles bid farewell to Gondolin; yet are they without much hope of further life beyond the hills, for how shall any slip from the hand of Melko?

Glad is Tuor when all have passed the entrance and his fear lightens; indeed by the luck of the Valar only can all the folk have got therein unspied of the Orcs. Some now are left who casting aside their arms labour with picks from within and block up the entry of the passage, faring then after the host as they might; but when that folk had descended the stairway to a level with the valley the heat grew to a torment for the fire of the dragons that were about the city; and they were indeed nigh, for the delving there was at no great depth in the earth. Boulders were loosened by the tremors of the ground and falling crushed many, and fumes were in the air so that their torches and lanterns went out. Here they fell over bodies of some that had gone before and perished, and Tuor was in fear for Eärendel; and they pressed on in great darkness and anguish. Nigh two hours were they in that tunnel of the earth, and towards its end it was scarce finished, but rugged at the sides and low.

Then came they at the last lessened by wellnigh a tithe to the tunnel's opening, and it debouched cunningly in a large basin where once water had lain, but it was now full of thick bushes. Here were gathered no small press of mingled folk whom Idril and Voronwë had sped down the hidden way before them, and they were weeping softly in weariness and sorrow, but Eärendel was not there. Thereat were Tuor and Idril in anguish of heart. Lamentation was there too among all those others, for amidmost of the plain about them loomed afar the hill of Amon Gwareth crowned with flames, where had stood the gleaming city of their home. Fire-drakes are about it and monsters of iron fare in and out of its gates, and great is that sack of the Balrogs and Orcs. Somewhat of comfort has this nonetheless for the leaders, for they judge the plain to be nigh empty of Melko's folk save hard by the city, for thither have fared all his evil ones to revel in that destruction.

'Now,' therefore said Galdor, 'we must get as far hence toward the Encircling Mountains as may be ere dawn come upon us, and that giveth no great space of time, for summer is at hand.' Thereat rose a dissension, for a number said that it were folly to make for Cristhorn as Tuor purposed. 'The sun,' say they, 'will be up long ere we win the foothills, and we shall be whelmed in the plain by those drakes and those demons. Let us fare to Bad Uthwen, the Way of Escape, for that is but half the journeying, and our weary and our wounded may hope to win so far if no further.'

Yet Idril spoke against this, and persuaded the lords that they trust not to the magic of that way that had aforetime shielded it from discovery: 'for what magic stands if Gondolin be fallen?' Nonetheless a large body of men and women sundered from Tuor and fared to Bad Uthwen, and there into the jaws of a monster who by the guile of Melko at Meglin's rede sat at the outer issue that none came through. But the others, led by Legolas Greenleaf of the house of the Tree, who knew all that plain by day or by dark, and was night-sighted, made much speed over the vale for all their weariness, and halted only after a great march. Then was all the Earth spread with the grey light of that sad dawn which looked no more on the beauty of Gondolin; but the plain was full of mists – and that was a marvel, for no mist or fog came there ever before, and this perchance had to do with the doom of the fountain of the king. Again they rose, and covered by the vapours fared long past dawn in safety, till they were already too far away for any to descry them in those misty airs from the hill or from the ruined walls.

Now the Mountains or rather their lowest hills were on that side seven leagues save a mile from Gondolin, and Cristhorn the Cleft of Eagles two leagues of upward going from the beginning of the Mountains, for it was at a great height; wherefore they had yet two leagues and part of a third to traverse amid the spurs and foothills, and they were very weary. By now the sun hung well above a saddle in the eastern hills, and she was very red and great; and the mists nigh them were lifted, but the ruins of Gondolin were utterly hidden as in a cloud. Behold then at the clearing of the airs they saw, but a few furlongs off, a knot of men that fled on foot, and these were pursued by a strange cavalry, for on great wolves rode Orcs, as they thought, brandishing spears. Then said Tuor: 'Lo! there is Eärendel my son; behold, his face shineth as a star in the waste, and my men of the Wing are about him, and they are in sore straits.' Forthwith he chose fifty of the men that were least weary, and leaving the main company to follow he fared over the plain with that troop as swiftly as they had strength left. Coming now to carry of voice Tuor shouted to the men about Eärendel to stand and flee not, for the wolfriders were scattering them and slaying them piecemeal, and the child was upon the shoulders of one Hendor, a house-carle of Idril's, and he seemed like to be left with his burden. Then they stood back to back and Hendor and Eärendel amidmost; but Tuor soon came up, though all his troop were breathless.

Of the wolfriders there were a score, and of the men that were about Eärendel but six living; therefore had Tuor opened his men into a crescent of but one rank, and hoped so to envelop the riders, lest any escaping bring tidings to the main foe and draw ruin upon the exiles. In this he succeeded, so that only two escaped, and therewithal wounded and without their beasts, wherefore were their tidings brought too late to the city.

Glad was Eärendel to greet Tuor, and Tuor most fain of his child; but said Eärendel: 'I am thirsty, father, for I have run far – nor had Hendor need to bear me.' Thereto his father said nought, having no water, and thinking of the need of all that company that he guided; but Eärendel said again: 'It was good to see Meglin die so, for he would set arms about my mother – and I liked him not; but I would travel in no tunnels for all Melko's wolfriders.' Then Tuor smiled and set him upon his shoulders. Soon after this the main company came up, and Tuor gave Eärendel to his mother who was in great joy; but Eärendel would not be borne in her arms, for he said: 'Mother Idril, thou art weary, and warriors in mail ride not among the Gondothlim, save it be old Salgant!' – and his mother laughed amid her sorrow; but Eärendel said: 'Nay, where is Salgant?' – for Salgant had told him quaint tales or played drolleries with him at times, and Eärendel had much laughter of the old Gnome in those days when he came many a day to the house of Tuor, loving the good wine and fair repast he there received. But none could say where Salgant was, nor can they now. Mayhap he was whelmed by fire upon his bed; yet some have it that he was taken captive to the halls of Melko and made his buffoon – and this is an ill fate for a noble of the good race of the Gnomes. Then was Eärendel sad at that, and walked beside his mother in silence.

Now came they to the foothills and it was full morning but still grey, and there nigh to the beginning of the upward road folk stretched them and rested in a little dale fringed with trees and with hazel-bushes, and many slept despite their peril, for they were utterly spent. Yet Tuor set a strict watch, and himself slept not. Here they made one meal of scanty food and broken meats; and Eärendel quenched his thirst and played beside a little brook. Then said he to his mother: 'Mother Idril, I would we had good Ecthelion of the Fountain here to play to me on his flute, or make me willow-whistles! Perchance he has gone on ahead?' But Idril said nay, and told what she had heard of his end. Then said Eärendel that he cared not ever to see the streets of Gondolin again, and he wept bitterly; but Tuor said that he would not again see those streets, 'for Gondolin is no more.'

Thereafter nigh to the hour of sundown behind the hills Tuor bade the company arise, and they pressed on by rugged paths. Soon now the grass faded and gave way to mossy stones, and trees fell away, and even the pines and firs grew sparse. About the set of the sun the way so wound behind a shoulder of the hills that they might not again look towards Gondolin. There all that company turned, and lo! the plain is clear and smiling in the last light as of old; but afar off as they gazed a great flare shot up against the darkened north – and that was the fall of the last tower of Gondolin, even that which had stood hard by the southern gate, and whose shadow fell oft across the walls of Tuor's house. Then sank the sun, and they saw Gondolin no more.

Now the pass of Cristhorn, that is the Eagles' Cleft, is one of dangerous going, and that host had not ventured it by dark, lanternless and without torches, and very weary and cumbered with women and children and sick and stricken men, had it not been for their great fear of Melko's scouts, for it was a great company and might not fare very secretly. Darkness gathered rapidly as they approached that high place, and they must string out into a long and straggling line. Galdor and a band of men spear-armed went ahead, and Legolas was with them, whose eyes were like cats' for the

dark, yet could they see further. Thereafter followed the
least weary of the women supporting the sick and the
wounded that could go on foot. Idril was with these, and
Eärendel who bore up well, but Tuor was in the midmost
behind them with all his men of the Wing, and they bare
some who were grievously hurt, and Egalmoth was with
him, but he had got a hurt in that sally from the square.
Behind again came many women with babes, and girls, and
lamed men, yet was the going slow enough for them. At the
rearmost went the largest band of men battle-whole, and
there was Glorfindel of the golden hair.

Thus were they come to Cristhorn, which is an ill place
by reason of its height, for this is so great that spring nor
summer come ever there, and it is very cold. Indeed while
the valley dances in the sun, there all the year snow dwells
in those bleak places, and even as they came there the wind
howled, coming from the north behind them, and it bit
sorely. Snow fell and whirled in wind-eddies and got into
their eyes, and this was not good, for there the path is
narrow, and of the right or westerly hand a sheer wall rises
nigh seven chains from the way, ere it bursts atop into jagged
pinnacles where are many eyries. There dwells Thorondor
King of Eagles, Lord of the Thornhoth, whom the Eldar
named Sorontur. But of the other hand is a fall not right
sheer yet dreadly steep, and it has long teeth of rock
up-pointing so that one may climb down – or fall maybe –
but by no means up. And from that deep is no escape at
either end any more than by the sides, and Thorn Sir runs
at bottom. He falls therein from the south over a great

precipice but with a slender water, for he is a thin stream in those heights, and he issues to the north after flowing but a rocky mile above ground down a narrow passage that goes into the mountain, and scarce a fish could squeeze through with him.

Galdor and his men were come now to the end nigh to where Thorn Sir falls into the abyss, and the others straggled, for all Tuor's efforts, back over most of the mile of the perilous way between chasm and cliff, so that Glorfindel's folk were scarce come to its beginning, when there was a yell in the night that echoed in that grim region. Behold, Galdor's men were beset in the dark suddenly by shapes leaping from behind rocks where they had lain hidden even from the glance of Legolas. It was Tuor's thought that they had fallen in with one of Melko's ranging companies, and he feared no more than a sharp brush in the dark, yet he sent the women and sick around him rearward and joined his men to Galdor's, and there was an affray upon the perilous path. But now rocks fell from above, and things looked ill, for they did grievous hurt; but matters seemed to Tuor yet worse when the noise of arms came from the rear, and tidings were said to him by a man of the Swallow that Glorfindel was ill bested by men from behind, and that a Balrog was with them.

Then was he sore afraid of a trap, and this was even what had in truth befallen, for watchers had been set by Melko all about the encircling hills. Yet so many did the valour of the Gondothlim draw off to the assault ere the city could be taken that these were but thinly spread, and were at the least here in the south. Nonetheless one of these had espied the company as they started the upward going from the dale of hazels, and as many bands were got together against them as might be, and devised to fall upon the exiles to front and rear even upon the perilous way of Cristhorn. Now Galdor and Glorfindel held their own despite the surprise of assault, and many of the Orcs were struck into the abyss; but the falling of the rocks was like to end all their valour, and the flight from Gondolin to come to ruin. The moon about that hour rose above the pass, and the gloom somewhat lifted, for his pale light filtered into dark places; yet it lit not the path for the height of the walls. Then arose Thorondor, King of Eagles, and he loved not Melko; for Melko had caught many of his kindred and chained them against sharp rocks to squeeze from them the magic words whereby he might learn to fly (for he dreamed of contending even against Manwë in the air); and when they would not tell he cut off their wings and sought to fashion therefrom a mighty pair for his use, but it availed not.

Now when the clamour from the pass rose to his great eyrie he said: 'Wherefore are these foul things, these Orcs of the hills, climbed near to my throne; and why do the sons of the Noldoli cry out in the low places for fear of the children of Melko the accursed? Arise O Thornhoth, whose beaks are of steel and whose talons swords!'

Thereupon there was a rushing like a great wind in rocky places, and the Thornhoth, the people of the Eagles, fell on those Orcs who had scaled above the path, and tore their faces and their hands and flung them to the rocks of Thorn Sir far below. Then were the Gondothlim glad, and they made in after days the Eagle a sign of their kindred in token of their joy, and Idril bore it, but Eärendel loved rather the Swan-wing of his father. Now unhampered Galdor's men bore back those that opposed them, for they were not very many and the onset of the Thornhoth affrighted them much; and the company fared forward again, though Glorfindel had fighting enough in the rear. Already the half had passed the perilous way and the falls of Thorn Sir, when that Balrog that was with the rearward foe leapt with great might on certain lofty rocks that stood into the path on the left side upon the lip of the chasm, and thence with a leap of fury he was past Glorfindel's men and among the women and the sick in front, lashing with his whip of flame. Then Glorfindel leapt forward upon him and his golden armour gleamed strangely in the moon, and he hewed at that demon that it leapt again upon a great boulder and Glorfindel after. Now there was a deadly combat upon that high rock above the folk; and these, pressed behind and hindered ahead, were grown so close that well nigh all could see, yet was it over ere Glorfindel's men could leap to his side. The ardour of Glorfindel drove that Balrog from point to point, and his mail fended him from its whip and claw. Now had he beaten a heavy swinge upon its iron helm, now hewn off the creature's whip-arm at the elbow. Then sprang the Balrog in the torment of his pain and fear full at Glorfindel, who stabbed like a dart of a snake; but he found only a shoulder, and was grappled, and they swayed to a fall upon the crag-top. Then Glorfindel's left hand sought a dirk, and this he thrust up that it pierced the Balrog's belly nigh his own face (for that demon was double his stature); and it shrieked, and fell backward from the rock, and falling clutched Glorfindel's yellow locks beneath his cap, and those twain fell into the abyss.

Now this was a very grievous thing, for Glorfindel was most dearly beloved – and lo! the dint of their fall echoed about the hills, and the abyss of Thorn Sir rang. Then at the death-cry of the Balrog the Orcs before and behind wavered and were slain or fled far away, and Thorondor himself, a mighty bird, descended to the abyss and brought up the body of Glorfindel; but the Balrog lay, and the water of Thorn Sir ran black for many a day far below in Tumladen.

Still do the Eldar say when they see good fighting at great odds of power against a fury of evil: 'Alas! It is Glorfindel and the Balrog', and their hearts are still sore for that fair one of the Noldoli. Because of their love, despite the haste and their fear of the advent of new foes, Tuor let raise a great stone-cairn over Glorfindel just there beyond the perilous way by the precipice of Eagle-stream, and Thorondor has let not yet any harm come thereto, but yellow flowers have fared thither and blow ever now about that mound in those unkindly places; but the folk of the Golden Flower wept at its building and might not dry their tears.

Now who shall tell of the wanderings of Tuor and the exiles of Gondolin in the wastes that lie beyond the mountains to the south of the vale of Tumladen? Miseries were theirs and death, colds and hungers, and ceaseless watches. That they won ever through those regions infested by

Melko's evil came from the great slaughter and damage done to his power in that assault, and from the speed and wariness with which Tuor led them; for of a certain Melko knew of that escape and was furious thereat. Ulmo had heard tidings in the far oceans of the deeds that were done, but he could not yet aid them for they were far from waters and rivers – and indeed they thirsted sorely, and they knew not the way.

But after a year and more of wandering, in which many a time they journeyed long tangled in the magic of those wastes only to come again upon their own tracks, once more the summer came, and nigh to its height they came at last upon a stream, and following this came to better lands and were a little comforted. Here did Voronwë guide them, for he had caught a whisper of Ulmo's in that stream one late summer's night – and he got ever much wisdom from the sound of waters. Now he led them even till they came down to Sirion which that stream fed, and then both Tuor and Voronwë saw that they were not far from the outer issue of old of the Way of Escape, and were once more in that deep dale of alders. Here were all the bushes trampled and the trees burnt, and the dale-wall scarred with flame, and they wept, for they thought they knew the fate of those who sundered aforetime from them at the tunnel-mouth.

Now they journeyed down that river but were again in fear from Melko, and fought affrays with his Orc-bands and were in peril from the wolfriders, but his firedrakes sought not at them, both for the great exhaustion of their fires in the taking of Gondolin, and the increasing power of Ulmo as the river grew. So came they after many days – for they went slowly and got their sustenance very hardly – to those great heaths and morasses above the Land of Willows, and Voronwë knew not those regions. Now here goes Sirion a very great way under earth, diving at the great cavern of the Tumultuous Winds, but running clear again above the Pools of Twilight, even where Tulkas after fought with Melko's self. Tuor had fared over these regions by night and dusk after Ulmo came to him amid the reeds, and he remembered not the ways. In places that land is full of deceits and very marshy; and here the host had long delay and was vexed by sore flies, for it was autumn still, and agues and fevers fared amongst them, and they cursed Melko.

Yet came they at last to the great pools and the edges of that most tender Land of Willows; and the very breath of the winds thereof brought rest and peace to them, and for the comfort of that place the grief was assuaged of those who mourned the dead in that great fall. There women and maids grew fair again and their sick were healed, and old wounds ceased to pain; yet they alone who of reason feared their folk living still in bitter thraldom in the Hells of Iron sang not, nor did they smile.

Here they abode very long indeed, and Eärendel was a grown boy ere the voice of Ulmo's conches drew the heart of Tuor, that his sea-longing returned with a thirst the deeper for years of stifling; and all that host arose at his bidding, and got them down Sirion to the Sea.

Now the folk that had passed into the Eagles' Cleft and who saw the fall of Glorfindel had been nigh eight hundreds – a large wayfaring, yet was it a sad remnant of so fair and numerous a city. But they who arose from the grasses of the Land of Willows in years after and fared away to sea, when spring set celandine in the meads and they had held sad festival in memorial of Glorfindel, these numbered but three hundreds and a score of men and man-children, and two hundreds and three score of women and maid-children. Now the number of women was few because of their hiding or being stowed by their kinsfolk in secret places in the city. There were they burned or slain or taken and enthralled, and the rescue-parties found them too seldom; and it is the greatest ruth to think of this, for the maids and women of the Gondothlim were as fair as the sun and as lovely as the moon and brighter than the stars. Glory dwelt in that city of Gondolin of the Seven Names, and its ruin was the most dread of all the sacks of cities upon the face of Earth. Nor Bablon, nor Ninwi, nor the towers of Trui, nor all the many takings of Rûm that is greatest among Men, saw such terror as fell that day upon Amon Gwareth in the kindred of the Gnomes; and this is esteemed the worst work that Melko has yet thought of in the world.

Yet now those exiles of Gondolin dwelt at the mouth of Sirion by the waves of the Great Sea. There they take the name of Lothlim, the people of the flower, for Gondothlim is a name too sore to their hearts; and fair among the Lothlim Eärendel grows in the house of his father, and the great tale of Tuor is come to its waning.'

Then said Littleheart son of Bronweg: 'Alas for Gondolin.'

*

THE EARLIEST TEXT

Important elements in the early evolution of the history of the Elder Days are my father's hurried notes. As I have described them elsewhere, these notes were for the most part pencilled at furious speed, the writing now rubbed and faint and in places after long study scarcely decipherable, on slips of paper, disordered and dateless, or in a little notebook; in these, during the years in which he was composing the *Lost Tales*, he jotted down thoughts and suggestions – many of them being no more than simple sentences, or mere isolated names, serving as reminders of work to be done, stories to be told, or changes to be made.

Among these notes is found what must be the earliest trace of the story of the fall of Gondolin:

Isfin daughter of Fingolma loved from afar by Eöl (Arval) of the Mole-kin of the Gnomes. He is strong and in favour with Fingolma and with the Sons of Fëanor (to whom he is akin) because he is a leader of the Miners and searches after hidden jewels, but he is illfavoured and Isfin loathes him.

For an explanation of the choice of the word 'Gnomes' see p.21 (footnote). *Fingolma* was an early name of the later *Finwë* (the leader of the second host of the Elves, the Noldor, on the Great Journey from Palisor, the land of their awakening). Isfin appears in the *Tale of the Fall of Gondolin* as the sister of Turgon King of Gondolin and the mother of Meglin, son of Eöl.

It is obvious that this note is a form of the story told in the Lost Tales, despite the major difference. In the note it is Eöl the miner of the 'Mole-kin' who is the suitor for the daughter of Fingolma, Isfin, who rejects him on account of his ugliness. In the 'Lost Tale', on the other hand, the rejected – and ugly – suitor is Meglin the *son* of Eöl and his mother is Isfin – the sister of Turgon King of Gondolin; and it is said expressly (p.61) that the tale of Isfin and Eöl 'may not here be told' – presumably because my father thought that it would go too far afield.

I think it most probable that the brief note given above was written before the *Tale of the Fall of Gondolin* and before the advent of Maeglin, and that the story in its origin had no association with Gondolin.

(Henceforward I shall usually refer to the 'Lost Tale' of *The Fall of Gondolin* (pp. 37–111) simply as 'the *Tale*'.)

*

TURLIN AND THE EXILES OF GONDOLIN

There is a loose page carrying a short prose piece, unquestionably preserved in its entirety, that bears the title *Turlin and the Exiles of Gondolin*. It can be placed chronologically *after* the *Tale of the Fall of Gondolin*, and was clearly the abandoned start of a new version of the *Tale*.

My father hesitated much over the name of the hero of Gondolin, and in this text he gave him the name *Turlin*, but altered it throughout to *Turgon*. Since this (not rare) interchange of names between characters can be needlessly confusing, I will name him *Tuor* in my text of the piece that follows.

The anger of the Gods (the Valar) against the Gnomes and the sealing of Valinor against all comers, with which this piece begins, arose from their rebellion and their evil deeds at the Haven of the Swans. This is known as the

Kinslaying, and is of importance in the story of the Fall of Gondolin, and indeed of the later history of the Elder Days.

Turlin [Tuor] and the Exiles of Gondolin

'Then' said Ilfiniol son of Bronweg 'know that Ulmo Lord of Waters forgot never the sorrows of the Elven kindreds beneath the power of Melko, but he might do little because of the anger of the other Gods who shut their hearts against the race of the Gnomes, and dwelt behind the veiled hills of Valinor heedless of the Outer World, so deep was their ruth and regret for the death of the Two Trees. Nor did any save Ulmo only dread the power of Melko that wrought ruin and sorrow over all the Earth; but Ulmo desired that Valinor should gather all its might to quench his evil ere it be too late, and it seemed to him that both purposes might perchance be achieved if messengers from the Gnomes should win to Valinor and plead for pardon and for pity upon the Earth; for the love of Palúrien and Oromë her son for those wide realms did but slumber still. Yet hard and evil was the road from the Outer Earth to Valinor, and the Gods themselves had meshed the ways with magic and veiled the encircling hills. Thus did Ulmo seek unceasingly to stir the Gnomes to send messengers unto Valinor, but Melko was cunning and very deep in wisdom, and unsleeping was his wariness in all things that touched the Elven kindreds, and their messengers overcame not the perils and temptations of that longest and most evil of all roads, and many that dared to set forth were lost for ever.

Now tells the tale how Ulmo despaired that any of the Elven race should surpass the dangers of the way, and of the deepest and the latest design that he then fashioned, and of those things which came of it.

In those days the greater part of the kindreds of Men dwelt after the Battle of Unnumbered Tears in that land of the North that has many names, but which the Elves of Kôr have named Hisilómë which is the Twilit Mist, and the Gnomes, who of the Elf-kin know it best, Dor-lómin the Land of Shadows. A people mighty in numbers were there, dwelling about the wide pale waters of Mithrim the great lake that lies in those regions, and other folk named them Tunglin or folk of the Harp, for their joy was in the wild music and minstrelsy of the fells and woodlands, but they knew not and sang not of the sea. Now this folk came into those places after the dread battle, being too late summoned thither from afar, and they bore no stain of treachery against the Elven kin; but indeed many among them clung to such friendship with the hidden Gnomes of the mountains and Dark Elves as might be still for the sorrow and mistrust born of those ruinous deeds in the Vale of Ninniach [the site of the Battle of Unnumbered Tears].

Tuor was a man of that folk, son of Peleg, son of Indor, son of Fengel who was their chief and hearing the summons had marched out of the deeps of the East with all his folk. But Tuor dwelt not much with his kindred, and loved rather solitude and the friendship of the Elves whose tongues he knew, and he wandered alone about the long shores of Mithrim, now hunting in its woods, now making sudden music in the rocks upon his rugged harp of wood strung with the sinews of bears. But he sang not for the ears of Men, and many hearing the power of his rough songs came from afar to hearken to his harping; but Tuor left his singing and departed to lonely places in the mountains.

Many strange things he learned there, broken tidings of far off things, and longing came upon him for deeper lore, but as yet his heart turned not from the long shores and the pale waters of Mithrim in the mists. Yet was he not fated to dwell for ever in those places, for it is said that magic and destiny led him on a day to a cavernous opening in the rocks, down which a hidden river flowed from Mithrim. And Tuor entered that cavern seeking to learn its secret, but having entered the waters of Mithrim drove him forward into the heart of the rock and he might not win back into the light. This men have said was not without the will of Ulmo, at whose prompting maybe the Gnomes had fashioned that deep and hidden way. Then came the Gnomes to Tuor and guided him along the dark passages amid the mountains until he came out once more into the light.

It will be seen that my father had the text of the *Tale* in front of him when he wrote this text (which I will call 'the *Turlin* version'), for phrases of the one reappear in the other (such as 'magic and destiny led him on a day to a cavernous opening', p.37); but in several features there are advances on the earlier text. The original genealogy of Tuor remains (son of Peleg, son of Indor), but more is told of his people: they were Men from the East who came to the aid of the Elves in the vast and ruinous battle against the forces of Melko that came to be known as *The Battle of Unnumbered Tears*. But they came too late; and they settled in great numbers in Hisilómë 'Twilit Mist' (Hithlum), called also Dor-lómin 'Land of Shadows'. An important and decisive element in the early conception of the history of the Elder Days was the overwhelming nature of the victory of Melko in that battle, so sweeping that a great part of the people named Noldoli became his imprisoned slaves; it is said in the *Tale* (p.49): 'Know then that the Gondothlim [the people of Gondolin] were that kin of the Noldoli who alone escaped Melko's power when at the Battle of Unnumbered Tears he slew and enslaved their folk and wove spells about them and caused them to dwell in the Hells of Iron, faring thence at his will and bidding only.'

Notable also is the account in this text of Ulmo's 'design and desire', as his purpose is described in the *Tale* (p.47): but in the *Tale* it is said that 'thereof Tuor understood little' – and we are told no more. In this further brief text, the *Turlin* version, on the other hand, Ulmo spoke of his inability to prevail against the other Valar, isolated in his fear of the power of Melko, and of his wish that Valinor should rise against that power; his attempts also to persuade the Noldoli to send messengers to Valinor to plead for compassion and help, while the Valar 'dwelt behind the veiled hills of Valinor heedless of the Outer World.' This was the time known as 'The Hiding of Valinor', when, as is said in the *Turlin* version (p.115), 'the Gods themselves had meshed the ways [to Valinor] with magic and veiled the encircling hills' (on this crucial element in the history see *The Evolution of the Story*, pp.223 ff.).

Most significant is this passage (p.116): 'Now tells the tale how Ulmo despaired that any of the Elven race should surpass the dangers of the way, and of the deepest and the latest design that he then fashioned, and of those things which came of it.'

THE STORY TOLD IN THE
SKETCH OF THE MYTHOLOGY

I give now the form of the story of the Fall of Gondolin that my father wrote in 1926 in a work called *Sketch of the Mythology*, identifying it later as *The Original Silmarillion*. A portion of the work was included and its nature explained in *Beren and Lúthien* (p.89), and I have used a further portion to serve as a prologue to this book. My father made later a number of corrections (almost all in the form of additions), and I include most of these in square brackets.

Ylmir is the Gnomish form for *Ulmo*.

The great river Sirion flowed through the lands south-west; at its mouth was a great delta, and its lower course ran through wide green and fertile lands, little peopled save by birds and beasts because of the Orc-raids; but they were not inhabited by Orcs, who preferred the northern woods, and feared the power of Ylmir – for Sirion's mouth was in the Western Seas.

Turgon Fingolfin's son had a sister Isfin. She was lost in Taur-na-Fuin after the Battle of Unnumbered Tears. There she was trapped by the Dark Elf Eöl. Their son was Meglin. The people of Turgon escaping, aided by the prowess of Húrin, were lost from the knowledge of Morgoth, and indeed of all in the world save Ylmir. In a secret place in the hills their scouts climbing to the tops [had] discovered a broad valley entirely encircled by the hills in rings ever lower as they came towards the centre. Amid this ring was a wide land without hills, except for one rocky hill that stuck up from the plain, not right at the centre, but nearest to that part of the outer wall which marched close to the edge of Sirion. [The hill nearest to Angband was guarded by Fingolfin's cairn.]

Ylmir's messages come up Sirion bidding them take refuge in this valley, and teaching them spells of enchantment to place upon all the hills about, to keep off foes and spies. He foretells that their fortress shall stand longest of all the refuges of the Elves against Morgoth, and like Doriath never be overthrown save by treachery from within. The spells are strongest near to Sirion, although here the encircling mountains are lowest. Here the Gnomes dig a mighty winding tunnel under the roots of the mountains, that issues at last in the Guarded Plain. Its outer entrance is guarded by the spells of Ylmir; its inner is watched unceasingly by the Gnomes. It is set there in case those within ever need to escape, and as a way of more rapid exit from the valley for scouts, wanderers, and messages, and also as an entrance for fugitives escaping from Morgoth.

Thorondor King of Eagles removes his eyries to the

northern heights of the encircling mountains and guards them against Orc-spies [sitting upon Fingolfin's cairn]. On the rocky hill Amon Gwareth, the hill of watching, whose sides they polish to the smoothness of glass, and whose top they level, the great city of Gondolin with gates of steel is built. The plain all about is levelled as flat and smooth as a lawn of clipped grass to the feet of the hills, so that nothing can creep over it unawares. The people of Gondolin grows mighty, and their armouries are filled with weapons. But Turgon does not march to the aid of Nargothrond, or Doriath, and after the slaying of Dior he has no more to do with the sons of Fëanor. Finally he closes the vale to all fugitives, and forbids the folk of Gondolin to leave the valley. Gondolin is the only stronghold of the Elves left. Morgoth has not forgotten Turgon, but his search is in vain. Nargothrond is destroyed; Doriath desolate; Húrin's children dead; and only scattered and fugitive Elves, Gnomes and Ilkorins left, except such as work in the smithies and mines in great numbers. His triumph is nearly complete.

Meglin son of Eöl and Isfin sister of Turgon was sent by his mother to Gondolin, and there received, although half of Ilkorin blood, and treated as a prince [last of the fugitives from without].

Húrin of Hithlum had a brother Huor. The son of Huor was Tuor, younger than [> cousin of] Túrin son of Húrin. Rían, Huor's wife, sought her husband's body among the slain on the field of Unnumbered Tears, and died there. Her son remaining in Hithlum fell into the hands of the faithless men whom Morgoth drove into Hithlum after that battle, and he was made a thrall. Growing wild and rough he fled into the woods, and became an outlaw, and a solitary, living alone and communing with none save rarely with wandering and hidden Elves. On a time Ylmir contrived that he should be led to a subterranean river-course leading out of Mithrim into a chasmed river that flowed at last into the Western Sea. In this way his going was unmarked by Man, Orc, or spy, and unknown of Morgoth. After long wanderings down the western shores he came to the mouths of Sirion, and there fell in with the Gnome Bronweg, who had once been in Gondolin. They journey secretly up Sirion together. Tuor lingers long in the sweet land Nan-tathrin 'Valley of Willows'; but there Ylmir himself comes up the river to visit him, and tells him of his mission. He is to bid Turgon to prepare for battle with Morgoth; for Ylmir will turn the hearts of the Valar to forgive the Gnomes and send them succour. If Turgon will do this, the battle will be terrible, but the race of Orcs will perish, and will not in after ages trouble Elves and Men. If not, the people of Gondolin are to prepare for flight to Sirion's mouth, where Ylmir will aid them to build a fleet and guide them back to Valinor. If Turgon does Ylmir's will Tuor is to abide a while in Gondolin and then go back to Hithlum with a force of Gnomes and draw Men once more into alliance with the Elves, for 'without Men the Elves shall not prevail against the Orcs and Balrogs'. This Ylmir does because he knows that ere seven full years are passed the doom of Gondolin will come through Meglin [if they sit still in their halls].

Tuor and Bronweg reach the secret way, [which they find

by grace of Ylmir] and come out upon the guarded plain. Taken captive by the watch they are led before Turgon. Turgon is grown old and very mighty and proud, and Gondolin so fair and beautiful, and its people so proud of it and confident in its secret and impregnable strength, that the king and most of the people do not wish to trouble about the Gnomes and Elves without, or care for Men, nor do they long any more for Valinor. Meglin approving, the king rejects Tuor's message in spite of the words of Idril the far-sighted (also called Idril Silverfoot, because she loved to walk barefoot) his daughter, and the wiser of his counsellors. Tuor lives on in Gondolin, and becomes a great chieftain. After three years he weds Idril – Tuor and Beren alone of all mortals ever wedded Elves, and since Elwing daughter of Dior Beren's son wedded Eärendel son of Tuor and Idril of them alone has come the strain of Elfinesse into mortal blood.

Not long after this Meglin going far afield over the mountains is taken by Orcs, and purchases his life when taken to Angband by revealing Gondolin and its secrets. Morgoth promises him the lordship of Gondolin, and possession of Idril. Lust for Idril led him the easier to his treachery, and added to his hatred for Tuor.

Morgoth sends him back to Gondolin. Eärendel is born, having the beauty and light and wisdom of Elfinesse, the hardihood and strength of Men, and the longing for the sea which captured Tuor and held him for ever when Ylmir spoke to him in the Land of Willows.

At last Morgoth is ready, and the attack is made on Gondolin with dragons, Balrogs, and Orcs. After a dreadful fight about the walls the city is stormed, and Turgon perishes with many of the most noble in the last fight in the great square. Tuor rescues Idril and Eärendel from Meglin, and hurls him from the battlements. He then leads the remnant of the people of Gondolin down a secret tunnel previously made by Idril's advice which comes out far in the north of the Plain. Those who would not come with him but fled to the old Way of Escape are caught by the dragon sent by Morgoth to watch that exit.

In the fume of the burning Tuor leads his company into the mountains into the cold pass of Cristhorn (Eagles' Cleft). There they are ambushed, but saved by the valour of Glorfindel (chief of the house of the Golden Flower of Gondolin, who dies in a duel with a Balrog upon a pinnacle) and the intervention of Thorondor. The remnant reaches Sirion and journeys to the land at its mouth – the Waters of Sirion. Morgoth's triumph is now complete.

The story told in this compressed form had not greatly changed from its form in the *Tale of the Fall of Gondolin*, but there are nonetheless significant developments. It is here that Tuor of the *Tale* is placed within the genealogy of the *Edain*, the Elf-friends: he has become the son of Huor the brother of Húrin – who was the father of the tragic hero Túrin Turambar. Thus Tuor was first cousin of Túrin. Here too emerges the story that Huor was slain in the Battle of Unnumbered Tears (see p.122), and that his wife Rían searched for his body on the battlefield, and died there. Tuor their son remained in Hithlum and was enslaved by 'the faithless men whom Morgoth drove into Hithlum after that battle' (p.122), but he escaped from them and took to a solitary life in the wilds.

A major difference in the early versions of the story, in respect of the wider history of the Elder Days, lies in what my father told of the discovery of the vale of Tumladen, hidden in the Encircling Mountains. In the *Sketch of the Mythology* (p.121) it is said that the people of Turgon escaping from the great battle (*Nirnaeth Arnoediad*, Unnumbered Tears) disappeared from the knowledge of Morgoth, because 'in a secret place in the hills their scouts climbing to the tops discovered a broad valley entirely encircled by the hills'. But in the days of the writing of the *Tale of the Fall of Gondolin* the story had been that there was a long age after the terrible battle before the destruction of Gondolin. It was said (p.58) that Tuor heard when he came there 'how unstaying labour through ages of years had not sufficed to its building and adornment whereat folk travailed yet'. The chronological difficulties led my father later to place the discovery of the site of Gondolin – by Turgon – and its building to a time many centuries *before* the Battle of Unnumbered Tears: Turgon led his people fleeing south down Sirion from the battlefield to the hidden city that he had founded a great age before. It was to a very ancient city that Tuor came.

A distinctive change in the story of the attack on Gondolin occurs, as I believe, in the *Sketch of the Mythology*. In the *Tale of The Fall of Gondolin* it was told that Morgoth had discovered Gondolin *before* Meglin was captured by Orcs (pp.63 ff.). He became very suspicious at the strange news that a Man had been seen 'wandering amid the dales of the waters of Sirion'; and to this end he gathered 'a mighty army of spies', of animals and birds and reptiles, who 'through the years untiring' brought back to him a mass of information. From the Encircling Mountains his spies had looked down on the plain of Tumladen; even the 'Way of Escape' had been revealed. When Eärendel was a year old tidings were brought to Gondolin of how the agents of Morgoth had 'encompassed the vale of Tumladen all around'; and Turgon strengthened the defences of the city. In *the Tale of The Fall of Gondolin* the *subsequent* treachery of Meglin lay in his describing in detail the plan of Gondolin and all the preparations for its defence (p.67); with Melko he 'devised a plan for the overthrow of Gondolin'.

But in the condensed account in the *Sketch* (p.124) it is said that when Meglin was captured by Orcs in the mountains 'he purchased his life when taken to Angband *by revealing Gondolin and its secrets*'. The words 'revealing Gondolin' seem to me to show clearly that the change had entered, and the later story was present: Morgoth did not know and could not discover where the Hidden Kingdom lay *until* the capture of Meglin by the Orcs. But there was yet another change to follow: see pp.292–3.

*

THE STORY TOLD IN THE
QUENTA NOLDORINWA

I come now to a major 'Silmarillion' text from which I took passages in *Beren and Lúthien*, and I repeat here a part of the explanatory note from that book.

After the *Sketch of the Mythology* this text, which I will refer to as 'the *Quenta*', was the only complete and finished version of 'The Silmarillion' that my father achieved: a typescript that he made in (as seems certain) 1930. No preliminary drafts or outlines, if there were any, survive; but it is plain that for a good part of its length he had the *Sketch* before him. It is longer than the *Sketch*, and the 'Silmarillion style' has clearly appeared, but it remains a compression, a compendious account.

In calling this text a compression I do not mean to suggest that it was a hasty piece of work, awaiting a more finished treatment at some later time. Comparison of the two versions Q I and Q II (explained below) shows how attentively he heard and weighed the rhythm of the phrases. But compression there was indeed: witness the twenty or so lines devoted to the battle in the *Quenta* compared with the twelve pages in the *Tale*.

Towards the end of the *Quenta* my father expanded and retyped portions of the text (while preserving the discarded pages); the text as it stood before this rewriting I will call 'Q I'. Near the end of the narrative Q I gives out, and only the rewritten version ('Q II') continues to the end. It seems clear from this that the rewriting (which concerns Gondolin and its destruction) belongs to the same time, and I have given the Q II text throughout, from the point where the tale of Gondolin begins. The name of the King of Eagles, *Thorndor*, was changed throughout the text to *Thorondor*.

It will be seen that in the *Quenta* manuscript as written the story told in the *Sketch* (see p.121) was still present: the vale of Gondolin was discovered by scouts of Turgon's people fleeing from the Battle of Unnumbered Tears. At some later but unidentifiable time, my father rewrote all the relevant passages, and I have shown these revisions in the text that follows here.

Here must be told of Gondolin. The great river Sirion, mightiest in Elvish song, flowed through all the land of Beleriand and its course was south-west; and at its mouth was a great delta and its lower course ran through green and fertile lands, little peopled save by birds and beasts. Yet the

Orcs came seldom there, for it was far from the northern woods and fells, and the power of Ulmo waxed ever in that water, as it drew nigh to the sea; for the mouths of that river were in the western sea, whose uttermost borders are the shores of Valinor.

Turgon, Fingolfin's son, had a sister, Isfin the white-handed. She was lost in Taur-na-Fuin after the Battle of Unnumbered Tears. There she was captured by the Dark-elf Eöl, and it is said that he was of gloomy mood, and had deserted the hosts ere the battle; yet he had not fought on Morgoth's side. But Isfin he took to wife, and their son was Meglin.

Now the people of Turgon escaping from the battle, aided by the prowess of Húrin, as has been told, escaped from the knowledge of Morgoth and vanished from all men's eyes; and Ulmo alone knew whither they had gone. [Their scouts climbing the heights had come upon a secret place in the mountains: a broad valley >] For they returned to the hidden city of Gondolin that Turgon had built. In a secret place in the mountains there was a broad valley entirely circled by the hills, ringed about in a fence unbroken, but falling ever lower as they came towards the middle. In the midmost of this marvellous ring was a wide land and a green plain, wherein was no hill, save for a single rocky height. This stood up dark upon the plain, not right at its centre, but nearest to that part of the outer wall that marched close to the borders of Sirion. Highest were the Encircling Mountains towards the North and the threat of Angband, and on their outer slopes to East and North began the shadow of dread Taur-na-Fuin; but they were crowned with the cairn of Fingolfin, and no evil came that way, as yet.

In this valley [the Gnomes took refuge >] Turgon had taken refuge and spells of hiding and enchantment were set on all the hills about, that foes and spies might never find it. In this Turgon had the aid of the messages of Ulmo, that came now up the river Sirion; for his voice is to be heard in many waters, and some of the Gnomes had yet the lore to harken. In those days Ulmo was filled with pity for the exiled Elves in their need, and in the ruin that had now almost overwhelmed them. He foretold that the fortress of Gondolin should stand longest of all the refuges of the Elves against the might of Morgoth, and like Doriath never be overthrown save by treachery from within. Because of his protecting might the spells of concealment were strongest in those parts nearest to Sirion, though there the Encircling Mountains were at their lowest. In that region the Gnomes dug a great winding tunnel under the roots of the hills, and its issue was in the steep side, tree-clad and dark, of a gorge through which the blissful river ran. There he was still a young stream, but strong, flowing down the narrow vale that lies between the shoulders of the Encircling Mountains and the Mountains of Shadow, Eryd-Lómin [> Eredweth-ion], the walls of Hithlum [*struck out*: in whose northern heights he took his rise].

That passage they made at first to be a way of return for fugitives and for such as escaped from the bondage of Morgoth; and most as an issue for their scouts and messengers. For Turgon deemed, when first they came into that vale after the dreadful battle,* that Morgoth Bauglir had grown too mighty for Elves and Men, and that it were better to seek the forgiveness and aid of the Valar, if either might be got, ere all was lost. Wherefore some of his folk went down the river Sirion at whiles, ere the shadow of Morgoth yet stretched into the uttermost parts of Beleriand, and a small and secret haven they made at his mouth; thence ever and anon ships would set forth into the West bearing the embassy of the Gnomish king. Some there were that came back driven by contrary winds; but the most never returned again, and none reached Valinor.

The issue of that Way of Escape was guarded and concealed by the mightiest spells they could contrive, and by the power that dwelt in Sirion beloved of Ulmo, and no thing of evil found it; yet its inner gate, which looked upon the vale of Gondolin, was watched unceasingly by the Gnomes.

In those days Thorondor King of Eagles removed his eyries from Thangorodrim, because of the power of Morgoth, and the stench and fumes, and the evil of the dark clouds that lay now ever upon the mountain-towers above his cavernous halls. But Thorondor dwelt upon the northward heights of the Encircling Mountains, and he kept watch and saw many things, sitting upon the cairn of King Fingolfin. And in the vale below dwelt Turgon Fingolfin's son. Upon Amon Gwareth, the Hill of Defence, the rocky height amidst the plain, was built Gondolin the great, whose fame

---

* This sentence marked with an X for rejection, but without replacement.

and glory is mightiest in song of all dwellings of the Elves in these Outer Lands. Of steel were its gates and of marble were its walls. The sides of the hill the Gnomes polished to the smoothness of dark glass, and its top they levelled for the building of their town, save amidmost where stood the tower and palace of the king. Many fountains there were in that city, and white waters fell shimmering down the glistening sides of Amon Gwareth. The plain all about they smoothed till it became as a lawn of shaven grass from the stairways before the gates unto the feet of the mountain wall, and nought might walk or creep across unseen.

In that city the folk waxed mighty, and their armouries were filled with weapons and with shields; for they purposed at first to come forth to war, when the hour was ripe. But as the years drew on, they grew to love that place, the work of their hands, as the Gnomes do, with a great love, and desired no better. Then seldom went any forth from Gondolin on errand of war or peace again. They sent no messengers more into the West, and Sirion's haven was desolate. They shut them behind their impenetrable and enchanted hills, and suffered none to enter, though he fled from Morgoth hate-pursued; tidings of the lands without came to them faint and far, and they heeded them little; and their dwelling became as a rumour, and a secret no man could find. They succoured not Nargothrond nor Doriath, and the wandering Elves sought them in vain; and Ulmo alone knew where the realm of Turgon could be found. Tidings Turgon heard of Thorondor concerning the slaying of Dior, Thingol's heir, and thereafter he shut his ear to word of the woes without;

and he vowed to march never at the side of any son of Fëanor; and his folk he forbade ever to pass the leaguer of the hills.

Gondolin now alone remained of all the strongholds of the Elves. Morgoth forgot not Turgon, and knew that without knowledge of that king his triumph could not be achieved; yet his search unceasing was in vain. Nargothrond was void, Doriath desolate, the sons of Fëanor driven away to a wild woodland life in the South and East, Hithlum was filled with evil men, and Taur-na-Fuin was a place of nameless dread: the race of Hador was at an end, and the house of Finrod; Beren came no more to war, and Huan was slain; and all Elves and Men bowed to his will, or laboured as slaves in the mines and smithies of Angband, save only the wild and wandering, and few there were of these save far in the East of once fair Beleriand. His triumph was near complete, and yet was not quite full.

On a time Eöl was lost in Taur-na-Fuin, and Isfin came through great peril and dread unto Gondolin, and after her coming none entered until the last messenger of Ulmo, of whom the tales speak more ere the end. With her came her son Meglin, and he was there received by Turgon as his sister-son, and though he was half of Dark-elven blood he was treated as a prince of Fingolfin's line. He was swart but comely, wise and eloquent, and cunning to win men's hearts and minds.

Now Húrin of Hithlum had a brother Huor. The son of Huor was Tuor. Rían Huor's wife sought her husband among the slain upon the field of Unnumbered Tears, and there bewailed him, ere she died. Her son was but a child, and remaining in Hithlum fell into the hands of the faithless Men whom Morgoth drove into that land after the battle; and he became a thrall. Growing of age, and he was fair of face and great of stature, and despite his grievous life valiant and wise, he escaped into the woods, and he became an outlaw and a solitary, living alone and communing with none save rarely wandering and hidden Elves.*

On a time Ulmo contrived, as is told in the *Tale of the Fall of Gondolin*, that he should be led to a river-course that flowed underground from Lake Mithrim in the midst of Hithlum into a great chasm, Cris-Ilfing [> Kirith Helvin] the Rainbow-cleft, through which a turbulent water ran at last into the western sea. And the name of this chasm was so devised by reason of the rainbow that shimmered ever in the sun in that place, because of the abundance of the spray of the rapids and the waterfalls.

In this way the flight of Tuor was marked by no Man nor Elf, neither was it known to the Orcs or any spy of Morgoth, with whom the land of Hithlum was filled.

Tuor wandered long by the western shores, journeying ever South; and he came at last to the mouths of Sirion, and

---

* The text here is somewhat confused by hasty changes. In this rewriting it is told that Rían 'went forth into the wild', where Tuor was born; and that 'he was fostered by the Dark-elves; but Rían laid herself down and died upon the Hill of Slain. But Tuor grew up in the woods of Hithlum, and he was fair of face and great of stature . . .' There is thus in the rewriting no mention of an enslavement of Tuor.

the sandy deltas peopled by many birds of the sea. There he fell in with a Gnome, Bronwë, who had escaped from Angband, and being of old of the people of Turgon, sought ever to find the path to the hidden places of his lord, of which rumour ran among all captives and fugitives. Now Bronwë had come thither by far and wandering paths to the East, and little though any step back nigher to the thraldom from which he had come was to his liking, he purposed now to go up Sirion and seek for Turgon in Beleriand. Fearful and very wary was he, and he aided Tuor in their secret march, by night and twilight, so that they were not discovered by the Orcs.

They came first into the fair Land of Willows, Nantathrin which is watered by the Narog and by Sirion; and there all things were yet green, and the meads were rich and full of flowers, and there was song of many birds; so that Tuor lingered there as one enchanted, and it seemed sweet to him to dwell there after the grim lands of the North and his weary wandering.

There Ulmo came and appeared before him, as he stood in the long grass at evening; and the might and majesty of that vision is told of in the song of Tuor that he made for his son Eärendel. Thereafter the sound of the sea and the longing for the sea was ever in Tuor's heart and ear; and an unquiet was on him at whiles that took him at last into the depths of the realm of Ulmo. But now Ulmo bade him make all speed to Gondolin, and gave him guidance for the finding of the hidden door; and a message he gave him to bear from Ulmo, friend of Elves, unto Turgon, bidding him to prepare for war, and battle with Morgoth ere all was lost; and to send again his messengers into the West. Summons too should he send into the East and gather, if he might, Men (who were now multiplying and spreading on the earth) unto his banners; and for that task Tuor was most fit. 'Forget,' counselled Ulmo, 'the treachery of Uldor the accursed, and remember Húrin; for without mortal Men the Elves shall not prevail against the Balrogs and the Orcs.' Nor should the feud with the sons of Fëanor be left unhealed; for this should be the last gathering of the hope of the Gnomes, when every sword should count. A terrible and mortal strife he foretold, but victory if Turgon would dare it, the breaking of Morgoth's power, and the healing of feuds, and friendship between Men and Elves, whereof the greatest good should come into the world, and the servants of Morgoth trouble it no more. But if Turgon would not go forth to this war, then he should abandon Gondolin and lead his people down Sirion, and build there his fleets and seek back to Valinor and the mercy of the Gods. But in this counsel there was danger more dire than in the other, though so it might not seem; and grievous thereafter would be the fate of the Hither Lands.

This errand Ulmo performed out of his love of the Elves, and because he knew that ere many years were passed the doom of Gondolin would come, if its people sat still behind its walls; not thus should anything of joy or beauty in the world be preserved from Morgoth's malice.

Obedient to Ulmo Tuor and Bronwë journeyed North, and came at last to the hidden door; and passing down the tunnel reached the inner gate, and were taken by the guard as prisoners. There they saw the fair vale of Tumladen set like a green jewel amid the hills; and amidst Tumladen Gondolin the great, the city of seven names, white, shining from afar, flushed with the rose of dawn upon the plain. Thither they were led and passed the gates of steel, and were brought before the steps of the palace of the king. There Tuor spoke the embassy of Ulmo, and something of the power and majesty of the Lord of Waters his voice had caught, so that all folk looked in wonder on him, and doubted that this were a Man of mortal race as he declared. But proud was Turgon become, and Gondolin as beautiful as a memory of Tûn, and he trusted in its secret and impregnable strength; so that he and the most part of his folk wished not to imperil it nor leave it, and they desired not to mingle in the woes of Elves and Men without; nor did they any longer desire to return through dread and danger to the West.

Meglin spoke ever against Tuor in the councils of the king, and his words seemed the more weighty in that they went with Turgon's heart. Wherefore Turgon rejected the bidding of Ulmo; though some there were of his wisest counsellors who were filled with disquiet. Wise-hearted even beyond the measure of the daughters of Elfinesse was the daughter of the king, and she spoke ever for Tuor, though it did not avail, and her heart was heavy. Very fair and tall was she, well nigh of warrior's stature, and her hair was a fountain of gold. Idril was she named, and called Celebrindal, Silver-foot, for the whiteness of her foot; and she walked and danced ever unshod in the white ways and green lawns of Gondolin.

Thereafter Tuor sojourned in Gondolin, and went not to summon the Men of the East, for the blissfulness of Gondolin, the beauty and wisdom of its folk, held him enthralled. And he grew high in the favour of Turgon; for he became a mighty man in stature and in mind, learning deeply of the lore of the Gnomes. The heart of Idril was turned to him, and his to her; at which Meglin ground his teeth, for he desired Idril, and despite his close kinship purposed to possess her; and she was the only heir of the king of Gondolin. Indeed in his heart he was already planning how he might oust Turgon and seize his throne; but Turgon loved and trusted him. Nonetheless Tuor took Idril to wife; and the folk of Gondolin made merry feast, for Tuor had won their hearts, all save Meglin and his secret following. Tuor and Beren alone of mortal Men had Elves to wife, and since Elwing daughter of Dior son of Beren after wedded Eärendel son of Tuor and Idril of Gondolin, of them alone has come the elven blood into mortal race. But as yet Eärendel was a little child: surpassing fair was he, a light was in his face as the light of heaven, and he had the beauty and the wisdom of Elfinesse and the strength and hardihood of the Men of old; and the sea spoke ever in his ear and heart, even as with Tuor his father.

On a time when Eärendel was yet young, and the days of Gondolin were full of joy and peace (and yet Idril's heart misgave her, and foreboding crept upon her spirit like a cloud), Meglin was lost. Now Meglin loved mining and quarrying after metals above other craft; and he was master and leader of the Gnomes who worked in the mountains distant from the city, seeking for metals for their smithying of things both of peace and war. But often Meglin went with few of his folk beyond the leaguer of the hills, though the king knew not that his bidding was defied; and so it came to pass, as fate willed, that Meglin was taken prisoner by the Orcs and taken before Morgoth. Meglin was no weakling or craven, but the torment wherewith he was threatened cowed his soul, and he purchased his life and freedom by revealing unto Morgoth the place of Gondolin and the ways whereby it might be found and assailed. Great indeed was the joy of Morgoth; and to Meglin he promised the lordship of Gondolin, as his vassal, and the possession of Idril, when that city should be taken. Lust for Idril and hatred of Tuor led Meglin the easier to his foul treachery. But Morgoth sent him back to Gondolin, lest men should suspect the betrayal, and so that Meglin should aid the assault from within when the hour came; and Meglin abode in the halls of the king with a smile on his face and evil in his heart, while the gloom gathered ever deeper upon Idril.

At last, and Eärendel was then seven years of age, Morgoth was ready, and he loosed upon Gondolin his Orcs and his Balrogs and his serpents; and of these, dragons of many and dire shapes were new devised for the taking of the city. The host of Morgoth came over the Northern hills where the height was greatest and the watch less vigilant, and it came at night at a time of festival, when all the folk of Gondolin were upon the walls to wait upon the rising sun and sing their songs at its uplifting, for the morrow was the feast which they named the Gates of Summer. But the red light mounted the hills in the North and not in the East; and there was no stay in the advance of the foe until they were beneath the very walls of Gondolin, and Gondolin was beleaguered without hope.

Of the deeds of desperate valour there done, by the chieftains of the noble houses and their warriors, and not least by Tuor, is much told in *The Fall of Gondolin*; of the death of Rog without the walls; and of the battle of Ecthelion of the Fountain with Gothmog lord of Balrogs in the very square of the king, where each slew the other; and of the defence of the tower of Turgon by the men of his household, until the tower was overthrown; and mighty was its fall and the fall of Turgon in its ruin.

Tuor sought to rescue Idril from the sack of the city, but Meglin had laid hands upon her and Eärendel; and Tuor fought on the walls with him, and cast him down to death. Then Tuor and Idril led such remnants of the folk of Gondolin as they could gather in the confusion of the burning, down a secret way that Idril had let prepare in the days of her foreboding. This was not yet complete, but its issue was already far beyond the walls and in the North of the plain where the mountains were long distant from Amon Gwareth. Those who would not come with them, but fled to the old Way of Escape that led into the gorge of Sirion, were caught and destroyed by a dragon that Morgoth had sent to watch that gate, being apprised of it by Meglin. But of the new passage Meglin had not heard, and it was not thought that fugitives would take a path towards the North and the highest parts of the mountains and the nighest to Angband.

The fume of the burning, and the steam of the fair

fountains of Gondolin withering in the flame of the dragons of the North, fell upon the vale in mournful mists, and thus was the escape of Tuor and his company aided, for there was still a long and open road to follow from the tunnel's mouth to the foothills of the mountains. They came nonetheless into the mountains, in woe and misery, for the high places were cold and terrible, and they had among them many women and children and many wounded men.

There is a dreadful pass, Cristhorn [> Kirith-thoronath] was it named, the Eagle's Cleft, where beneath the shadow of the highest peaks a narrow path winds its way, walled by a precipice to the right and on the left a dreadful fall leaps into emptiness. Along that narrow way their march was strung when it was ambushed by an outpost of Morgoth's power; and a Balrog was their leader. Then dreadful was their plight, and hardly would it have been saved by the deathless valour of yellow-haired Glorfindel, chief of the House of the Golden Flower of Gondolin, had not Thorondor come timely to their aid.

Songs have been sung of the duel of Glorfindel with the Balrog upon a pinnacle of rock in that high place; and both fell to ruin in the abyss. But Thorondor bore up Glorfindel's body and he was buried in a mound of stones beside the pass, and there came after a turf of green and small flowers like yellow stars bloomed there amid the barrenness of stone. And the birds of Thorondor stooped upon the Orcs and drove them shrieking back; and all were slain or cast into the deeps, and rumour of the escape from Gondolin came not until long after to Morgoth's ears.

Thus by weary and dangerous marches the remnant of Gondolin came unto Nan-tathrin and there rested a while, and were healed of their hurts and weariness, but their sorrow could not be cured. There they made feast in memory of Gondolin and those that had perished, fair maidens, wives, and warriors and their king; but for Glorfindel the well-beloved many and sweet were the songs they sang. And there Tuor spoke in song to Eärendel his son of the coming of Ulmo aforetime, the sea-vision in the midst of the land, and the sea-longing awoke in his heart and in his son's. Wherefore they removed with the most part of the people to the mouths of Sirion by the sea, and there they dwelt, and joined their folk to the slender company of Elwing daughter of Dior, that had fled thither little while before.

Then Morgoth thought in his heart that his triumph was fulfilled, recking little of the sons of Fëanor, and of their oath, which had harmed him never and turned always to his mightiest aid. And in his black thought he laughed, regretting not the one Silmaril he had lost, for by it he deemed the last shreds of the Elvish race should vanish yet from the earth and trouble it no more. If he knew of the dwelling by the waters of Sirion he made no sign, biding his time, and waiting upon the working of oath and lie.

Yet by Sirion and the sea there grew up an elven folk, the gleanings of Gondolin and Doriath, and they took to the waves and to the making of fair ships, dwelling ever nigh unto the shores and under the shadow of Ulmo's hand.

We are now at the same place in the story of Gondolin in the *Quenta Noldorinwa* as that reached in the *Sketch of the Mythology* on p.125. Here I will leave the *Quenta* and turn to the last major text of the story of Gondolin, which is also the last account of the foundation of Gondolin and of how Tuor came to enter the city.

THE LAST VERSION

Many years passed between the story of Gondolin as told in the *Quenta Noldorinwa* and this text, entitled *Of Tuor and the Fall of Gondolin*. It is certain that it was written in 1951 (see *The Evolution of the Story* p.207).

Rían, wife of Huor, dwelt with the people of the house of Hador; but when rumour came to Dor-lómin of the Nirnaeth Arnoediad [the Battle of Unnumbered Tears], and yet she could hear no news of her lord, she became distraught and wandered forth into the wild alone. There she would have perished, but the Grey-elves came to her aid. For there was a dwelling of this people in the mountains westward of Lake Mithrim; and thither they led her, and she was there delivered of a son before the end of the Year of Lamentation.

And Rían said to the Elves: 'Let him be called *Tuor*, for that name his father chose, ere war came between us. And I beg of you to foster him, and to keep him hidden in your care; for I forebode that great good, for Elves and Men, shall come from him. But I must go in search of Huor, my lord.'

Then the Elves pitied her; but one Annael, who alone of all that went to war from that people had returned from the Nirnaeth, said to her: 'Alas, lady, it is known now that Huor fell at the side of Húrin his brother; and he lies, I deem, in the great hill of slain that the Orcs have raised upon the field of battle.'

Therefore Rían arose and left the dwelling of the Elves, and she passed through the land of Mithrim and came at last to the Haudh-en-Ndengin in the waste of Anfauglith, and there she laid her down and died. But the Elves cared for the infant son of Huor, and Tuor grew up among them; and he was fair of face, and golden-haired after the manner of his father's kin, and he became strong and tall and valiant, and being fostered by the Elves he had lore and skill no less than the princes of the Edain, ere ruin came upon the North.

But with the passing of the years the life of the former folk of Hithlum, such as still remained, Elves or Men, became ever harder and more perilous. For as is elsewhere told, Morgoth broke his pledges to the Easterlings that had served him, and he denied to them the rich lands of Beleriand which they had coveted, and he drove away these evil folk into Hithlum, and there commanded them to dwell. And though they loved Morgoth no longer, they served him still in fear, and hated all the Elven-folk; and they despised the remnant of the House of Hador (the aged and women and children, for the most part), and they oppressed them, and wedded their women by force, and took their lands and goods, and enslaved their children. Orcs came and went about the land as they would, pursuing the lingering Elves into the fastnesses of the mountains, and taking many captive to the mines of Angband to labour as the thralls of Morgoth.

Therefore Annael led his small people to the caves of Androth, and there they lived a hard and wary life, until Tuor was sixteen years of age and was become strong and able to wield arms, the axe and bow of the Grey-elves; and his heart grew hot within him at the tale of the griefs of his people, and he wished to go forth and avenge them on the Orcs and Easterlings. But Annael forbade this.

'Far hence, I deem, your doom lies, Tuor son of Huor,' he said. 'And this land shall not be freed from the shadow of Morgoth until Thangorodrim itself be overthrown. There-fore we are resolved at last to forsake it, and to depart into the South; and with us you shall go.'

'But how shall we escape the net of our enemies?' said Tuor. 'For the marching of so many together will surely be marked.'

'We shall not march through the land openly,' said Annael; 'and if our fortune is good we shall come to the secret way which we call Annon-in-Gelydh, the Gate of the Noldor; for it was made by the skill of that people, long ago in the days of Turgon.'

At that name Tuor was stirred, though he knew not why; and he questioned Annael concerning Turgon. 'He is a son of Fingolfin,' said Annael, 'and is now accounted High King of the Noldor, since the fall of Fingon. For he lives yet, most feared of the foes of Morgoth, and he escaped from the ruin of the Nirnaeth, when Húrin of Dor-lómin and Huor your father held the passes of Sirion behind him.'

'Then I will go and seek Turgon,' said Tuor; 'for surely he will lend me aid for my father's sake?'

'That you cannot,' said Annael. 'For his stronghold is hidden from the eyes of Elves and Men, and we know not where it stands. Of the Noldor some, maybe, know the way thither, but they will speak of it to none. Yet if you would have speech with them, then come with me, as I bid you; for in the far havens of the South you may meet with wanderers from the Hidden Kingdom.'

Thus it came to pass that the Elves forsook the caves of Androth, and Tuor went with them. But their enemies kept watch upon their dwellings, and were soon aware of their march; and they had not gone far from the hills into the plain before they were assailed by a great force of Orcs and Easterlings, and they were scattered far and wide, fleeing into the gathering night. But Tuor's heart was kindled with the fire of battle, and he would not flee, but boy as he was he wielded the axe as his father before him, and for long he stood his ground and slew many that assailed him; but at the last he was overwhelmed and taken captive and led before Lorgan the Easterling. Now this Lorgan was held the chief of the Easterlings and claimed to rule all Dor-lómin as a fief under Morgoth; and he took Tuor to be his slave. Hard and bitter then was his life; for it pleased Lorgan to treat Tuor the more evilly as he was of the kin of the former lords, and he sought to break, if he could, the pride of the house of Hador. But Tuor saw wisdom, and endured all pains and taunts with watchful patience; so that in time his lot was somewhat lightened, and at the least he was not starved, as were many of Lorgan's unhappy thralls. For he was strong and skilful, and Lorgan fed his beasts of burden well, while they were young and could work.

But after three years of thraldom Tuor saw at last a chance of escape. He was come now almost to his full stature, taller and swifter than any of the Easterlings; and being sent with other thralls on an errand of labour into the woods he turned suddenly on the guards and slew them with an axe, and fled into the hills. The Easterlings hunted him with dogs, but without avail; for wellnigh all the hounds of Lorgan were his friends, and if they came up with him they would fawn upon him, and then run homeward at his command. Thus he came back at last to the caves of Androth and dwelt there alone. And for four years he was an outlaw in the land of his fathers, grim and solitary; and his name was feared, for he went often abroad, and slew many of the Easterlings that he came upon. Then they set a great price upon his head; but they did not dare to come to his hiding-place, even with strength of men, for they feared the Elven-folk, and shunned the caves where they had dwelt. Yet it is said that Tuor's journeys were not made for the purpose of vengeance; rather he sought ever for the Gate of the Noldor, of which Annael had spoken. But he found it not, for he knew not where to look, and such few of the Elves as lingered in the mountains had not heard of it.

Now Tuor knew that, though fortune still favoured him, yet in the end the days of an outlaw are numbered, and are ever few and without hope. Nor was he willing to live thus for ever a wild man in the houseless hills, and his heart urged him ever to great deeds. Herein, it is said, the power of Ulmo was shown. For he gathered tidings of all that passed in Beleriand, and every stream that flowed from Middle-earth to the Great Sea was to him a messenger, both to and fro; and he remained also in friendship, as of old, with Círdan and the Shipwrights at the Mouths of Sirion. And at this time most of all Ulmo gave heed to the fates of the House of Hador, for in his deep counsels he purposed that they should play great part in his designs for the succour of the Exiles; and he knew well of the plight of Tuor, for Annael and many of his folk had indeed escaped from Dor-lómin and come at last to Círdan in the far South.*

Thus it came to pass that on a day in the beginning of the year (twenty and three since the Nirnaeth) Tuor sat by a spring that trickled forth near to the door of the cave where he dwelt; and he looked out westward towards the cloudy sunset. Then suddenly it came into his heart that he would wait no longer, but would arise and go. 'I will leave now the grey land of my kin that are no more,' he cried, 'and I will go in search of my doom! But whither shall I turn? Long have I sought the Gate and found it not.'

---

* This is Círdan the Shipwright who appears in *The Lord of the Rings* as the lord of the Grey Havens at the end of the Third Age.

Then he took up the harp which he bore ever with him, being skilled in playing upon its strings, and heedless of the peril of his clear voice alone in the waste he sang an elven song of the North for the uplifting of hearts. And even as he sang the well at his feet began to boil with great increase of water, and it overflowed, and a rill ran noisily down the rocky hillside before him. And Tuor took this as a sign, and he arose at once and followed after it. Thus he came down from the tall hills of Mithrim and passed out into the northward plain of Dor-lómin; and ever the stream grew as he followed it westward, until after three days he could descry in the west the long grey ridges of Ered Lómin that in those regions marched north and south, fencing off the far coastlands of the Western Shores. To those hills in all his journeys Tuor had never come.

Now the land became more broken and stony again, as it approached the hills, and soon it began to rise before Tuor's feet, and the stream went down into a cloven bed. But even as dim dusk came on the third day of his journey, Tuor found before him a wall of rock, and there was an opening therein like a great arch; and the stream passed in and was lost. Then Tuor was dismayed, and he said: 'So my hope has cheated me! The sign in the hills has led me only to a dark end in the midst of the land of my enemies.' And grey at heart he sat among the rocks on the high bank of the stream, keeping watch through a bitter fireless night; for it was yet but the month of Súlimë, and no stir of spring had come to that far northern land, and a shrill wind blew from the East.

But even as the light of the coming sun shone pale in the far mists of Mithrim, Tuor heard voices, and looking down he saw in amazement two Elves that waded in the shallow water; and as they climbed up steps hewn in the bank, Tuor stood up and called to them. At once they drew their bright swords and sprang towards him. Then he saw that they were grey-cloaked but mail-clad under; and he marvelled, for they were fairer and more fell to look upon, because of the light of their eyes, than any of the Elven-folk that he yet had known. He stood to his full height and awaited them; but when they saw that he drew no weapon, but stood alone and greeted them in the Elven-tongue, they sheathed their swords and spoke courteously to him. And one said: 'Gelmir and Arminas we are, of Finarfin's people. Are you not one of the Edain of old that dwelt in these lands ere the Nirnaeth? And indeed of the kindred of Hador and Húrin I deem you; for so the gold of your head declares you.'

And Tuor answered: 'Yea, I am Tuor, son of Huor, son of Galdor, son of Hador; but now at last I desire to leave this land where I am outlawed and kinless.'

'Then,' said Gelmir, 'if you would escape and find the havens in the South, already your feet have been guided on the right road.'

'So I thought,' said Tuor. 'For I followed a sudden spring of water in the hills, until it joined this treacherous stream. But now I know not whither to turn, for it has gone into darkness.'

'Through darkness one may come to the light,' said Gelmir.

'Yet one will walk under the Sun while one may,' said Tuor. 'But since you are of that people, tell me if you can where lies the Gate of the Noldor. For I have sought it long, ever since Annael my foster-father of the Grey-elves spoke of it to me.'

Then the Elves laughed, and said: 'Your search is ended; for we have ourselves just passed that Gate. There it stands before you!' And they pointed to the arch into which the water flowed. 'Come now! Through darkness you shall come to the light. We will set your feet on the road, but we cannot guide you far; for we are sent back to the lands whence we fled upon an urgent errand.' 'But fear not,' said Gelmir: 'a great doom is written upon your brow, and it shall lead you far from these lands, far indeed from Middle-earth, as I guess.'

Then Tuor followed the Noldor down the steps and waded in the cold water, until they passed into the shadow beyond the arch of stone. And then Gelmir brought forth one of those lamps for which the Noldor were renowned; for they were made of old in Valinor, and neither wind nor water could quench them, and when they were unhooded they sent forth a clear blue light from a flame imprisoned in white crystal. Now by the light that Gelmir held above his head Tuor saw that the river began to go suddenly down a smooth slope into a great tunnel, but beside its rock-hewn course there ran long flights of steps leading on and downward into a deep gloom beyond the beam of the lamp.

When they had come to the foot of the rapids they stood under a great dome of rock, and there the river rushed over a steep fall with a great noise that echoed in the vault, and it passed then on again under another arch into a further tunnel. Beside the falls the Noldor halted, and bade Tuor farewell.

'Now we must return and go our ways with all speed,' said Gelmir; 'for matters of great peril are moving in Beleriand.'

'Is then the hour come when Turgon shall come forth?' said Tuor.

Then the Elves looked at him in amazement. 'That is a matter which concerns the Noldor rather than the sons of Men,' said Arminas. 'What know you of Turgon?'

'Little,' said Tuor; 'save that my father aided his escape from the Nirnaeth, and that in his stronghold dwells the hope of the Noldor. Yet, though I know not why, ever his name stirs in my heart, and comes to my lips. And had I my will, I would go in search of him, rather than tread this dark way of dread. Unless, perhaps, this secret road is the way to his dwelling?'

'Who shall say?' answered the Elf. 'For since the dwelling of Turgon is hidden, so also are the ways thither. I know them not, though I have sought them long. Yet if I knew them, I would not reveal them to you, nor to any among Men.'

But Gelmir said: 'I have heard that your House has the favour of the Lord of Waters. And if his counsels lead you to Turgon, then surely shall you come to him, whithersoever you turn. Follow now the road to which the water has brought you from the hills, and fear not! You shall not walk long in darkness. Farewell! And think not that our meeting was by chance; for the Dweller in the Deep moves many things in this land still. *Anar kaluva tielyanna!* [The sun will shine upon your path!]'

With that the Noldor turned and went back up the long stairs; but Tuor stood still, until the light of their lamp was lost, and he was alone in a darkness deeper than night amid the roaring of the falls. Then summoning his courage he set his left hand to the rock-wall, and felt his way forward, slowly at first, and then more quickly, as he became more used to the darkness and found nothing to hinder him. And after a great while, as it seemed to him, when he was weary and yet unwilling to rest in the black tunnel, he saw far before him a light; and hastening on he came to a tall and narrow cleft, and followed the noisy stream between its leaning walls out into a golden evening. For he was come into a deep ravine with tall sheer sides, and it ran straight towards the West; and before him the setting sun, going down through a clear sky, shone into the ravine and kindled its walls with yellow fire, and the waters of the river glittered like gold as they broke and foamed upon many gleaming stones.

In that deep place Tuor went on now in great hope and delight, finding a path beneath the southern wall, where there lay a long and narrow strand. And when night came, and the river rushed on unseen, save for a glint of high stars mirrored in dark pools, then he rested, and slept; for he felt no fear beside that water, in which the power of Ulmo ran.

With the coming of day he went on again without haste. The sun rose behind his back and set before his face, and where the water foamed among the boulders or rushed over sudden falls, at morning and evening rainbows were woven across the stream. Wherefore he named that stream Cirith Ninniach [Rainbow Cleft].

Thus Tuor journeyed slowly for three days, drinking the cold water but desiring no food, though there were many fish that shone as gold or silver, or gleamed with colours like to the rainbows in the spray above. And on the fourth day the channel grew wider, and its walls lower and less sheer; but the river ran deeper and more strongly, for high hills now marched on either side, and fresh waters spilled from them into Cirith Ninniach over shimmering falls. There long while Tuor sat, watching the swirling of the stream and listening to its endless voice, until night came again and stars shone cold and white in the dark lane of sky above him. Then he lifted up his voice, and plucked the strings of his harp, and above the noise of the water the sound of his song and the sweet thrilling of the harp were echoed in the stone and multiplied, and went forth and rang in the night-clad hills, until all the empty land was filled with music beneath the stars. For though he knew it not, Tuor was now come to the Echoing Mountains of Lammoth about the Firth of Drengist. There once long ago Fëanor had landed from the sea, and the voices of his host were swelled to a mighty clamour upon the coasts of the North ere the rising of the Moon.

Then Tuor was filled with wonder and stayed his song, and slowly the music died in the hills, and there was silence. And then amid the silence he heard in the air above him a strange cry; and he knew not of what creature that cry came. Now he said: 'It is a fay-voice', now: 'Nay, it is a small beast that is wailing in the waste'; and then, hearing it again, he said: 'Surely, it is the cry of some nightfaring bird that I know not.' And it seemed to him a mournful sound, and yet he desired nonetheless to hear it and follow it, for it called him, he knew not whither.

The next morning he heard the same voice above his head, and looking up he saw three great white birds beating down the ravine against the westerly wind, and their strong wings shone in the new-risen sun, and as they passed over him they wailed aloud. Thus for the first time he beheld the great gulls, beloved of the Teleri. Then Tuor arose to follow them, and so that he might better mark whither they flew he climbed the cliff upon his left hand, and stood upon the top, and felt a great wind out of the West rush against his face; and his hair streamed from his head. And he drank deep of that new air, and said: 'This uplifts the heart like the drinking of cool wine!' But he knew not that the wind came fresh from the Great Sea.

Now Tuor went on once more, seeking the gulls, high above the river; and as he went the sides of the ravine drew together again, and he came to a narrow channel, and it was filled with a great noise of water. And looking down Tuor saw a great marvel, as it seemed to him; for a wild flood came up the narrows and strove with the river that would still press on, and a wave like a wall rose up almost to the cliff-top, crowned with foam-crests flying in the wind. Then the river was thrust back, and the incoming flood swept roaring up the channel, drowning it in deep water, and the rolling of the boulders was like thunder as it passed. Thus Tuor was saved by the call of the sea-birds from death in the rising tide; and that was very great because of the season of the year and of the high wind from the sea.

But now Tuor was dismayed by the fury of the strange waters, and he turned aside and went away southward, and so came not to the long shores of the Firth of Drengist, but wandered still for some days in a rugged country bare of trees; and it was swept by a wind from the sea, and all that grew there, herb or bush, leaned ever to the dawn because of the prevalence of that wind from the West. In this way Tuor passed into the borders of Nevrast, where once Turgon had dwelt; and at last at unawares (for the cliff-tops at the margin of the land were higher than the slopes behind) he came suddenly to the black brink of Middle-earth, and saw the Great Sea, Belegaer the Shoreless. And at that hour the sun went down beyond the rim of the world, as a mighty fire; and Tuor stood alone upon the cliff with outspread arms, and a great yearning filled his heart. It is said that he was the first of Men to reach the Great Sea, and that none, save the Eldar, have ever felt more deeply the longing that it brings.

Tuor tarried many days in Nevrast, and it seemed good to him, for that land, being fenced by mountains from the North and East and nigh to the sea, was milder and more kindly than the plains of Hithlum. He was long used to dwell alone as a hunter in the wild, and he found no lack of food; for spring was busy in Nevrast, and the air was filled with the noise of birds, both those that dwelt in multitudes upon the shores, and those that teemed in the marshes of Linaewen in the midst of the hollow land, but in those days no voice of Elves or Men was heard in all the solitude.

To the borders of the great mere Tuor came, but its waters were beyond his reach, because of the wide mires and the pathless forests of reeds that lay all about; and soon he turned away, and went back to the coast, for the Sea drew him, and he was not willing to dwell long where he could not hear the sound of its waves. And in the shorelands Tuor first found traces of the Noldor of old. For among the tall and sea-hewn cliffs south of Drengist there were many coves and sheltered inlets, with beaches of white sand among the black gleaming rocks, and leading down to such places Tuor found often winding stairs cut in the living stone; and by the water-edge were ruined quays, built of great blocks hewn from the cliffs, where elven ships had once been moored. In those regions Tuor long remained, watching the ever-changing sea, while through spring and summer the slow year wore on, and darkness deepened in Beleriand, and the autumn of the doom of Nargothrond drew near.

And, maybe, birds saw from afar the fell winter that was to come; for those that were wont to go south gathered early to depart, and others that used to dwell in the North came from their homes to Nevrast. And one day, as Tuor sat upon the shore, he heard the rush and whine of great wings, and he looked up and saw seven white swans flying in a swift wedge southward. But as they came above him they wheeled and flew suddenly down, and alighted with a great plash and churning of water.

Now Tuor loved swans, which he knew on the grey pools of Mithrim; and the swan moreover had been the token of Annael and his foster-folk. He rose therefore to greet the birds, and called to them, marvelling to behold that they were greater and prouder than any of their kind that he had seen before; but they beat their wings and uttered harsh cries, as if they were wroth with him and would drive him from the shore. Then with a great noise they rose again from the water and flew above his head, so that the rush of their wings blew upon him as a whistling wind; and wheeling in a wide circle they ascended into the high air and went away south.

Then Tuor cried aloud: 'Here now comes another sign that I have tarried too long!' And straightway he climbed to the cliff-top, and there he beheld the swans still wheeling on high, but when he turned southward and set out to follow them, they flew swiftly away.

Now Tuor journeyed south along the coast for full seven days, and each morning he was aroused by the rush of wings above him in the dawn and each day the swans flew on as he followed after. And as he went the great cliffs became lower, and their tops were clothed deep with flowering turf; and away eastward there were woods turning yellow in the waning of the year. But before him, drawing ever nearer, he saw a line of great hills that barred his way, marching westward until they ended in a tall mountain: a dark and cloud-helmed tower reared upon mighty shoulders above a great green cape thrust out into the sea.

Those grey hills were indeed the western outliers of Ered Wethrin, the north fence of Beleriand, and the mountain was Mount Taras, westernmost of all the towers of that land, whose head a mariner would first descry across the miles of the sea, as he drew near to the mortal shores. Beneath its long slopes in bygone days Turgon had dwelt in the halls of Vinyamar, eldest of all the works of stone that the Noldor built in the lands of their exile. There it still stood, desolate but enduring, high upon great terraces that looked towards the sea. The years had not shaken it, and the servants of Morgoth had passed it by; but wind and rain and frost had graven it, and upon the coping of its walls and the great shingles of its roof there was a deep growth of grey-green plants that, living upon the salt air, throve even in the cracks of barren stone.

Now Tuor came to the ruins of a lost road, and he passed amid green mounds and leaning stones, and so came as the day was waning to the old hall and its high and windy courts. No shadow of fear or evil lurked there, but an awe fell upon him, thinking of those that had dwelt there and had gone, none knew whither: the proud people, deathless but doomed, from far beyond the Sea. And he turned and looked, as often their eyes had looked, out across the glitter of the unquiet waters to the end of sight. Then he turned back again, and saw that the swans had alighted on the highest terrace, and stood before the west-door of the hall; and they beat their wings, and it seemed to him that they beckoned him to enter. Then Tuor went up the wide stairs, now half-hidden in thrift and campion, and he passed under the mighty lintel and entered the shadows of the house of Turgon; and he came at last to a high-pillared hall. If great it had appeared from without, now vast and wonderful it seemed to Tuor from within, and for awe he wished not to awake the echoes in its emptiness. Nothing could he see there, save at the eastern end a high seat upon a dais, and softly as he might he paced towards it; but the sound of his feet rang upon the paved floor as the steps of doom, and echoes ran before him along the pillared aisles.

As he stood before the great chair in the gloom, and saw that it was hewn of a single stone and written with strange signs, the sinking sun drew level with a high window under the westward gable, and a shaft of light smote the wall before him, and glittered as it were upon burnished metal. Then Tuor marvelling saw that on the wall behind the throne there hung a shield and a great hauberk, and a helm and a long sword in a sheath. The hauberk shone as it were wrought of silver untarnished, and the sunbeam gilded it with sparks of gold. But the shield was of a shape strange to Tuor's eyes, for it was long and tapering; and its field was blue, in the midst of which was wrought an emblem of a white swan's wing. Then Tuor spoke, and his voice rang as a challenge in the roof: 'By this token I will take these arms unto myself, and upon myself whatsoever doom they bear.' And he lifted down the shield and found it light and wieldy beyond his guess; for it was wrought, it seemed, of wood, but overlaid by the craft of elven-smiths with plates of metal, strong yet thin as foil, whereby it had been preserved from worm and weather.

Then Tuor arrayed himself in the hauberk, and set the helm upon his head, and he girt himself with the sword; black were sheath and belt with clasps of silver. Thus armed he went forth from Turgon's hall, and stood upon the high terraces of Taras in the red light of the sun. None were there to see him, as he gazed westward, gleaming in silver and gold, and he knew not that in that hour he appeared as one of the Mighty of the West, and fit to be the father of the kings of the Kings of Men beyond the Sea, as it was indeed his doom to be; but in the taking of those arms a change came upon Tuor son of Huor, and his heart grew great within him. And, as he stepped down from the doors the swans did him reverence, and plucking each a great feather from their wings they proffered them to him, laying their long necks upon the stone before his feet; and he took the seven feathers and set them in the crest of his helm, and straightway the swans arose and flew north in the sunset, and Tuor saw them no more.

Now Tuor felt his feet drawn to the sea-strand, and he went down by long stairs to a wide shore upon the north side of Taras-ness; and as he went he saw that the sun was sinking low into a great black cloud that came up over the rim of the darkening sea; and it grew cold, and there was a stirring and murmur as of a storm to come. And Tuor stood upon the shore, and the sun was like a smoky fire behind the menace of the sky; and it seemed to him that a great wave rose far off and rolled towards the land, but wonder held him, and he remained there unmoved. And the wave came towards him, and upon it lay a mist of shadow. Then suddenly as it drew near it curled, and broke, and rushed forward in long arms of foam; but where it had broken there stood dark against the rising storm a living shape of great height and majesty.

Then Tuor bowed in reverence, for it seemed to him that he beheld a mighty king. A tall crown he wore like silver, from which his long hair fell down as foam glimmering in the dusk; and as he cast back the grey mantle that hung about him like a mist, behold! he was clad in a gleaming coat, close-fitted as the mail of a mighty fish, and in a kirtle of deep green that flashed and flickered with sea-fire as he strode slowly towards the land. In this manner the Dweller of the Deep, whom the Noldor name Ulmo, Lord of Waters, showed himself to Tuor son of Huor of the House of Hador beneath Vinyamar.

He set no foot upon the shore, but standing knee-deep in the shadowy sea he spoke to Tuor, and then for the light of his eyes and for the sound of his deep voice that came as it seemed from the foundations of the world, fear fell upon Tuor and he cast himself down upon the sand.

'Arise, Tuor son of Huor!' said Ulmo. 'Fear not my wrath, though long have I called to thee unheard; and setting out at last thou hast tarried on thy journey hither. In the Spring thou shouldst have stood here; but now a fell winter cometh soon from the land of the Enemy. Haste thou must learn, and the pleasant road that I designed for thee must be changed. For my counsels have been scorned, and a great evil creeps upon the Valley of Sirion, and already a host of foes is come between thee and thy goal.'

'What then is my goal, Lord?' said Tuor.

'That which thy heart hath ever sought,' answered Ulmo: 'to find Turgon, and look upon the hidden city. For thou art arrayed thus to be my messenger, even in the arms which long ago I decreed for thee. Yet now thou must under shadow pass through peril. Wrap thyself therefore in this cloak, and cast it never aside, until thou come to thy journey's end.'

Then it seemed to Tuor that Ulmo parted his grey mantle, and cast to him a lappet, and as it fell about him it was for him a great cloak wherein he might wrap himself over all, from head to foot.

'Thus thou shalt walk under my shadow,' said Ulmo. 'But tarry no more; for in the lands of Anar and in the fires of Melkor it will not endure. Wilt thou take up my errand?'

'I will, Lord,' said Tuor.

'Then I will set words in thy mouth to say unto Turgon,' said Ulmo. 'But first I will teach thee, and some things thou shalt hear which no man else hath heard, nay, not even the mighty among the Eldar.' And Ulmo spoke to Tuor of Valinor and its darkening, and the Exile of the Noldor, and the Doom of Mandos, and the hiding of the Blessed Realm. 'But behold!' said he, 'in the armour of Fate (as the Children of Earth name it) there is ever a rift, and in the walls of Doom a breach, until the full-making, which ye call the End. So it shall be while I endure, a secret voice that gainsayeth, and a light where darkness was decreed. Therefore, though in the days of this darkness I seem to oppose the will of my brethren, the Lords of the West, that is my part among them, to which I was appointed ere the making of the World. Yet Doom is strong, and the shadow of the Enemy lengthens; and I am diminished, until in Middle-earth I am become now no more than a secret whisper. The waters that run westward wither, and their springs are poisoned, and my power withdraws from the land; for Elves and Men grow blind and deaf to me because of the might of Melkor. And now the Curse of Mandos hastens to its fulfilment, and all the works of the Noldor shall perish, and every hope which they build shall crumble. The last hope alone is left, the hope that they have not looked for and have not prepared. And that hope lieth in thee; for so I have chosen.'

'Then shall Turgon not stand against Morgoth, as all the Eldar yet hope?' said Tuor. 'And what wouldst thou of me, Lord, if I come now to Turgon? For though I am indeed willing to do as my father and stand by that king in his need, yet of little avail shall I be, a mortal man alone, among so many and so valiant of the High Folk of the West.'

'If I choose to send thee, Tuor son of Huor, then believe not that thy one sword is not worth the sending. For the valour of the Edain the Elves shall ever remember as the ages lengthen, marvelling that they gave life so freely of which on earth they had so little. But it is not for thy valour only that I send thee, but to bring into the world a hope beyond thy sight, and a light that shall pierce the darkness.'

And as Ulmo said these things the mutter of the storm

rose to a great cry, and the wind mounted, and the sky grew black; and the mantle of the Lord of Waters streamed out like a flying cloud. 'Go now,' said Ulmo, 'lest the Sea devour thee! For Ossë obeys the will of Mandos, and he is wroth, being a servant of the Doom.'

'As thou commandest,' said Tuor. 'But if I escape the Doom, what words shall I say unto Turgon?'

'If thou come to him,' answered Ulmo, 'then the words shall arise in thy mind, and thy mouth shall speak as I would. Speak and fear not! And thereafter do as thy heart and valour lead thee. Hold fast to my mantle, for thus shalt thou be guarded. And I will send one to thee out of the wrath of Ossë, and thus shalt thou be guided: yea, the last mariner of the last ship that shall seek into the West until the rising of the Star. Go now back to the land!'

Then there was a noise of thunder, and lightning flared over the sea; and Tuor beheld Ulmo standing among the waves as a tower of silver flickering with darting flames; and he cried against the wind: 'I go, Lord! Yet now my heart yearneth rather to the Sea.'

And thereupon Ulmo lifted up a mighty horn, and blew upon it a single great note, to which the roaring of the storm was but a wind-flaw upon a lake. And as he heard that note, and was encompassed by it, and filled with it, it seemed to Tuor that the coasts of Middle-earth vanished, and he surveyed all the waters of the world in a great vision: from the veins of the lands to the mouths of the rivers, and from the strands and estuaries out into the deep. The Great Sea he saw through its unquiet regions teeming with strange forms, even to its lightless depths, in which amid the everlasting darkness there echoed voices terrible to mortal ears. Its measureless plains he surveyed with the swift sight of the Valar, lying windless under the eye of Anar, or glittering under the horned Moon, or lifted in hills of wrath that broke upon the Shadowy Isles, until remote upon the edge of sight, and beyond the count of leagues, he glimpsed a mountain, rising beyond his mind's reach into a shining cloud, and at its feet a long surf glimmering. And even as he strained to hear the sound of those far waves, and to see clearer that distant light, the note ended, and he stood beneath the thunder of the storm, and lightning many-branched rent asunder the heavens above him. And Ulmo was gone, and the sea was in tumult, as the wild waves of Ossë rode against the walls of Nevrast.

Then Tuor fled from the fury of the sea, and with labour he won his way back to the high terraces; for the wind drove him against the cliff, and when he came out upon the top it bent him to his knees. Therefore he entered again the dark and empty hall for shelter, and he sat nightlong in the stone seat of Turgon. The very pillars trembled for the violence of the storm, and it seemed to Tuor that the wind was full of wailing and wild cries. Yet being weary he slept at times, and his sleep was troubled with many dreams, of which naught remained in waking memory save one: a vision of an isle, and in the midst of it was a steep mountain, and behind it the sun went down, and shadows sprang into the sky; but above it there shone a single dazzling star.

After this dream Tuor fell into a deep sleep, for before the night was over the tempest passed, driving the black clouds into the East of the world. He awoke at length in the grey light, and arose, and left the high seat, and as he went down the dim hall he saw that it was filled with sea-birds driven in by the storm; and he went out as the last stars were fading in the West before the coming day. Then he saw that the great waves in the night had ridden high upon the land, and had cast their crests above the cliff-tops, and weed and shingle-drift were flung even upon the terraces before the doors. And Tuor looked down from the lowest terrace and saw, leaning against its wall among the stones and the sea-wrack, an Elf, clad in a grey cloak sodden with the sea. Silent he sat, gazing beyond the ruin of the beaches out over the long ridges of the waves. All was still, and there was no sound save the roaring of the surf below.

As Tuor stood and looked at the silent grey figure he remembered the words of Ulmo, and a name untaught came to his lips, and he called aloud: 'Welcome, Voronwë! I await you.'

Then the Elf turned and looked up, and Tuor met the piercing glance of his sea-grey eyes, and knew that he was of the high folk of the Noldor. But fear and wonder grew in his gaze as he saw Tuor standing high upon the wall above him, clad in his great cloak like a shadow out of which the elven-mail gleamed upon his breast.

A moment thus they stayed, each searching the face of the other, and then the Elf stood up and bowed low before Tuor's feet. 'Who are you, lord?' he said. 'Long have I laboured in the unrelenting sea. Tell me: have great tidings befallen since

I walked the land? Is the Shadow overthrown? Have the Hidden People come forth?'

'Nay,' Tuor answered. 'The Shadow lengthens, and the Hidden remain hid.'

Then Voronwë looked at him long in silence. 'But who are you?' he asked again. 'For many years ago my people left this land, and none have dwelt here since. And now I perceive that despite your raiment you are not of them, as I thought, but are of the kindred of Men.'

'I am,' said Tuor. 'And are you not the last mariner of the last ship that sought the West from the Havens of Círdan?'

'I am,' said the Elf. 'Voronwë son of Aranwë am I. But how you know my name and fate I understand not.'

'I know, for the Lord of Waters spoke to me yestereve,' answered Tuor, 'and he said that he would save you from the wrath of Ossë, and send you hither to be my guide.'

Then in fear and wonder Voronwë cried: 'You have spoken with Ulmo the Mighty? Then great indeed must be your worth and doom! But whither should I guide you, lord? For surely a king of Men you must be, and many must wait upon your word.'

'Nay, I am an escaped thrall,' said Tuor, 'and I am an outlaw alone in an empty land. But I have an errand to Turgon the Hidden King. Know you by what road I should find him?'

'Many are outlaw and thrall in these days who were not born so,' answered Voronwë. 'A lord of Men by right you are, I deem. But were you the highest of all your folk, no right would you have to seek Turgon, and vain would be your quest. For even were I to lead you to his gates, you could not enter in.'

'I do not bid you to lead me further than the gate,' said Tuor. 'There Doom shall strive with the Counsel of Ulmo. And if Turgon will not receive me, then my errand will be ended, and Doom shall prevail. But as for my right to seek Turgon: I am Tuor son of Huor and kin to Húrin, whose names Turgon will not forget. And I seek also by the command of Ulmo. Will Turgon forget that which he spoke to him of old: *Remember that the last hope of the Noldor cometh from the Sea*? Or again: *When peril is nigh one shall come from Nevrast to warn thee*? I am he that should come, and I am arrayed thus in the gear that was prepared for me.'

Tuor marvelled to hear himself speak so, for the words of Ulmo to Turgon at his going from Nevrast were not known to him before, nor to any save the Hidden People. Therefore the more amazed was Voronwë; but he turned away, and looked toward the Sea, and he sighed.

'Alas!' he said. 'I wish never again to return. And often have I vowed in the deeps of the sea that, if ever I set foot on land again, I would dwell at rest far from the Shadow in the North, or by the Havens of Círdan, or maybe in the fair fields of Nan-tathrin, where the spring is sweeter than the heart's desire. But if evil has grown while I have wandered, and the last peril approaches them, then I must go to my people.' He turned back to Tuor. 'I will lead you to the hidden gates,' he said; 'for the wise will not gainsay the counsels of Ulmo.'

'Then we will go together, as we are counselled,' said

Tuor. 'But mourn not, Voronwë! For my heart says to you that far from the Shadow your long road shall lead you, and your hope shall return to the Sea.'

'And yours also,' said Voronwë. 'But now we must leave it, and go in haste.'

'Yea,' said Tuor. 'But whither will you lead me, and how far? Shall we not first take thought how we may fare in the wild, or if the way be long, how pass the harbourless winter?'

But Voronwë would answer nothing clearly concerning the road. 'You know the strength of Men,' he said. 'As for me, I am of the Noldor, and long must be the hunger and cold the winter that shall slay the kin of those who passed the Grinding Ice. Yet how think you that we could labour countless days in the salt wastes of the sea? Or have you not heard of the waybread of the Elves? And I keep still that which all mariners hold until the last.' Then he showed beneath his cloak a sealed wallet clasped upon his belt. 'No water nor weather will harm it while it is sealed. But we must husband it until great need; and doubtless an outlaw and hunter may find other food ere the year worsens.'

'Maybe,' said Tuor. 'But not in all lands is it safe to hunt, be the game never so plentiful. And hunters tarry on the road.'

Now Tuor and Voronwë made ready to depart. Tuor took with him the small bow and arrows that he had brought, beside the gear that he had taken from the hall; but his spear, upon which his name was written in the elven-runes of the

North, he set upon the wall in token that he had passed. No arms had Voronwë save a short sword only.

Before the day was broad they left the ancient dwelling of Turgon, and Voronwë led Tuor about, westward of the steep slopes of Taras, and across the great cape. There once the road from Nevrast to Brithombar had passed, that now was but a green track between old turf-clad dikes. So they came into Beleriand, and the north region of the Falas; and turning eastward they sought the dark eaves of Ered Wethrin, and there they lay hid and rested until day had waned to dusk. For though the ancient dwellings of the Falathrim, Brithombar and Eglarest, were still far distant, Orcs now dwelt there and all the land was infested by the spies of Morgoth: he feared the ships of Círdan that would come at times raiding to the shores, and join with the forays sent forth from Nargothrond.

Now as they sat shrouded in their cloaks as shadows under the hills, Tuor and Voronwë spoke much together. And Tuor questioned Voronwë concerning Turgon, but Voronwë would tell little of such matters, and spoke rather of the dwellings upon the Isle of Balar, and of the Lisgardh, the land of reeds at the Mouths of Sirion.

'There now the numbers of the Eldar increase,' he said, 'for ever more flee thither of either kin from the fear of Morgoth, weary of war. But I forsook not my people of my own choice. For after the Bragollach and the breaking of the Siege of Angband doubt first came into Turgon's heart that Morgoth might prove too strong. In that year he sent out the first of his folk that passed his gates from within: a few only, upon a secret errand. They went down Sirion to the shores about the Mouths, and there built ships. But it availed them nothing, save to come to the great Isle of Balar and there establish lonely dwellings, far from the reach of Morgoth. For the Noldor have not the art of building ships that will long endure the waves of Belegaer the Great.

'But when later Turgon heard of the ravaging of the Falas and the sack of the ancient Havens of the Shipwrights that lie away there before us, and it was told that Círdan had saved a remnant of his people and sailed away south to the Bay of Balar, then he sent out messengers anew. That was but a little while ago, yet it seems in memory the longest portion of my life. For I was one of those that he sent, being young in years among the Eldar. I was born here in Middle-earth in the land of Nevrast. My mother was of the Grey-elves of the Falas, and akin to Círdan himself – there was much mingling of the peoples in Nevrast in the first days of Turgon's kingship – and I have the sea-heart of my mother's people. Therefore I was among the chosen, since our errand was to Círdan, to seek his aid in our shipbuilding, that some message and prayer for aid might come to the Lords of the West ere all was lost. But I tarried on the way. For I had seen little of the lands of Middle-earth, and we came to Nan-tathrin in the spring of the year. Lovely to heart's enchantment is that land, Tuor, as you shall find, if ever your feet go upon the southward roads down Sirion. There is the cure of all sea-longing, save for those whom Doom will not release. There Ulmo is but the servant of Yavanna, and the earth has brought to life a wealth of fair things that is beyond the thought of hearts in the hard hills of the North. In that land Narog joins Sirion, and they haste no more, but flow broad and quiet through living meads; and all about the shining river are flaglilies like a blossoming forest, and the grass is filled with flowers, like gems, like bells, like flames of red and gold, like a waste of many-coloured stars in a firmament of green. Yet fairest of all are the willows of Nan-tathrin, pale green, or silver in the wind, and the rustle of their innumerable leaves is a spell of music: day and night would flicker by uncounted, while still I stood knee-deep in grass and listened. There I was enchanted, and forgot the Sea in my heart. There I wandered, naming new flowers, or lay adream amid the singing of the birds, and the humming of bees and flies; and there I might still dwell in delight, forsaking all my kin, whether the ships of the Teleri or the swords of the Noldor, but my doom would not so. Or the Lord of Waters himself, maybe; for he was strong in that land.

'Thus it came into my heart to make a raft of willow-boughs and move upon the bright bosom of Sirion; and so I did, and so I was taken. For on a day, as I was in the midst of the river, a sudden wind came and caught me, and bore me away out of the Land of Willows down to the Sea. Thus I came last of the messengers to Círdan; and of the seven ships that he built at Turgon's asking all but one were then full-wrought. And one by one they set sail into the West, and none yet has ever returned, nor has any news of them been heard.

'But the salt air of the sea now stirred anew the heart of

my mother's kin within me, and I rejoiced in the waves, learning all ship-lore, as were it already stored in the mind. So when the last ship, and the greatest, was made ready, I was eager to be gone, saying within my thought: "If the words of the Noldor be true, then in the West there are meads with which the Land of Willows cannot compare. There is no withering nor any end of Spring. And perhaps even I, Voronwë, may come thither. And at the worst to wander on the waters is better far than the Shadow in the North." And I feared not, for the ships of the Teleri no water may drown.

'But the Great Sea is terrible, Tuor son of Huor; and it hates the Noldor, for it works the Doom of the Valar. Worse things it holds than to sink into the abyss and so perish: loathing, and loneliness, and madness; terror of wind and tumult, and silence, and shadows where all hope is lost and all living shapes pass away. And many shores evil and strange it washes, and many islands of danger and fear infest it. I will not darken your heart, son of Middle-earth, with the tale of my labour seven years in the Great Sea from the North even into the South, but never to the West. For that is shut against us.

'At the last, in black despair, weary of all the world, we turned and fled from the doom that so long had spared us, only to strike us more cruelly. For even as we descried a mountain from afar, and I cried: "Lo! There is Taras, the land of my birth," the wind awoke, and great clouds thunder-laden came up from the West. Then the waves hunted us like living things filled with malice, and the light-nings smote us; and when we were broken down to a helpless hull the seas leaped upon us in fury. But as you see, I was spared; for it seemed to me that there came a wave, greater and yet calmer than all the others, and it took me and lifted me from the ship, and bore me high upon its shoulders, and rolling to the land it cast me upon the turf, and then drained away, pouring back over the cliff in a great waterfall. There but one hour had I sat when you came upon me, still dazed by the sea. And still I feel the fear of it, and the bitter loss of all my friends that went with me so long and so far, beyond the sight of mortal lands.'

Voronwë sighed, and spoke then softly as if to himself. 'But very bright were the stars upon the margin of the world, when at times the clouds about the West were drawn aside. Yet whether we saw only clouds still more remote, or glimpsed indeed, as some held, the Mountains of the Pelóri about the lost strands of our long home, I know not. Far, far away they stand, and none from mortal lands shall come there ever again, I deem.' Then Voronwë fell silent; for night had come, and the stars shone white and cold.

Soon after Tuor and Voronwë arose and turned their backs toward the sea, and set out upon their long journey in the dark; of which there is little to tell, for the shadow of Ulmo was on Tuor, and none saw them pass, by wood or stone, by field or fen, between the setting and the rising of the sun. But ever warily they went, shunning the night-eyed hunters of Morgoth, and forsaking the trodden ways of Elves and Men. Voronwë chose their path and Tuor followed. He asked no vain questions, but noted well that they went ever eastward along the march of the rising mountains, and turned never southward: at which he wondered, for he believed, as did well nigh all Elves and Men, that Turgon dwelt far from the battles of the North.

Slow was their going by twilight or by night in the pathless wilds, and the fell winter came down swiftly from the realm of Morgoth. Despite the shelter of the hills the winds were strong and bitter, and soon the snow lay deep upon the heights, or whirled through the passes, and fell upon the woods of Núath ere the full-shedding of their withered leaves. Thus though they set out before the middle of Narquelië, the Hísimë came in with biting frost even as they drew nigh to the Sources of Narog.

There at the end of a weary night in the grey of dawn they halted, and Voronwë was dismayed, looking about him in grief and fear. Where once the fair pool of Ivrin had lain in its great stone basin carved by falling waters, and all about it had been a tree-clad hollow under the hills, now he saw a land defiled and desolate. The trees were burned or uprooted; and the stone-marges of the pool were broken, so that the waters of Ivrin strayed and wrought a great barren marsh amid the ruin. All now was but a welter of frozen mire, and a reek of decay lay like a foul mist upon the ground.

'Alas! Has the evil come even here?' Voronwë cried. 'Once far from the threat of Angband was this place; but ever the fingers of Morgoth grope further.'

'It is even as Ulmo spoke to me,' said Tuor: *The springs are poisoned, and my power withdraws from the waters of the land.'*

'Yet,' said Voronwë, 'a malice has been here with strength greater than that of Orcs. Fear lingers in this place.' And he searched about the edges of the mire, until suddenly he stood still and cried again: 'Yea, a great evil!' And he beckoned to Tuor, and Tuor coming saw a slot like a huge furrow that passed away southward, and at either side, now blurred, now sealed hard and clear by frost, the marks of great clawed feet. 'See!' said Voronwë, and his face was pale with dread and loathing, 'Here not long since was the Great Worm of Angband, most fell of all the creatures of the Enemy! Late already is our errand to Turgon. There is need of haste.'

Even as he spoke thus, they heard a cry in the woods, and they stood still as grey stones, listening. But the voice was a fair voice, though filled with grief, and it seemed that it called ever upon a name, as one that searches for another who is lost. And as they waited one came through the trees, and they saw that he was a tall Man, armed, clad in black, with a long sword drawn; and they wondered, for the blade of the sword also was black, but the edges shone bright and cold. Woe was graven in his face, and when he beheld the ruin of Ivrin he cried aloud in grief, saying: 'Ivrin, Faelivrin! Gwindor and Beleg! Here once I was healed. But now never shall I drink the draught of peace again.'

Then he went swiftly away towards the North, as one in pursuit, or on an errand of great haste, and they heard him cry *Faelivrin, Finduilas!* until his voice died away in the woods. But they knew not that Nargothrond had fallen, and this was Túrin son of Húrin, the Blacksword. Thus only for a moment, and never again, did the paths of those kinsmen, Túrin and Tuor, draw together.

When the Blacksword had passed, Tuor and Voronwë held on their way for a while, though day had come; for the memory of his grief was heavy upon them, and they could not endure to remain beside the defilement of Ivrin. But before long they sought a hiding-place, for all the land was filled now with a foreboding of evil. They slept little and uneasily, and as the day wore it grew dark and a great snow fell, and with the night came a grinding frost. Thereafter the snow and ice relented not at all, and for five months the Fell Winter, long remembered, held the North in bonds. Now Tuor and Voronwë were tormented by the cold, and feared to be revealed by the snow to hunting enemies, or to fall into hidden dangers treacherously cloaked. Nine days they held on, ever slower and more painfully, and Voronwë turned somewhat north, until they crossed the three well-streams of Teiglin; and then he bore eastward again, leaving the mountains, and went warily, until they passed Glithui and came to the stream of Malduin, and it was frozen black.

Then Tuor said to Voronwë: 'Fell is this frost, and death draws near to me, if not to you.' For they were now in evil case: it was long since they had found any food in the wild, and the waybread was dwindling; and they were cold and weary. 'Ill is it to be trapped between the Doom of the Valar and the Malice of the Enemy,' said Voronwë. 'Have I escaped the mouths of the sea but to lie under the snow?'

But Tuor said: 'How far is now to go? For at last, Voronwë, you must forgo your secrecy with me. Do you lead me straight, and whither? For if I must spend my last strength, I would know to what that may avail.'

'I have led you as straight as I safely might,' answered Voronwë. 'Know then now that Turgon dwells still in the north of the land of the Eldar, though that is believed by few. Already we draw nigh to him. Yet there are many leagues still to go, even as a bird might fly; and for us Sirion is yet to cross, and great evil, maybe, lies between. For we must come soon to the Highway that ran of old down from the Minas of King Finrod to Nargothrond. There the servants of the Enemy will walk and watch.'

'I counted myself the hardiest of Men,' said Tuor, 'and I have endured many winters' woe in the mountains; but I had a cave at my back and fire then, and I doubt now my strength to go much further thus hungry through the fell weather. But let us go on as far as we may before hope fails.'

'No other choice have we,' said Voronwë, 'unless it be to lay us down here and seek the snow-sleep.'

Therefore all through that bitter day they toiled on, deeming the peril of foes less than the winter; but ever as they went they found less snow, for they were now going southward again down into the Vale of Sirion, and the Mountains of Dor-lómin were left far behind. In the deepening dusk they came to the Highway at the bottom of a tall wooded bank. Suddenly they were aware of voices, and looking out warily from the trees they saw a red light below. A company of Orcs was encamped in the midst of the road, huddled about a large wood-fire.

'*Gurth an Glamhoth!* [Death to the Orcs!]' Tuor

muttered. 'Now the sword shall come from under the cloak. I will risk death for mastery of that fire, and even the meat of Orcs would be a prize.'

'Nay!' said Voronwë. 'On this quest only the cloak will serve. You must forgo the fire, or else forgo Turgon. This band is not alone in the wild: cannot your mortal sight see the far flame of other posts to the north and to the south? A tumult will bring a host upon us. Hearken to me, Tuor! It is against the law of the Hidden Kingdom that any should approach the gates with foes at their heels; and that law I will not break, neither for Ulmo's bidding, nor for death. Rouse the Orcs, and I leave you.'

'Then let them be,' said Tuor. 'But may I live yet to see the day when I need not sneak aside from a handful of Orcs like a cowed dog.'

'Come then!' said Voronwë. 'Debate no more, or they will scent us. Follow me!'

He crept then away through the trees, southward down the wind, until they were midway between that Orc-fire and the next upon the road. There he stood a long while listening.

'I hear none moving on the road,' he said, 'but we know not what may be lurking in the shadows.' He peered forward into the gloom and shuddered. 'The air is evil,' he muttered. 'Alas! Yonder lies the land of our quest and hope of life, but death walks between.'

'Death is all about us,' said Tuor. 'But I have strength left only for the shortest road. Here I must cross, or perish. I will trust to the mantle of Ulmo, and you also it shall cover. Now I will lead!'

So saying he stole to the border of the road. Then clasping
Voronwë close he cast about them both the folds of the grey
cloak of the Lord of Waters, and stepped forth.

All was still. The cold wind sighed as it swept down the
ancient road. Then suddenly it too fell silent. In the pause
Tuor felt a change in the air as if the breath from the land
of Morgoth had failed a while, and faint as a memory of the
Sea came a breeze from the West. As a grey mist on the wind
they passed over the stony street and entered a thicket on its
eastern brink.

All at once from near at hand there came a wild cry, and
many others along the borders of the road answered it. A
harsh horn blared, and there was the sound of running feet.
But Tuor held on. He had learned enough of the tongue of
the Orcs in his captivity to know the meaning of those cries:
the watchers had scented them and heard them, but they
were not seen. The hunt was out. Desperately he stumbled
and crept forward with Voronwë at his side, up a long slope
deep in whin and whortleberry among knots of rowan
and low birch. At the top of the ridge they halted, listening
to the shouts behind and the crashing of the Orcs in the
undergrowth below.

Beside them was a boulder that reared its head out of a
tangle of heath and brambles, and beneath it was such a lair
as a hunted beast might seek and hope there to escape pursuit, or at the least with its back to stone to sell its life dearly.
Down into the dark shadow Tuor drew Voronwë, and side
by side under the grey cloak they lay and panted like tired

foxes. No word they spoke; all their heed was in their ears.

The cries of the hunters grew fainter; for the Orcs thrust never deep into the wild lands at either hand, but swept rather down and up the road. They recked little of stray fugitives, but spies they feared and the scouts of armed foes; for Morgoth had set a guard on the highway, not to ensnare Tuor and Voronwë (of whom as yet he knew nothing) nor any coming from the West, but to watch for the Blacksword, lest he should escape and pursue the captives of Nargothrond, bringing help, it might be, out of Doriath.

The night passed, and the brooding silence lay again upon the empty lands. Weary and spent Tuor slept beneath Ulmo's cloak; but Voronwë crept forth and stood like a stone silent, unmoving, piercing the shadows with his Elvish eyes. At the break of day he woke Tuor, and he creeping out saw that the weather had indeed for a time relented, and the black clouds were rolled aside. There was a red dawn, and he could see far before him the tops of strange mountains glinting against the eastern fire.

Then Voronwë said in a low voice: '*Alae! Ered en Echoriath, ered e·mbar nín!* [the Encircling Mountains, the mountains of my home]'. For he knew that he looked on the Encircling Mountains and the walls of the realm of Turgon. Below them, eastward, in a deep and shadowy vale lay Sirion the fair, renowned in song; and beyond, wrapped in mist, a grey land climbed from the river to the broken hills at the mountains' feet. 'Yonder lies Dimbar,' said Voronwë. 'Would we were there! For there our foes seldom dare to walk. Or so it was, while the power of Ulmo was strong in

Sirion. But all may now be changed – save the peril of the river: it is already deep and swift, and even for the Eldar dangerous to cross. But I have led you well; for there gleams the Ford of Brithiach, yet a little southward, where the East Road that of old ran all the way from Taras in the West made the passage of the river. None now dare to use it save in desperate need, neither Elf nor Man nor Orc, since that road leads to Dungortheb and the land of dread between the Gorgoroth and the Girdle of Melian; and long since has it faded into the wild, or dwindled to a track among weeds and trailing thorns.'

Then Tuor looked as Voronwë pointed, and far away he caught the glimmer as of open waters under the brief light of dawn; but beyond loomed a darkness, where the great forest of Brethil climbed away southward into a distant highland. Now warily they made their way down the valley-side, until at last they came to the ancient road descending from the waymeet on the borders of Brethil, where it crossed the highway from Nargothrond. Then Tuor saw that they were come close to Sirion. The banks of its deep channel fell away in that place, and its waters, choked by a great waste of stones, were spread out into broad shallows, full of the murmur of fretting streams. Then after a little the river gath-ered together again, and delving a new bed flowed away toward the forest, and far off vanished into a deep mist that his eye could not pierce; for there lay, though he knew it not, the north march of Doriath within the shadow of the Girdle of Melian.

At once Tuor would hasten to the ford, but Voronwë

restrained him, saying: 'Over the Brithiach we may not go in open day, nor while any doubt of pursuit remains.'

'Then shall we sit here and rot?' said Tuor. 'For such doubt will remain while the realm of Morgoth endures. Come! Under the shadow of the cloak of Ulmo we must go forward.'

Still Voronwë hesitated, and looked back westward; but the track behind was deserted, and all about was quiet save for the rush of the waters. He looked up, and the sky was grey and empty, for not even a bird was moving. Then suddenly his face brightened with joy, and he cried aloud: 'It is well! The Brithiach is guarded still by the enemies of the Enemy. The Orcs will not follow us here; and under the cloak we may pass now without more doubt.'

'What new thing have you seen?' said Tuor.

'Short is the sight of Mortal Men!' said Voronwë. 'I see the Eagles of the Crissaegrim; and they are coming hither. Watch a while!'

Then Tuor stood at gaze; and soon high in the air he saw three shapes beating on strong wings down from the distant mountain-peaks now wreathed again in cloud. Slowly they descended in great circles, and then stooped suddenly upon the wayfarers; but before Voronwë could call to them they turned with a wide sweep and rush, and flew northward along the line of the river.

'Now let us go,' said Voronwë. 'If there be any Orc nearby, he will lie cowering nose to ground, until the eagles have gone far away.'

Swiftly down a long slope they hastened, and passed over

the Brithiach, walking often dryfoot upon shelves of shingle, or wading in the shoals no more than knee-deep. The water was clear and very cold, and there was ice upon the shallow pools, where the wandering streams had lost their way among the stones; but never, not even in the Fell Winter of the Fall of Nargothrond, could the deadly breath of the North freeze the main flood of Sirion.

On the far side of the ford they came to a gully, as it were the bed of an old stream, in which no water now flowed; yet once, it seemed, a torrent had cloven its deep channel, coming down from the north out of the mountains of the Echoriath, and bearing thence all the stones of the Brithiach down into Sirion.

'At last beyond hope we find it!' cried Voronwë. 'See! Here is the mouth of the Dry River, and that is the road we must take.' Then they passed into the gully, and as it turned north and the slopes of the land went steeply up, so its sides rose on either hand, and Tuor stumbled in the dim light among the stones with which its rough bed was strewn. 'If this is a road,' he said, 'it is an evil one for the weary.'

'Yet it is the road to Turgon,' said Voronwë.

'Then the more do I marvel,' said Tuor, 'that its entrance lies open and unguarded. I had looked to find a great gate, and strength of guard.'

'That you shall yet see,' said Voronwë. 'This is but the approach. A road I named it; yet upon it none have passed for more than three hundred years, save messengers few and secret, and all the craft of the Noldor has been expended to conceal it, since the Hidden People entered in. Does it lie open? Would you have known it, if you had not had one of the Hidden Kingdom for a guide? Or would you have guessed it to be but the work of the weathers and the waters of the wilderness? And are there not the Eagles, as you have seen? They are the folk of Thorondor, who dwelt once even on Thangorodrim ere Morgoth grew so mighty, and dwell now in the Mountains of Turgon since the fall of Fingolfin. They alone save the Noldor know the Hidden Kingdom and guard the skies above it, though as yet no servant of the Enemy has dared to fly into the high airs; and they bring much news to the King of all that moves in the lands without. Had we been Orcs, doubt not that we should have been seized, and cast from a great height upon the pitiless rocks.'

'I doubt it not,' said Tuor. 'But it comes into my mind to wonder also whether news will not now come to Turgon of our approach swifter than we. And if that be good or ill, you alone can say.'

'Neither good nor ill,' said Voronwë. 'For we cannot pass the Guarded Gate unmarked, be we looked for or no; and if we come there the Guards will need no report that we are not Orcs. But to pass we shall need a greater plea than that. For you do not guess, Tuor, the peril that we then shall face. Blame me not, as one unwarned, for what may then betide; may the power of the Lord of Waters be shown indeed! For in that hope alone have I been willing to guide you, and if it fails then more surely shall we die than by all the perils of wild and winter.'

But Tuor said: 'Forebode no more. Death in the wild is

certain; and death at the Gate is yet in doubt to me, for all your words. Lead me still on!'

Many miles they toiled on in the stones of the Dry River, until they could go no further, and the evening brought darkness into the deep cleft; they climbed out then onto the east bank, and they had now come into the tumbled hills that lay at the feet of the mountains. And looking up Tuor saw that they towered up in a fashion other than that of any mountains that he had seen; for their sides were like sheer walls, piled each one above and behind the lower, as were they great towers of many-storeyed precipices. But the day had waned, and all the lands were grey and misty, and the Vale of Sirion was shrouded in shadow. Then Voronwë led him to a shallow cave in a hillside that looked out over the lonely slopes of Dimbar, and they crept within, and there they lay hid; and they ate their last crumbs of food, and were cold, and weary, but slept not. Thus did Tuor and Voronwë come in the dusk of the eighteenth day of Hísimë, the thirty-seventh of their journey, to the towers of the Echoriath and the threshold of Turgon, and by the power of Ulmo escaped both the Doom and the Malice.

When the first glimmer of day filtered grey amid the mists of Dimbar they crept back into the Dry River, and soon after its course turned eastward, winding up to the very walls of the mountains; and straight before them there loomed a great precipice, rising sheer and sudden from a steep slope upon which grew a tangled thicket of thorn-trees. Into this thicket the stony channel entered, and there it was still dark as night; and they halted, for the thorns grew far down the sides of the gully, and their lacing branches were a dense roof above it, so low that often Tuor and Voronwë must crawl under like beasts stealing back to their lair.

But at last, as with great labour they came to the very foot of the cliff, they found an opening, as it were the mouth of a tunnel worn in the hard rock by waters flowing from the heart of the mountains. They entered, and within there was no light, but Voronwë went steadily forward, while Tuor followed with his hand upon his shoulder, bending a little, for the roof was low. Thus for a time they went on blindly, step by step, until presently they felt the ground beneath their feet had become level and free from loose stones. Then they halted and breathed deeply, as they stood listening. The air seemed fresh and wholesome, and they were aware of a great space around and above them; but all was silent, and not even the drip of water could be heard. It seemed to Tuor that Voronwë was troubled and in doubt, and he whispered: 'Where then is the Guarded Gate? Or have we indeed now passed it?'

'Nay,' said Voronwë. 'Yet I wonder, for it is strange that any incomer should creep thus far unchallenged. I fear some stroke in the dark.'

But their whispers aroused the sleeping echoes, and they were enlarged and multiplied, and ran in the roof and the unseen walls, hissing and murmuring as the sound of many stealthy voices. And even as the echoes died in the stone, Tuor heard out of the darkness a voice speak in the

Elven-tongues: first in the High Speech of the Noldor, which he knew not; and then in the tongue of Beleriand, though in a manner somewhat strange to his ears, as of a people long sundered from their kin.

'Stand!' it said. 'Stir not! Or you will die, be you foes or friends.'

'We are friends,' said Voronwë.

'Then do as we bid,' said the voice.

The echo of their voices rolled into silence. Voronwë and Tuor stood still, and it seemed to Tuor that many slow minutes passed, and a fear was in his heart such as no other peril of his road had brought. Then there came the beat of feet, growing to a tramping loud as the march of trolls in that hollow place. Suddenly an elven lantern was unhooded, and its bright ray was turned upon Voronwë before him, but nothing else could Tuor see save a dazzling star in the darkness; and he knew that while that beam was upon him he could not move, neither to flee nor to run forward.

For a moment they were held thus in the eye of the light, and then the voice spoke again, saying: 'Show your faces!' And Voronwë cast back his hood, and his face shone in the ray, hard and clear, as if graven in stone; and Tuor marvelled to see its beauty. Then he spoke proudly, saying: 'Know you not whom you see? I am Voronwë son of Aranwë of the House of Fingolfin. Or am I forgotten in my own land after a few years? Far beyond the thought of Middle-earth I have wandered, yet I remember your voice, Elemmakil.'

'Then Voronwë will remember also the laws of his land,' said the voice. 'Since by command he went forth, he has the right to return. But not to lead hither any stranger. By that deed his right is void, and he must be led as a prisoner to the king's judgement. As for the stranger, he shall be slain or held captive at the judgement of the Guard. Lead him hither that I may judge.'

Then Voronwë led Tuor towards the light, and as they drew near many Noldor, mail-clad and armed, stepped forward out of the darkness and surrounded them with drawn swords. And Elemmakil, captain of the Guard, who bore the bright lamp, looked long and closely at them.

'This is strange in you, Voronwë,' he said. 'We were long friends. Why then would you set me thus cruelly between the law and my friendship? If you had led hither unbidden one of the other houses of the Noldor, that were enough. But you have brought to knowledge of the Way a mortal Man – for by his eyes I perceive his kin. Yet free can he never again go, knowing the secret; and as one of alien kin that has dared to enter, I should slay him – even though he be your friend and dear to you.'

'In the wide lands without, Elemmakil, many strange things may befall one, and tasks unlooked for be laid on one,' Voronwë answered. 'Other shall the wanderer return than as he set forth. What I have done, I have done under command greater than the law of the Guard. The King alone should judge me, and him that comes with me.'

Then Tuor spoke, and feared no longer. 'I come with Voronwë son of Aranwë, because he was appointed to be my guide by the Lord of Waters. To this end was he delivered from the wrath of the Sea and the Doom of the Valar. For

I bear from Ulmo an errand to the son of Fingolfin, and to him will I speak it.'

Thereat Elemmakil looked in wonder upon Tuor. 'Who then are you?' he said. 'And whence come you?'

'I am Tuor son of Huor of the House of Hador and the kindred of Húrin, and these names, I am told, are not unknown in the Hidden Kingdom. From Nevrast I have come through many perils to seek it.'

'From Nevrast?' said Elemmakil. 'It is said that none dwell there, since our people departed.'

'It is said truly,' answered Tuor. 'Empty and cold stand the courts of Vinyamar. Yet thence I come. Bring me now to him that built those halls of old.'

'In matters so great judgement is not mine,' said Elemmakil. 'Therefore I will lead you to the light where more may be revealed, and I will deliver you to the Warden of the Great Gate.'

Then he spoke in command, and Tuor and Voronwë were set between tall guards, two before and three behind them; and their captain led them from the cavern of the Outer Guard, and they passed, as it seemed, into a straight passage, and there walked long upon a level floor until a pale light gleamed ahead. Thus they came at length to a wide arch with tall pillars upon either hand, hewn in the rock, and between hung a great portcullis of crossed wooden bars, marvellously carved and studded with nails of iron.

Elemmakil touched it, and it rose silently, and they passed through; and Tuor saw that they stood at the end of a ravine, the like of which he had never before beheld or imagined in his thought, long though he had walked in the wild mountains of the North; for beside the Orfalch Echor Cirith Ninniach was but a groove in the rock. Here the hands of the Valar themselves, in ancient wars of the world's beginning, had wrested the great mountains asunder, and the sides of the rift were sheer as if axe-cloven, and they towered up to heights unguessable. There far aloft ran a ribbon of sky, and against its deep blue stood black peaks and jagged pinnacles, remote but hard, cruel as spears. Too high were those mighty walls for the winter sun to overlook, and though it was now full morning faint stars glimmered above the mountain-tops, and down below all was dim, but for the pale light of lamps set beside the climbing road. For the floor of the ravine sloped steeply up, eastward, and upon the left hand Tuor saw beside the stream-bed a wide way, laid and paved with stone, winding upward till it vanished into shadow.

'You have passed the First Gate, the Gate of Wood,' said Elemmakil. 'There lies the way. We must hasten.'

How far that deep road ran Tuor could not guess, and as he stared onward a great weariness came upon him like a cloud. A chill wind hissed over the faces of the stones, and he drew his cloak about him. 'Cold blows the wind from the Hidden Kingdom!' he said.

'Yea, indeed,' said Voronwë; 'to a stranger it might seem that pride has made the servants of Turgon pitiless. Long and hard seem the leagues of the Seven Gates to the hungry and wayworn.'

'If our law were less stern, long ago guile and hatred

would have entered and destroyed us. That you know well,' said Elemmakil. 'But we are not pitiless. Here there is no food, and the stranger may not go back through a gate that he has passed. Endure then a little, and at the Second Gate you shall be eased.'

'It is well,' said Tuor, and he went forward as he was bidden. After a little he turned, and saw that Elemmakil alone followed with Voronwë. 'There is no need more of guards,' said Elemmakil, reading his thought. 'From the Orfalch there is no escape for Elf or Man, and no returning.'

Thus they went on up the steep way, sometimes by long stairs, sometimes by winding slopes, under the daunting shadow of the cliff, until some half-league from the Wooden Gate Tuor saw that the way was barred by a great wall built across the ravine from side to side, with stout towers of stone at either hand. In the wall was a great archway above the road, but it seemed that masons had blocked it with a single mighty stone. As they drew near its dark and polished face gleamed in the light of a white lamp that hung above the midst of the arch.

'Here stands the Second Gate, the Gate of Stone,' said Elemmakil; and going up to it he thrust lightly upon it. It turned upon an unseen pivot, until its edge was towards them, and the way was open upon either side; and they passed through, into a court where stood many armed guards clad in grey. No word was spoken, but Elemmakil led his charges to a chamber beneath the northern tower; and there food and wine was brought to them, and they were permitted to rest a while.

'Scant may the fare seem,' said Elemmakil to Tuor. 'But if your claim be proved, hereafter it shall richly be amended.'

'It is enough,' said Tuor. 'Faint were the heart that needed better healing.' And indeed such refreshment did he find in the drink and food of the Noldor that soon he was eager to go on.

After a little space they came to a wall yet higher and stronger than before, and in it was set the Third Gate, the Gate of Bronze: a great twofold door hung with shields and plates of bronze, wherein were wrought many figures and strange signs. Upon the wall above its lintel were three square towers, roofed and clad with copper that by some device of smith-craft were ever bright and gleamed as fire in the rays of the red lamps ranged like torches along the wall. Again silently they passed the gate, and saw in the court beyond a yet greater company of guards in mail that glowed like dull fire; and the blades of their axes were red. Of the kindred of the Sindar of Nevrast for the most part were those that held this gate.

Now they came to the most toilsome road, for in the midst of the Orfalch the slope was at the steepest, and as they climbed Tuor saw the mightiest of the walls looming dark above him. Thus at last they drew near the fourth Gate, the Gate of Writhen Iron. High and black was the wall, and lit with no lamps. Four towers of iron stood upon it, and between the two inner towers was set an image of a great eagle wrought in iron, even the likeness of King Thorondor himself, as he would alight upon a mountain from the high airs. But as Tuor stood before the gate it seemed to his wonder that he was looking through boughs and stems of imperishable trees into a pale glade of the Moon. For a light came through the traceries of the gate, which were wrought and hammered into the shapes of trees with writhing roots and woven branches laden with leaves and flowers. And as he passed through he saw how this could be; for the wall was of great thickness, and there was not one grill, but three in line, so set that to one who approached in the middle of the way each formed part of the device; but the light beyond was the light of day.

For they had climbed now to a great height above the lowlands where they began, and beyond the Iron Gate the road ran almost level. Moreover, they had passed the crown and heart of the Echoriath, and the mountain-towers now fell swiftly down towards the inner hills, and the ravine opened wider, and its sides became less sheer. Its long shoulders were mantled with white snow, and the light of the sky snow-mirrored came white as moonlight through a glimmering mist that filled the air.

Now they passed through the lines of the Iron Guards that stood behind the Gate; black were their mantles and their mail and long shields, and their faces were masked with vizors bearing each an eagle's beak. Then Elemmakil went before them and they followed him into the pale light; and Tuor saw beside the way a sward of grass, where like stars bloomed the white flowers of *uilos*, the Evermind that knows no season and withers not; and thus in wonder and lightening of heart he was brought to the Gate of Silver.

The wall of the Fifth Gate was built of white marble, and

was low and broad, and its parapet was a trellis of silver between five great globes of marble; and there stood many archers robed in white. The gate was in shape as three parts of a circle, and wrought of silver and pearl of Nevrast in likenesses of the Moon; but above the Gate upon the midmost globe stood an image of the White Tree Telperion, wrought of silver and malachite, with flowers made of great pearls of Balar. And beyond the Gate in a wide court paved with marble, green and white, stood archers in silver mail and white-crested helms, a hundred upon either hand. Then Elemmakil led Tuor and Voronwë through their silent ranks, and they entered upon a long white road, that ran straight towards the Sixth Gate; and as they went the grass-sward became wider, and among the white stars of *uilos* there opened many small flowers like eyes of gold.

So they came to the Golden Gate, the last of the ancient gates of Turgon that were wrought before the Nirnaeth; and it was much like the Gate of Silver, save that the wall was built of yellow marble, and the globes and parapet were of red gold; and there were six globes, and in the midst upon a golden pyramid was set an image of Laurelin, the Tree of the Sun, with flowers wrought of topaz in long clusters upon chains of gold. And the Gate itself was adorned with discs of gold, many-rayed, in likenesses of the Sun, set amid devices of garnet and topaz and yellow diamonds. In the court beyond were arrayed three hundred archers with long bows, and their mail was gilded, and tall golden plumes rose from their helmets; and their great round shields were red as flame.

Now sunlight fell upon the further road, for the walls of the hills were low on either side, and green, but for the snows upon their tops; and Elemmakil hastened forward, for the way was short to the Seventh Gate, named the Great, the Gate of Steel that Maeglin wrought after the return from the Nirnaeth, across the wide entrance to the Orfalch Echor.

No wall stood there, but on either hand were two round towers of great height, many-windowed, tapering in seven storeys to a turret of bright steel, and between the towers there stood a mighty fence of steel that rusted not, but glittered cold and white. Seven great pillars of steel there were, tall with the height and girth of strong young trees, but ending in a bitter spike that rose to the sharpness of a needle; and between the pillars were seven cross-bars of steel, and in each space seven times seven rods of steel upright with heads like the broad blades of spears. But in the centre, above the midmost pillar and the greatest, was raised a mighty image of the king-helm of Turgon, the Crown of the Hidden Kingdom, set about with diamonds.

No gate or door could Tuor see in this mighty hedge of steel, but as he drew near through the spaces between the bars there came, as it seemed to him, a dazzling light, and he shaded his eyes, and stood still in dread and wonder. But Elemmakil went forward, and no gate opened to his touch; but he struck upon a bar, and the fence rang like a harp of many strings, giving forth clear notes in harmony that ran from tower to tower.

Straightway there issued riders from the towers, but before those of the north tower came one upon a white horse; and he dismounted and strode towards them. And high and noble as was Elemmakil, greater and more lordly was Ecthelion, Lord of the Fountains, at that time Warden of the Great Gate. All in silver was he clad, and upon his shining helm was set a spike of steel pointed with a diamond; and as his esquire took his shield it shimmered as if it were bedewed with drops of rain, that were indeed a thousand studs of crystal.

Elemmakil saluted him and said: 'Here have I brought Voronwë Aranwion, returning from Balar; and here is the stranger that he has led hither, who demands to see the King.'

Then Ecthelion turned to Tuor, but he drew his cloak about him and stood silent, facing him; and it seemed to Voronwë that a mist mantled Tuor and his stature was increased, so that the peak of his high hood over-topped the helm of the Elf-lord, as it were the crest of a grey sea-wave riding to the land. But Ecthelion bent his bright glance upon Tuor, and after a silence he spoke gravely, saying:* 'You have come to the Last Gate. Know then that no stranger who passes it shall ever go out again, save by the door of death.'

'Speak not ill-boding! If the messenger of the Lord of Waters go by that door, then all those who dwell here will follow him. Lord of the Fountains, hinder not the messenger of the Lord of Waters!'

Then Voronwë and all those who stood near looked again

---

* At this point the carefully written manuscript ends, and there follows only a rough text scribbled on a scrap of paper.

in wonder at Tuor, marvelling at his words and voice. And to Voronwë it seemed as if he heard a great voice, but as of one who called from afar off. But to Tuor it seemed that he listened to himself speaking, as if another spoke with his mouth.

For a while Ecthelion stood silent, looking at Tuor, and slowly awe filled his face, as if in the grey shadow of Tuor's cloak he saw visions from far away. Then he bowed, and went to the fence and laid hands upon it, and gates opened inward on either side of the pillar of the Crown. Then Tuor passed through, and coming to a high sward that looked out over the valley beyond, he beheld a vision of Gondolin amid the white snow. And so entranced was he that for long he could look at nothing else; for he saw before him at last the vision of his desire out of dreams of longing.

Thus he stood and spoke no word. Silent upon either hand stood a host of the army of Gondolin; all of the seven kinds of the Seven Gates were there represented; but their captains and chieftains were upon horses, white and grey. Then even as they gazed on Tuor in wonder, his cloak fell, and he stood there before them in the mighty livery of Nevrast. And many were there who had seen Turgon himself set these things upon the wall behind the High Seat of Vinyamar.

Then Ecthelion said at last: 'Now no further proof is needed; and even the name he claims as son of Huor matters less than this clear proof, that he comes from Ulmo himself.'

*

Here this text comes to an end, but there follow some rapidly written notes sketching out elements of the narrative as my father at that time foresaw it. Tuor asked the name of the city, and was told its seven names (see *The Tale of The Fall of Gondolin* p.51). Ecthelion gave orders for the sounding of the signal, and trumpets were blown on the towers of the Great Gate; then answering trumpets were heard blown far off on the city walls.

On horseback they rode to the city, of which a description was to follow: of the Great Gate, the trees, the Place of the Fountain, and of the King's house; and then would be described the welcome of Tuor by Turgon. Beside the throne would be seen Maeglin on the right and Idril on the left; and Tuor would declare the message of Ulmo. There is also a note saying that there was to be a description of the city as Tuor saw it from afar; and that it was to be recounted why there was no queen of Gondolin.

THE EVOLUTION OF THE STORY

These notes (i.e. at the end of the 'latest Tuor' manuscript) are of slight significance in the history of the legend of *The Fall of Gondolin*, but they show at least that my father did not abandon this work in some sudden unlooked for haste never to take it up again. But any idea that a further fully evolved continuation of the story, after Ecthelion's words to Tuor at the Seventh Gate of Gondolin, has been lost is out of the question.

So there we have it. My father did indeed abandon this essential, and (one may say) definitive, form and treatment of the legend, at the very moment when he had brought Tuor at long last to 'behold a vision of Gondolin amid the white snow.' For me it is perhaps the most grievous of his many abandonments. Why did he stop there? An answer, of a kind, can be found.

This was a deeply distressing time for him, a time of intense frustration. It can be said with certainty that when

The Lord of the Rings was at last completed, he returned to the legends of the Elder days with a strong new energy. I will cite here parts of a remarkable letter that he wrote to Sir Stanley Unwin, the Chairman of Allen and Unwin, on 24 February 1950, for it clearly presents the prospect of publishing as he saw it at that time.

In one of your more recent letters you expressed a desire still to see the MS of my proposed work, *The Lord of the Rings*, originally expected to be a sequel to *The Hobbit*? For eighteen months now I have been hoping for the day when I could call it finished. But it was not until after Christmas [1949] that this goal was reached at last. It is finished, if still partly unrevised, and is, I suppose, in a condition which a reader could read, if he did not wilt at the sight of it.

As the estimate for typing a fair copy was in the neighbourhood of £100 (which I have not to spare), I was obliged to do nearly all myself. And now I look at it, the magnitude of the disaster is apparent to me. My work has escaped from my control, and I have produced a monster: an immensely long, complex, rather bitter, and very terrifying romance, quite unfit for children (if fit for anybody); and it is not really a sequel to *The Hobbit*, but to *The Silmarillion*. My estimate is that it contains, even without certain necessary adjuncts, about 600,000 words. One typist put it even higher. I can see only too clearly how impracticable this is. But I am tired. It is off my chest, and I do not feel that I can do anything more about it, beyond a little revision of inaccuracies. Worse still: I feel that it is tied to the *Silmarillion*.

You may, perhaps, remember about that work, a long legendary of imaginary times in a 'high style', and full of Elves (of a sort). It was rejected on the advice of your reader many years ago. As far as my memory goes he allowed it a kind of Celtic beauty intolerable to Anglo-Saxons in large doses.* He was probably perfectly right and just. And you commented that it was a work to be drawn upon rather than published.

Unfortunately I am not an Anglo-Saxon, and though shelved (until a year ago) the *Silmarillion* and all that has refused to be suppressed. It has bubbled up, infiltrated, and probably spoiled everything (that even remotely approached 'Faery') which I have tried to write since. It was kept out of *Farmer Giles* with an effort, but stopped the continuation. Its shadow was deep on the later parts of *The Hobbit*. It has captured *The Lord of the Rings* so that that has become simply its continuation and completion, requiring *The Silmarillion* to be fully intelligible – without a lot of references and explanations that clutter it in one or two places.

---

* The reader had in fact only seen a few pages of *The Silmarillion*, although he did not know this. As I have mentioned in *Beren and Lúthien* (p.220), he contrasted those pages greatly to the detriment of *The Lay of Leithian*, having no understanding of their relationship; and in his enthusiasm for the *Silmarillion* pages he said absurdly that the tale is 'told with a picturesque brevity and dignity that holds the reader's interest in spite of its eye-splitting Celtic names. It has something of that mad, bright-eyed beauty that perplexes all Anglo-Saxons in the face of Celtic art.'

Ridiculous and tiresome as you may think me, I want to publish them both – *The Silmarillion* and *The Lord of the Rings* – in conjunction or in connexion. 'I want to' – it would be wiser to say 'I should like to', since a little packet of, say, a million words, of matter set out in extenso, that Anglo-Saxons (or the English-speaking public) can only endure in moderation, is not very likely to see the light, even if paper were available at will.

All the same that is what I should like. Or I will let it all be. I cannot contemplate any drastic re-writing or compression. Of course being a writer I should like to see my words printed; but there they are. For me the chief thing is that I feel that the whole matter is now 'exorcized', and rides me no more. I can turn now to other things ...

I will not follow the intricate and painful history through the next two years. My father never relinquished his opinion, in his words in another letter, that '*The Silmarillion* etc. and *The Lord of the Rings* went together, as one long Saga of the Jewels and the Rings': 'I was resolved to treat them as one thing, however they might formally be issued'.

But the costs of production of such a huge work in the years after the War were hopelessly against him. On 22 June 1952 he wrote to Rayner Unwin:

As for *The Lord of the Rings* and *The Silmarillion*, they are where they were. The one finished (and the end revised), and the other still unfinished (or unrevised), and both gathering dust. I have been off and on too unwell, and too burdened to do much about them, and too downhearted. Watching paper-shortages and costs mounting against me. But I have rather modified my views. Better something than nothing! Although to me all are one, and *The Lord of the Rings* would be better far (and eased) as part of the whole, I would gladly consider the publication of any part of this stuff. Years are becoming precious. And retirement (not far off) will, as far as I can see, bring not leisure but a poverty that will necessitate scraping a living by 'examining' and suchlike tasks.

As I said in *Morgoth's Ring* (1993): 'Thus he bowed to necessity, but it was a grief to him'.

I believe that the explanation of his abandonment of 'the Last Version' is to be found in the extracts of correspondence given above. In the first place, there are his words in his letter to Stanley Unwin of 24 February 1950. He announced firmly that *The Lord of the Rings* was finished: 'after Christmas this goal was reached at last.' And he said: 'For me the chief thing is that I feel that the whole matter is now "exorcized", and rides me no more. I can turn now to other things ...'

In the second place, there is an essential date. The page of the manuscript of the Last Version of *Of Tuor and the Fall of Gondolin*, carrying notes of elements in the story that were never reached in that text (p.202), was a page of an engagement calendar for September 1951; and other pages from this calendar were used for rewriting passages.

In the Foreword to *Morgoth's Ring* I wrote:

But little of all the work begun at that time was completed. The new *Lay of Leithian*, the new tale of Tuor and the Fall of Gondolin, the *Grey Annals* (of Beleriand), the revision of the *Quenta Silmarillion*, were all abandoned. I have little doubt that despair of publication, at least in the form that he regarded as essential, was the prime cause.

As he said in the letter to Rayner Unwin of 22 June 1952 cited above: 'As for *The Lord of the Rings* and *The Silmarillion*, they are where they were. I have been off and on been too unwell, and too burdened to do much about them, and too downhearted.'

It remains therefore to look back at what we do possess of this last story, which never became 'the Fall of Gondolin', but is nevertheless unique among the evocations of Middle-earth in the Elder Days, most especially perhaps in my father's intense awareness of the detail, of the atmosphere, of successive scenes. Reading his account of the coming to Tuor of the God Ulmo, Lord of Waters, of his appearance and of his 'standing knee-deep in the shadowy sea', one may wonder what descriptions there might have been of the colossal encounters in the battle for Gondolin.

As it stands – and stops – it is the story of a journey – a journey on an extraordinary mission, conceived and ordained by one of the greatest of the Valar, and expressly imposed upon Tuor, of a great house of Men, to whom the God ultimately appears at the ocean's edge in the midst of a vast storm. That extraordinary mission is to have a yet more extraordinary outcome, that would change the history of the imagined world.

The profound importance of the journey presses down upon Tuor and Voronwë, the Noldorin Elf who becomes his companion, at every step, and my father felt their growing deadly weariness, in the Fell Winter of that year, as if he himself had in dreams trudged from Vinyamar to Gondolin in hunger and exhaustion, and the fear of Orcs, in the last years of the Elder Days in Middle-earth.

The story of Gondolin has now been repeated from its origin in 1916 to this final but strangely abandoned version of some thirty-five years later. In what follows I will usually refer to the original story as 'the Lost Tale', or for brevity simply as 'the Tale', and the abandoned text as 'the Last Version', or abbreviated 'LV'. Of these two widely separated texts this may be said at once. It seems unquestionable either that my father had the manuscript of the Lost Tale in front of him, or at any rate that he had been reading it not long before, when he wrote the Last Version. This conclusion derives from the very close similarity or even near identity of passages here and there in either text. To cite a single example:

(*The Lost Tale* p.40)
Then Tuor found himself in a rugged country bare of trees, and swept by a wind coming from the set of the sun, and all the shrubs and bushes leaned to the dawn because of the prevalence of that wind.

(*The Last Version* p.158)

[Tuor] wandered still for some days in a rugged country
bare of trees; and it was swept by a wind from the sea, and
all that grew there, herb or bush, leaned ever to the dawn
because of the prevalence of that wind from the West.

All the more interesting is it to compare the two texts, in so
far as they are comparable, and observe how essential features of the old story are retained but transformed in their
significance, while wholly new elements and dimensions
have entered.

In the *Tale* Tuor announces his name and lineage thus
(p.54):

I am Tuor son of Peleg son of Indor of the house of the
Swan of the sons of the Men of the North who live far
hence.

It was also said of him in the *Tale* (p.41) that when he made a
dwelling for himself in the cove of Falasquil on the coast of
the ocean he adorned it with many carvings, 'and ever among
them was the Swan the chief, for Tuor loved this emblem and
it became the sign of himself, his kindred and folk thereafter.' Moreover, again in the *Tale*, it was said of him (p.60)
that when in Gondolin a suit of armour was made for Tuor
'his helm was adorned with a device of metals and jewels
like to two swan-wings, one on either side, and a swan's
wing was wrought on his shield.'

And again, at the time of the attack on Gondolin, all the

warriors of Tuor who stood around him 'wore wings as it were of swans or gulls upon their helms, and the emblem of the White Wing was upon their shields' (p.73); they were 'the folk of the Wing'.

Already in the *Sketch of the Mythology*, however, Tuor had been drawn into the evolving *Silmarillion*. The house of the Swan of the Men of the North had disappeared. He had become a member of the House of Hador, the son of Huor who was killed in the Battle of Unnumbered Tears and the cousin of Túrin Turambar. Yet the association of Tuor with the Swan and the Swan's wing was by no means lost in this transformation. It was said in the *Last Version* (p.160):

Now Tuor loved swans, which he knew on the grey pools of Mithrim; and the swan moreover had been the token of Annael and his foster-folk [for Annael see the *Last Version* p.146].

Then in Vinyamar, the ancient house of Turgon before the discovery of Gondolin, the shield that Tuor found bore upon it the emblem of a white swan's wing, and he said: '*By this token* I will take these arms unto myself, and upon myself whatsoever doom they bear' (LV p.162).

The original *Tale* opened (p.37) with no more than a very slight introduction concerning Tuor, 'who dwelt in very ancient days in that land of the North called Dor-lómin or the Land of Shadows.' He lived alone, a hunter in the lands about Lake Mithrim, singing the songs that he made and playing on his harp; and he became acquainted with 'the wandering Noldoli', from whom he learned greatly and not least much of their language.

But 'it is said that magic and destiny led him on a day to a cavernous opening down which a hidden river flowed from Mithrim', and Tuor entered in. This, it is said, 'was the will of Ulmo Lord of Waters at whose prompting the Noldoli had made that hidden way.'

When Tuor was unable against the strength of the river to retreat from the cavern the Noldoli came and guided him along dark passages amid the mountains until he came out in the light once more.

In the *Sketch* of 1926, where as noted above Tuor's lineage as a descendant of the house of Hador emerged, it is told (pp.122–3) that after the death of Rían his mother he became a slave of the faithless men whom Morgoth drove into Hithlum after the Battle of Unnumbered Tears; but he escaped from them, and Ulmo contrived that he should be led to a subterranean river-course leading out of Mithrim into a chasmed river that flowed at last into the Western Sea. In the *Quenta* of 1930 (pp.134–5) this account was closely followed, and in both texts the only significance in the story that is ascribed to it is the secrecy that it afforded to Tuor's escape, totally unknown to any spy of Morgoth. But both these texts were of their nature largely condensed.

Returning to the *Tale*, Tuor's passage of the river-chasm was told at length, to the point where the incoming tide met the river flowing down swiftly from Lake Mithrim in frightening tumult to one standing in the path: 'but the Ainur [Valar] put it into his heart to climb from the gully when he did, or had he been whelmed in the incoming tide' (p.40). It seems that the guiding Noldoli left Tuor when he came out of the dark cavern: '[The Noldoli] guided him along dark passages amid the mountains until he came out in the light once more' (p.38).

Leaving the river and standing above its ravine Tuor for the first time set his eyes upon the sea. Finding in the coast a sheltered cove (which came to be called *Falasquil*) he built there a dwelling of timber floated down the river to him by the Noldoli (on the Swan amid the carvings of his dwelling see p.210 above). In Falasquil he 'passed a very great while' (*Tale* p.41) until he wearied of his loneliness, and here again the Ainur are said to bear a part ('for Ulmo loved Tuor', *Tale* p.41); he left Falasquil and followed a flight of three swans passing southward down the coast and plainly leading him. His great journey through winter to spring is described, until he reached the Sirion. Thence he went further until he reached the Land of Willows (*Nan-tathrin*, *Tasarinan*), where the butterflies and the bees, the flowers and the singing birds enthralled him, and he gave names to them, and lingered there through spring and summer (*Tale* pp.44–5).

The accounts in the *Sketch* and the *Quenta* are extremely brief, as is to be expected. In the *Sketch* (p.123) it is said of Tuor only that 'after long wanderings down the western shores he came to the mouths of Sirion, and there fell in with the Gnome Bronweg [Voronwë] who had once been in Gondolin. They journey secretly up Sirion together. Tuor lingers long in the sweet land Nan-tathrin "Valley of Willows".' The passage in the *Quenta* (p.135–6) is in content essentially the same. The Gnome, spelled Bronwë, is now said to have escaped from Angband, and 'being of old of the people of Turgon sought ever to find the path to the hidden places of his lord', and so he and Tuor went up Sirion and came to the Land of Willows.

It is curious that in these texts the entry of Voronwë into the narrative takes place before the coming of Tuor to the Land of Willows: for in the primary source, the *Tale*, Voronwë had appeared much later, under wholly different circumstances, *after* the appearance of Ulmo. In the *Tale* (p.45) Tuor's long rapture in Nan-tathrin led Ulmo to fear that he would never leave it; and in his instruction to Tuor he said that the Noldoli would escort him secretly to the city of the people named *Gondothlim* or 'dwellers in stone' (this being the first reference to Gondolin in the *Tale*: in both the *Sketch* and the *Quenta* some account of the hidden city is given before there is any mention of Tuor). In the event, according to the *Tale* (p.48), the Noldoli guiding Tuor on his eastbound journey deserted him out of fear of Melko, and he became lost. But one of the Elves came back to him, and offered to accompany him in his search for Gondolin, of which this Noldo had heard rumour, but nothing else. He was Voronwë.

Advancing now through many years we come to the Last Version (LV), and what is told of Tuor's youth. Neither in the *Sketch* nor the *Quenta* is there any reference to Tuor's fostering by the Grey-elves of Hithlum, but in this final version there enters an extensive account (pp.145–9). This tells of his upbringing among the Elves under Annael, of their oppressed lives and southward flight by the secret way known as Annon-in-Gelydh 'the Gate of the Noldor, for it was made by the skill of that people long ago in the days of Turgon'. There is here also an account of Tuor's slavery and his escape, with the years following as a much feared outlaw.

The most significant development in all this arises from Tuor's determination to flee the land. Following what he had learned from Annael he sought far and wide for the Gate of the Noldor, and the mysterious hidden kingdom of Turgon (LV p.149). This was Tuor's express aim; but he did not know what that 'Gate' might be. He came to the spring of a stream that rose in the hills of Mithrim, and it was here that he made his final decision to depart from Hithlum 'the grey land of my kin', though his search for the Gate of the Noldor had failed. He followed the stream down until he came to a rock wall where it disappeared in 'an opening like a great arch'. There he sat in despair through the night, until at sunrise he saw two Elves climbing up from the arch.

They were Noldorin Elves named Gelmir and Arminas, engaged on an urgent errand which they did not define. From them he learned that the great arch was indeed the Gate of the Noldor, and all unknowing he had found it. Taking the place of the Noldoli who guided him in the old *Tale* (p.38), Gelmir and Arminas guided him through the tunnel to a place where they halted, and he questioned them about Turgon, saying that that name strangely moved him whenever he heard it. To this they gave him no reply, but bade him farewell and went back up the long stairs in the darkness (p.155).

The Last Version introduced little alteration to the narrative of the *Tale* in the account of Tuor's journey, after he had emerged from the tunnel, down the steep-sided ravine. It is notable, however, that whereas in the *Tale* (p.40) 'the Ainur put it into his heart to climb from the gully when he did, or had he been whelmed in the incoming tide', in LV (pp.157–8) he climbed up because he wished to follow the three great gulls, and he 'was saved by the call of the sea-birds from death in the rising tide'. The sea-cove named Falasquil (*Tale* p.41) where Tuor built himself a dwelling and 'passed a very great while', 'by slow labour' adorning it with carvings, had disappeared in the Last Version.

In that text Tuor, dismayed by the fury of the strange waters (LV p.158), set off southwards from the ravine of the river, and passed into the borders of the region of Nevrast in the far west 'where once Turgon had dwelt'; and at last he came at sunset to the shores of Middle-earth and saw the Great Sea. Here the Last Version departs radically from the history of Tuor as told hitherto.

Returning to the *Tale*, and the coming of Ulmo to meet Tuor in the Land of Willows (p.45), there enters my father's original description of the appearance of the great Vala

(*Tale* p.45). The Lord of all seas and rivers, he came to urge Tuor to tarry no longer in that place. This description is an elaborate and sharply defined picture of the god himself, come on a vast voyage across the ocean. He dwells in a 'palace' below the waters of the Outer Sea, he rides in his 'car', made in the fashion of a whale, at a stupendous speed. His hair and his great beard are observed, his mail 'like the scales of blue and silver fishes', his kirtle (coat) of 'shimmering greens', his girdle of great pearls, his shoes of stone. Leaving his 'car' at the mouth of the Sirion he strode up beside the great river, and 'he sat among the reeds at twilight' near the place where Tuor 'stood knee-deep in the grass'; he played upon his strange instrument of music, which was 'made of many long twisted shells pierced with holes' (*Tale* pp.45–6).

Perhaps most notable of all the characters of Ulmo was the fathomless depth of his eyes and his voice when he spoke to Tuor, filling him with fear. Leaving the Land of Willows Tuor, escorted secretly by Noldoli, must seek out the city of the Gondothlim (see p.46 above). In the *Tale* (p.46) Ulmo said 'Words I will set to your mouth there, and there you shall abide awhile.' Of what his words to Turgon would be there is in this version no indication – but it is said that Ulmo spoke to Tuor 'some of his design and desire', which he scarcely understood. Ulmo uttered also an extraordinary prophecy concerning Tuor's child to be, 'than whom no man shall know more of the uttermost deeps, be it of the sea or of the firmament of heaven.' That child was Eärendel.

*

In the *Sketch* of 1926, on the other hand, there is a clear statement (p.123) of Ulmo's purpose that Tuor is to assert in Gondolin: in brief, Turgon must prepare for a terrible battle with Morgoth, in which 'the race of Orcs will perish'; but if Turgon will not accept this, then the people of Gondolin must flee their city and go to the mouth of Sirion, where Ulmo 'will aid them to build a fleet and guide them back to Valinor'. In the *Quenta Noldorinwa* of 1930 (p.137) the prospects held out by Ulmo are essentially the same, though the outcome of such a battle, 'a terrible and mortal strife', is presented as the breaking of Morgoth's power and much else, 'whereof the greatest good should come into the world, and the servants of Morgoth trouble it no more'.

It is convenient at this point to turn to the important manuscript of the later 1930s entitled *Quenta Silmarillion*. This was to be a new prose version of the history of the Elder Days following the *Quenta Noldorinwa* of 1930; but it came to an abrupt end in 1937 with the advent of the 'new story about hobbits' (I have given an account of this strange history in *Beren and Lúthien*, pp.219–21).

From this work I append here passages that bear on the early history of Turgon, his discovery of Tumladen and the building of Gondolin, but which do not appear in the texts of *The Fall of Gondolin*.

It is told in the *Quenta Silmarillion* that Turgon, a leader of the Noldor who dared the terror of the *Helkaraksë* (the Grinding Ice) in the crossing to Middle-earth, dwelt in Nevrast. In this text occurs this passage:

On a time Turgon left Nevrast where he dwelt and went to visit Inglor his friend, and they journeyed southward along Sirion, being weary for a while of the northern mountains, and as they journeyed night came upon them beyond the Meres of Twilight beside the waters of Sirion, and they slept upon his banks beneath the summer stars. But Ulmo coming up the river laid a profound sleep upon them and heavy dreams; and the trouble of the dreams remained after they awoke, but neither said aught to the other, for their memory was not clear, and each deemed that Ulmo had sent a message to him alone. But unquiet was upon them ever after and doubt of what should befall, and they wandered often alone in unexplored country, seeking far and wide for places of hidden strength; for it seemed to each that he was bidden to prepare for a day of evil, and to establish a retreat, lest Morgoth should burst from Angband and overthrow the armies of the North.

Thus it came to pass that Inglor found the deep gorge of Narog and the caves in its western side; and he built there a stronghold and armouries after the fashion of the deep mansions of Menegroth. And he called this place Nargothrond, and made there his home with many of his folk; and the Gnomes of the North, at first in merriment, called him on this account Felagund, or Lord of Caves, and that name he bore thereafter until his end. But Turgon went alone into hidden places, and by the guidance of Ulmo found the secret vale of Gondolin; and of this he said nought as yet, but returned to Nevrast and his folk.

In a further passage of the *Quenta Silmarillion* it is told of Turgon, the second son of Fingolfin, that he ruled over a numerous people, but 'the unquiet of Ulmo increased upon him;'

> he arose, and took with him a great host of Gnomes, even to a third of the people of Fingolfin, and their goods and wives and children, and departed eastward. His going was by night and his march swift and silent, and he vanished out of knowledge of his kindred. But he came to Gondolin, and built there a city like unto Tûn of Valinor, and fortified the surrounding hills; and Gondolin lay hidden for many years.

A third, and essential, citation comes from a different source. There are two texts, bearing the titles *The Annals of Beleriand* and *The Annals of Valinor*. These were begun about 1930, and are extant in subsequent versions. I have said of them: 'The Annals began, perhaps, in parallel with the *Quenta* as a convenient way of driving abreast, and keeping track of, the different elements in the ever more complex narrative web.' The final text of *The Annals of Beleriand*, also named the *Grey Annals*, derive from the time in the early 1950s when my father turned again to the matter of the Elder Days after the completion of *The Lord of the Rings*. It was a major source for the published *Silmarillion*.

There follows here a passage from the *Grey Annals*; it refers to the year 'in which Gondolin was full-wrought, after fifty and two years of secret toil'.

Now therefore Turgon prepared to depart from Nevrast, and leave his fair halls in Vinyamar beneath Mount Taras; and then Ulmo came to him a second time and said: 'Now thou shalt go at last to Gondolin, Turgon; and I will set my power in the Vale of Sirion, so that none shall mark thy going, nor shall any find there the hidden entrance to thy land against thy will. Longest of all the realms of the Eldalië shall Gondolin stand against Melkor. But love it not too well, and remember that the true hope of the Noldor lieth in the West and cometh from the Sea.'*

And Ulmo warned Turgon that he also lay under the Doom of Mandos, which Ulmo had no power to remove. 'Thus it may come to pass,' he said, 'that the curse of the Noldor shall find thee too ere the end, and treason shall awake within thy walls. Then shall they be in peril of fire. But if this peril draweth nigh, then even from Nevrast one shall come to warn thee, and from him beyond ruin and fire hope shall be born for Elves and Men. Leave, therefore, in this house arms and a sword, that in years to come he may find them, and thus shalt thou know him and be not deceived.' And Ulmo showed to Turgon of what kind and stature should be the mail and helm and sword that he left behind.

Then Ulmo returned to the Sea; and Turgon sent forth all his folk ... and they passed away, company by company, secretly, under the shadows of Eryd Wethion, and came unseen with their wives and goods to Gondolin, and none

---

* These words, slightly changed, were spoken by Tuor to Voronwë at Vinyamar, LV p.171.

knew whither they were gone. And last of all Turgon arose and went with his lords and household silently through the hills and passed the gates in the mountains, and they were shut. But Nevrast was empty of folk and so remained until the ruin of Beleriand.

In this last passage is seen the explanation of the shield and sword, the hauberk and helm, that Tuor found when he entered the great hall of Vinyamar (LV p.162).

After the conclusion of the meeting of Ulmo with Tuor in the Land of Willows all the early texts (the *Tale*, the *Sketch*, the *Quenta Noldorinwa*) move on to the journey of Tuor and Voronwë in search of Gondolin. Of the eastward journey itself there is indeed scarcely any mention, the mystery of the hidden city residing in the secret of entry to Tumladen (to which in the *Sketch* and *Quenta Noldorinwa* Ulmo gives them aid).

But here we will return to the Last Version, which I left in this discussion at the coming of Tuor to the coast of the Sea in the region of Nevrast (LV p.158). Here we see the great abandoned house of Vinyamar beneath Mount Taras ('eldest of all the works of stone that the Noldor built in the lands of their exile') where Turgon first dwelt, and which Tuor now entered. Of all that follows ('Tuor in Vinyamar', LV pp.161 ff.) there is no hint or preceding trace in the early texts – save of course the advent of Ulmo, told again after a lapse of thirty-five years.

*

I pause here to observe what is told elsewhere concerning the guidance, indeed the urging, of Tuor in the furtherance of Ulmo's designs.

The origin of his 'designs' that came to be centred on Tuor arose from the massive and far-reaching event that came to be called *The Hiding of Valinor*. There exists an early story, one of the *Lost Tales*, that bears that title, and describes the origin and nature of this alteration of the world in the Elder Days. It arose from the rebellion of the Noldoli (Noldor) under the leadership of Fëanor, maker of the Silmarils, against the Valar, and their intent to leave Valinor. I have described very briefly the consequence of that decision in *Beren and Lúthien*, p.23, and I repeat that here.

Before their departure from Valinor there took place the dreadful event that marred the history of the Noldor in Middle-earth. Fëanor demanded of those Teleri, the third host of the Eldar on the Great Journey [from the place of their Awakening], who dwelt now on the coast of Aman, that they give up to the Noldor their fleet of ships, their great pride, for without ships the crossing to Middle-earth by such a host would not be possible. This the Teleri refused utterly. Then Fëanor and his people attacked the Teleri in their city of Alqualondë, the Haven of the Swans, and took the fleet by force. In that battle, which was known as the Kinslaying, many of the Teleri were slain.

In *The Hiding of Valinor* there is a remarkable description of a very heated and indeed extraordinary meeting of the Valar that bears on the present subject. On this occasion there was present an Elf of Alqualondë named Ainairos whose kin had perished in the battle of the Haven, 'and he sought unceasingly with his words to persuade the [Teleri] to greater bitterness of heart.' This Ainairos spoke at the debate, and his words are recorded in *The Hiding of Valinor*.

He laid before the Gods the mind of the Elves [i.e. the Teleri] concerning the Noldoli and of the nakedness of the land of Valinor toward the world beyond. Thereat arose much tumult and many of the Valar and their folk supported him loudly, and some others of the Eldar cried out that Manwë and Varda had caused their kindred to dwell in Valinor promising them unfailing joy therein – now let the Gods see to it that their gladness was not minished to a little thing, seeing that Melko held the world and they dared not fare forth to the places of their awakening even if they would.

The most of the Valar moreover were fain of their ancient ease and desired only peace, wishing neither rumour of Melko and his violence nor murmur of the restless Gnomes to come ever again among them to disturb their happiness; and for such reasons they also clamoured for the concealment of the land. Not the least among these were Vána and Nessa, albeit most even of the great Gods were of one mind. In vain did Ulmo of his foreknowing plead before them for pity and pardon on the Noldoli, or Manwë unfold the secrets of the Music of the Ainur and the purpose of the world; and long and very full of that noise was that council, and more filled with bitterness and burning words than any that had been; wherefore did Manwë Súlimo depart at length from among them, saying that no walls or bulwarks might now fend Melko's evil from them which lived already among them and clouded all their minds.

So came it that the enemies of the Gnomes carried the council of the Gods and the blood of [the Haven of the Swans] began already its fell work; for now began that which is named the Hiding of Valinor, and Manwë and Varda and Ulmo of the Seas had no part therein, but none others of the Valar or the Elves held aloof therefrom . . .

Now Lórien and Vána led the Gods and Aulë lent his skill and Tulkas his strength, and the Valar went not at that time forth to conquer Melko, and the greatest ruth was that to them thereafter, and yet is; for the great glory of the Valar by reason of that error came not to its fullness in many ages of the Earth, and still doth the world await it.

Very striking is this last passage, with its clear representation of the Gods as indolently regarding only their own security and well-being, and expression of the view that they had committed a colossal 'error', for in failing to make war on Melko they left Middle-earth open to the destructive ambitions and hatreds of the arch-enemy. But such condemnation of the Valar is not found in later writing. The Hiding of Valinor is present only as a great fact of legendary antiquity.

There follows in *The Hiding of Valinor* a passage in which the gigantic and manifold works of defence are described –

'new and mighty labours such as had not been seen among them since the days of the first building of Valinor', such as the making of the encircling mountains more utterly impassable on their eastern sides.

From North to South marched the enchantments and inaccessible magic of the Gods, yet were they not content; and they said: 'Behold, we will cause all the paths that fare to Valinor, both known and secret, to fade utterly from the world, or wander treacherously into blind confusion.'

This then they did, and no channel in the seas was left that was not beset with perilous eddies or with streams of overmastering strength for the confusion of all ships. And spirits of sudden storms and winds unlooked for brooded there by Ossë's will, and others of inextricable mist.

To read of the effects of the Hiding of Valinor on Gondolin one may look ahead to Turgon's words to Tuor in the *Tale*, speaking of the fate of the many messengers that had been sent from Gondolin to build ships for the voyage to Valinor (p.57):

'... but the paths thereto are forgotten and the highways faded from the world, and the seas and mountains are about it, and they that sit within in mirth reck little of the dread of Melko or the sorrow of the world, but hide their land and weave about it inaccessible magic, that no tidings of evil come ever to their ears. Nay, enough of my people have for years untold gone out to the wide waters never to return, but have perished in the deep places or wander now lost in the shadows that have no paths; and at the coming of next year no more shall fare to the sea . . .'

(It is a very curious fact that Turgon's words here were uttered in ironic repetition of Tuor's, spoken as Ulmo bade him, immediately preceding (*Tale* p.56):

'. . . lo! the paths thereto are forgotten and the highways faded from the world, and the seas and mountains are about it, yet still dwell there the Elves on the hill of Kôr and the Gods sit in Valinor, though their mirth is minished for sorrow and fear of Melko, and they hide their land and weave about it inaccessible magic that no evil come to its shores.')

On pp.115–17 (*Turlin and the Exiles of Gondolin*) I have given a brief text that was soon abandoned, but was clearly intended as the beginning of a new version of the *Tale* (but still with the old version of the genealogy of Tuor, which was replaced by that of the house of Hador in the *Sketch* of 1926). It is a remarkable feature of this piece that Ulmo is explicitly represented as altogether alone among the Valar in his concern for the Elves who lived under the power of Melko, 'nor did any save Ulmo only dread the power of Melko that wrought ruin and sorrow over all the Earth; but Ulmo desired that Valinor should gather all its might to quench his evil ere it be too late, and it seemed to him that both his purposes might perchance be achieved if messengers from the Gnomes should win to Valinor and plead for pardon and for pity upon the Earth.'

It was here that the 'isolation' of Ulmo among the Valar first appears, for there is no suggestion of it in the *Tale*. I will conclude this account with a repetition of how Ulmo saw it in his words to Tuor as he stood at the water's edge in the rising storm at Vinyamar (LV pp.165–6).

And Ulmo spoke to Tuor of Valinor and its darkening, and the Exile of the Noldor, and the Doom of Mandos, and the hiding of the Blessed Realm. 'But behold!' said he, 'in the armour of Fate (as the Children of Earth name it) there is ever a rift, and in the walls of Doom a breach, until the full-making, which ye call the End. So it shall be while I endure, a secret voice that gainsayeth, and a light where darkness was decreed. Therefore, though in the days of this darkness I seem to oppose the will of my brethren, the Lords of the West, that is my part among them, to which I was appointed ere the making of the World. Yet Doom is strong, and the shadow of the Enemy lengthens; and I am diminished, until in Middle-earth I am become now no more than a secret whisper. The waters that run westward wither, and their springs are poisoned, and my power withdraws from the land; for Elves and Men grow blind and deaf to me because of the might of Melkor. And now the Curse of Mandos hastens to its fulfilment, and all the works of the Noldor shall perish, and every hope that they build will crumble. The last hope alone is left, the hope that they have not looked for and have not prepared. And that hope lieth in thee; for so I have chosen.'

This leads to a further question: why did he choose Tuor? Or even, why did he choose a Man? To this latter question an answer is given in the *Tale*, p.62:

Behold now many years have gone since Tuor was lost amid the foothills and deserted by those Noldoli; yet many years too have gone since to Melko's ears came first those strange tidings – faint were they and various in form – of a man wandering amid the dales of the waters of Sirion. Now Melko was not much afraid of the race of Men in those days of his great power, and for this reason did Ulmo work through one of this kindred for the better deceiving of Melko, seeing that no Valar and scarce any of the Eldar or Noldoli might stir unmarked of his vigilance.

But to the far more significant question I think that the answer lies in the words of Ulmo to Tuor at Vinyamar (LV p.166), when Tuor said to him: 'Of little avail shall I be, a mortal man alone, among so many and so valiant of the High Folk of West.' To this Ulmo replied:

'If I choose to send thee, *Tuor son of Huor*, then believe not that thy one sword is not worth the sending. For the valour of the Edain the Elves shall ever remember as the ages lengthen, marvelling that they gave life so freely of which on earth they had so little. But it is not for thy valour only that I send thee, but to bring into the world a hope beyond thy sight, and a light that shall pierce the darkness.'

What was that hope? I believe that it was the event that Ulmo declared with such miraculous foresight to Tuor in the *Tale* (p.47):

'... of a surety a child shall come of thee than whom no man shall know more of the uttermost deeps, be it of the sea or of the firmament of heaven.'

As I have observed (p.217 above), the child was Eärendel.

It cannot be doubted that Ulmo's prophetic words 'a light that shall pierce the darkness', sent by Ulmo himself, and brought into the world by Tuor, is Eärendel. But strange indeed as it appears, there is a passage elsewhere showing that Ulmo's 'miraculous foresight', as I have called it, had emerged many years before, independently of Ulmo.

This passage occurs in the version of the text *The Annals of Beleriand* known as the *Grey Annals*, from the period following the completion of *The Lord of the Rings*, on which see *The Evolution of the Story* p.220. The scene is the Battle of Unnumbered Tears, towards its end with the death of Fingon the Elvenking.

The day was lost, but still Húrin and Huor with the men of Hador stood firm, and the Orcs could not yet win the passes of Sirion ... The last stand of Húrin and Huor is the deed of war most renowned among the Eldar that the

Fathers of Men wrought in their behalf. For Húrin spoke to Turgon saying: 'Go now, lord, while time is! For last art thou of the House of Fingolfin, and in thee lives the last hope of the Noldor. While Gondolin stands, strong and guarded, Morgoth shall still know fear in his heart.'

'Yet not long now can Gondolin be hidden, and being discovered it must fall,' said Turgon.

'Yet if it stands but a little while,' said Huor, 'then out of thy house shall come the hope of Elves and Men. This I say to thee, lord, with the eyes of death; though here we part for ever, and I shall never look on thy white walls, from thee and me shall a new star arise.'

Turgon accepted the counsel of Húrin and Huor. He withdrew with all such warriors as he could gather from the host of Fingon and from Gondolin and vanished into the mountains, while Húrin and Huor held the pass behind them against the swarming host of Morgoth. Huor fell with a poisoned arrow in the eye.

We cannot overestimate the divine powers of Ulmo – mightiest of the Gods after Manwë alone: in his vast knowledge and foreknowledge, and in his inconceivable ability to enter the minds of other beings and influence their thoughts and even their understanding from far away. Most notable of course is his speaking through Tuor when he came to Gondolin. This goes back to the *Tale*: 'Words I will set to your mouth there' (p.46); and in the Last Version (p.167), when Tuor asks 'What words shall I say unto

Turgon?', Ulmo replies: 'If thou come to him, then the words shall arise in thy mind, then thy mouth shall speak as I would.' In the *Tale* (p.55) this capacity of Ulmo goes even further: 'Then spoke Tuor, and Ulmo set power in his heart and majesty in his voice.'

In this discursive discussion of Ulmo's designs for Tuor we have come to Vinyamar, and to the second appearance of the God in this narrative that differs profoundly from that in the *Tale* (p.45 and p.216 above). No longer does he come up the great river Sirion and make music sitting in the reeds, but as a great storm of the sea draws near he strides out of a wave, 'a living shape of great height and majesty', seeming to Tuor a mighty king wearing a tall crown; and the God speaks to the Man 'standing knee-deep in the shadowy sea'. But the entire episode of Tuor's coming to Vinyamar was absent from the story as it previously existed; and thus likewise the essential element, in the Last Version, of the arms left for him in the house of Turgon (see LV p.162 and p.221 above).

It is conceivable, however, that the germ of this story was present as far back as the *Tale*, p.55, when Turgon greets Tuor before the doors of his palace: 'Welcome, O Man of the Land of Shadows. Lo! thy coming was set in our books of wisdom, and it has been written that there would come to pass many great things in the homes of the Gondothlim whenso thou faredst hither.'

In the Last Version there appears (p.169) the Noldorin Elf Voronwë in a role that binds him from his first appearance in the narrative to the tale of Tuor and Ulmo, wholly distinct from his entry in earlier texts (see p.48). After the departure of Ulmo

> Tuor looked down from the lowest terrace [of Vinyamar] and saw, leaning against its wall among the stones and the sea-wrack, an Elf, clad in a grey cloak sodden with the sea … As Tuor stood and looked at the silent grey figure he remembered the words of Ulmo, and a name untaught came to his lips, and he called aloud: 'Welcome, Voronwë! I await you.'

These words of Ulmo were his last to Tuor before his departure (LV p. 167):

> 'I will send one to thee out of the wrath of Ossë, and thus shalt thou be guided: yea, the last mariner of the last ship that shall seek into the West until the rising of the Star.'

And this mariner was Voronwë, who told his story to Tuor beside the sea at Vinyamar (LV pp.173–7). His account of his voyaging over seven years in the Great Sea was a grim one to give to Tuor, so greatly enamoured of the ocean. But before setting forth on his mission, he said (LV p.174 ff.):

> I tarried on the way. For I had seen little of the lands of Middle-earth, and we came to Nan-tathrin in the spring of the year. Lovely to heart's enchantment is that land, Tuor,

as you shall find, if ever your feet go upon the southward roads down Sirion. There is the cure of all sea-longing . . .

The story in the *Tale* of Tuor's overlong stay in Nan-tathrin, the Land of Willows, the cause of Ulmo's visitation as originally told, bewitched by its beauty, had now of course disappeared from the narrative; but it was not lost. In the last version it was Voronwë, speaking to Tuor at Vinyamar, who had passed a while in Nan-tathrin, and become enthralled as he 'stood knee-deep in grass' (LV p.175); in the old story it had been Tuor who 'stood knee-deep in the grass' in the Land of Willows (*Tale* p.46). Both Tuor and Voronwë gave names of their own to the flowers and birds and butterflies unknown to them.

Since we shall not in this 'Evolution of the Story' meet again Ulmo in person I attach here a portrait of the great Vala that my father wrote in his work *The Music of the Ainur* (late 1930s):

Ulmo has dwelt ever in the Outer Ocean, and governed the flowing of all waters, and the courses of all rivers, the replenishment of springs and the distilling of rain and dew throughout the world. In the deep places he gives thought to music great and terrible; and the echo thereof runs through all the veins of the world, and its joy is as the joy of a fountain in the sun whose wells are the wells of unfathomed sorrow at the foundations of the world. The Teleri learned much of him, and for this reason their music has both sadness and enchantment.

We come now to the journey of Tuor and Voronwë from Vinyamar in Nevrast, beside the sea in the far West, to find Gondolin. This would take them eastward along the southern side of the great mountain range Ered Wethrin, the Mountains of Shadow, that formed a vast barrier between Hithlum and West Beleriand, and bring them at last to the great river Sirion running from north to south.

The earliest reference, in the *Tale* (p.49), says no more than that 'Long time did Tuor and Voronwë [who in the old story had never been there] seek for the city of that folk [the Gondothlim], until after many days they came upon a deep dale amid the hills'. Likewise the *Sketch*, not surprisingly, says very simply (pp.123–4) that 'Tuor and Bronweg reach the secret way ... and come out upon the guarded plain.' And the *Quenta Noldorinwa* (p.137) is equally brief: 'Obedient to Ulmo Tuor and Bronwë journeyed North, and came at last to the hidden door.'

Beside these terse glances the account in the Last Version of the fearful days passed by Tuor and Voronwë in the bitter winds and biting frosts of the houseless country, their escape from the bands of Orcs and their encampments, the coming of the eagles, may be seen as a significant element in the history of Gondolin. (On the presence of the eagles in that region see *Quenta Noldorinwa* p.132 and LV p.188.) Most notable is their coming to the Pool of Ivrin (p.178), the lake where the river Narog rose, now defiled and made desolate by the passage of the dragon Glaurung (called by Voronwë 'the Great Worm of Angband'). Here the seekers of Gondolin touched the greatest story of the Elder Days: for they saw a tall man passing, bearing a long sword drawn, and the blade was long and black. They did not speak to this man clad in black; and they did not know that he was Túrin Turambar, the Blacksword, fleeing north from the sack of Nargothrond, of which they had not heard. 'Thus only for a moment, and never again, did the paths of those kinsmen, Túrin and Tuor, draw together.' (Húrin the father of Túrin was the brother of Huor the father of Tuor.)

We come now to the last step in the 'Evolution of the Story' (because the Last Version extends no further): the first sight of Gondolin, by way of the hidden and guarded entry into the plain of Tumladen – a 'door' or 'gate' of renown in the history of Middle-earth. In the *Tale* (p.49) Tuor and Voronwë came to a place where the river (Sirion) 'went over a very stony bed'. This was the Ford of Brithiach, not yet so named; 'it was curtained with a heavy growth of alders', but the banks were sheer-sided. There in the 'green wall' Voronwë found 'an opening like a great door with sloping sides, and this was cloaked with thick bushes and long-tangled undergrowth'.

Passing through this opening (p.49) they found themselves in a dark and wandering tunnel. In this they groped their way until they saw a distant light, 'and making for this gleam they came to a gate like that by which they had entered'. Here they were surrounded by armed guards, and found themselves in the sunlight at the feet of steep hills bordering in a circle a wide plain, and in this there stood a city, at the summit of a great hill standing alone.

In the *Sketch* there is of course no description of the entry; but in the *Quenta Noldorinwa* (p.131) this is said of the Way of Escape: in the region where the Encircling Mountains were at their lowest the Elves of Gondolin 'dug a great winding tunnel under the roots of the hills, and its issue was in the steep side, tree-clad and dark, of a gorge through which the blissful river [Sirion] ran.' It is said in the *Quenta* (p.137) that when Tuor and Bronwë (Voronwë) came to the hidden door they passed down the tunnel and 'reached the inner gate', where they were taken prisoner.

The two 'gates' and the tunnel between them were thus present when my father wrote the *Quenta Noldorinwa* in 1930, and on this conception he based the final version of 1951. This is where the resemblance ends.

But it will be seen that in the final version (LV pp.187 ff.) my father introduced a sharp difference into the topography. The entrance was no longer in the eastern bank of the Sirion; it was from a tributary stream. But the dangerous crossing of the Brithiach they made, being fortified by the appearance of the eagles.

On the far side of the ford they came to a gully, as it were the bed of an old stream, in which no water now flowed; yet once, it seemed, a torrent had cloven its deep channel, coming down from the north out of the mountains of the Echoriath, and bearing thence all the stones of the Brithiach down into Sirion.

'At last beyond hope we find it!' cried Voronwë. 'See!

Here is the mouth of the Dry River, and that is the road we must take.'

But the 'road' was full of stones and went sharply up, and Tuor expressed to Voronwë his disgust, and his amazement that this wretched track should be the way of entry to the city of Gondolin.

After many miles, and a night spent, in the Dry River it led them to the walls of the Encircling Mountains, and entering by an opening they were brought at length to what they felt to be a great silent space, in which they could see nothing. The sinister reception of Tuor and Voronwë can scarcely be equalled in the writings of Middle-earth: the dazzling light turned on Voronwë in the huge darkness, the cold menacing, questioning voice. That dreadful interview over, they were led to another entry, or exit.

In the *Quenta Noldorinwa* (p.138) Tuor and Voronwë stepped out from the long twisting black tunnel, where they were taken prisoner by the guard, and saw Gondolin 'shining from afar, flushed with the rose of dawn upon the plain'. Thus the conception at that time was readily described: the wide plain Tumladen wholly encircled by the mountains, the Echoriath, and a tunnel from the outer world running through them. But in the Last Version, when they left the place of their inquisition, Tuor found that they were standing 'at the end of a ravine, the like of which he had never before beheld or imagined in his thought'. Up this ravine, named the Orfalch Echor, a long road climbed through a succession of huge gates magnificently adorned until the top of the rift was reached at the seventh, the Great Gate. It was only then that Tuor 'beheld a vision of Gondolin amid the white snow'; and it was there that Ecthelion said of Tuor that it was certain that 'he comes from Ulmo himself' – the words with which the last text of *The Fall of Gondolin* ends.

CONCLUSION

I mentioned (p.23) that the original title of the *Tale, Tuor and the Exiles of Gondolin*, was followed by the words 'which bringeth in the Great Tale of Eärendel.' Further, the 'Last Tale' that followed *The Fall of Gondolin*, was the *Tale of the Nauglafring* (The Necklace of the Dwarves, on which was set the Silmaril) of which I cited the concluding words in *Beren and Lúthien*, p.246:

> And thus did all the fates of the fairies weave then to one strand, and that strand is the great tale of Eärendel; and to that tale's true beginning are we now come.

We may suppose that the 'true beginning' of the *Tale of Eärendel* was to follow the words with which the *Tale of The Fall of Gondolin* ended (p.111):

Yet now those exiles of Gondolin dwelt at the mouth of Sirion by the waves of the Great Sea ... and fair among the Lothlim Eärendel grows in the house of his father, and the great tale of Tuor is come to its waning.

But the Lost Tale of Eärendel was never written. There are many notes and outlines from the early period, and several very early poems: but there is nothing remotely corresponding to the Tale of *The Fall of Gondolin*. To set out and discuss these often contradictory outlines in their clipped phrases would be contrary to the purpose of these two books: the comparative histories of *narratives* as they evolved. On the other hand, the story of the destruction of Gondolin is very fully told in the original *Tale*; the history of the survivors is an essential continuation of the history of the Elder Days. I have decided therefore to return to the two early narratives in which the tale of the end of the Elder Days is told: the *Sketch of the Mythology* and the *Quenta Noldorinwa*. (As I have remarked elsewhere, 'It will seem strange indeed that the *Quenta Noldorinwa* was the only completed text (after the *Sketch*) that he ever made.')

For this reason there follows here the conclusion of the *Sketch* of 1926, following on the words (p.125): 'The remnant [of the people of Gondolin] reaches Sirion and journeys to the land at its mouth – the Waters of Sirion. Morgoth's triumph is now complete.'

THE CONCLUSION OF THE
SKETCH OF THE MYTHOLOGY

At Sirion's mouth Elwing daughter of Dior dwelt, and received the survivors of Gondolin. These become a seafaring folk, building many boats and living far out on the delta, whither the Orcs dare not come.

Ylmir [Ulmo] reproaches the Valar, and bids them rescue the remnants of the Noldoli and the Silmarils in which alone now lives the light of the old days of bliss when the Trees were shining.

The sons of the Valar led by Fionwë Manwë's son lead forth a host, in which all the Quendi march, but remembering Swanhaven few of the Teleri go with them. Côr is deserted.

Tuor growing old cannot forbear the call of the sea, and builds Eärámë and sails West with Idril and is heard of no more. Eärendel weds Elwing. The call of the sea is born also in him. He builds Wingelot and wishes to sail in search of his father. Here follow the marvellous adventures of

Wingelot in the seas and isles, and of how Eärendel slew Ungoliant in the South. He returned home and found the Waters of Sirion desolate. The sons of Fëanor learning of the dwelling of Elwing and the Nauglafring [on which was set the Silmaril of Beren] had come down on the people of Gondolin. In a battle all the sons of Fëanor save Maidros and Maglor were slain, but the last folk of Gondolin were destroyed or forced to go away and join the people of Maidros. Maglor sat and sang by the sea in repentance. Elwing cast the Nauglafring into the sea and leapt after it, but was changed into a white sea-bird by Ylmir, and flew to seek Eärendel, seeking about all the shores of the world.

Their son Elrond who is part mortal and part elven, a child, was saved however by Maidros. When later the Elves return to the West, bound by his mortal half he elects to stay on earth ...

Eärendel learning of these things from Bronweg, who dwelt in a hut, a solitary, at the mouth of Sirion, is overcome with sorrow. With Bronweg he sets sail in Wingelot once more in search of Elwing and of Valinor.

He comes to the magic isles, and to the Lonely Isle, and at last to the Bay of Faërie. He climbs the hill of Kôr, and walks in the deserted ways of Tûn, and his raiment becomes encrusted with the dust of diamonds and of jewels. He dares not go further into Valinor. He builds a tower on an isle in the northern seas, to which all the seabirds of the world repair. He sails by the aid of their wings even over the airs in search of Elwing, but is scorched by the Sun and hunted from the sky by the Moon, and for a long while he wanders the sky as a fugitive star.

The march of Fionwë into the North is then told, and of the Terrible or Last Battle. The Balrogs are all destroyed, and the Orcs destroyed or scattered. Morgoth himself makes a last sally with all his dragons; but they are destroyed, all save two which escape, by the sons of the Valar, and Morgoth is overthrown and bound by the chain Angainor, and his iron crown is made into a collar for his neck. The two Silmarils are rescued. The Northern and Western parts of the world are rent and broken in the struggle, and the fashion of their lands altered.

The Gods and Elves release Men from Hithlum, and march through the lands summoning the remnants of the Gnomes and Ilkorins to join them. All do so except the people of Maidros. Maidros prepares to perform his oath, though now at last weighed down by sorrow because of it. He sends to Fionwë reminding him of the oath and begging for the Silmarils. Fionwë replies that he has lost his right to them because of the evil deeds of Fëanor, and of the slaying of Dior, and of the plundering of Sirion. He must submit, and come back to Valinor; in Valinor only and at the judgement of the Gods shall they be handed over ...

On the last march Maglor says to Maidros that there are two sons of Fëanor left, and two Silmarils; one is his. He steals it, and flies, but it burns him so that he knows he no longer has a right to it. He wanders in pain over the earth and casts it into a fiery pit. One Silmaril is now in the sea, and one in the earth. Maglor sings now ever in sorrow by the sea.

The judgement of the Gods takes place. The earth is to be for Men, and the Elves who do not set sail for the Lonely Isle or Valinor shall slowly fade and fail. For a while the last dragons and Orcs shall grieve the earth, but in the end all shall perish by the valour of Men.

Morgoth is thrust through the Door of Night into the outer dark beyond the Walls of the World, and a guard set for ever on that Door. The lies that he sowed in the hearts of Men and Elves do not die and cannot all be slain by the Gods, but live on and bring much evil even to this day. Some say also that secretly Morgoth or his black shadow and spirit in spite of the Valar creeps back over the Walls of the World in the North and East and visits the world, others that this is Thû his great chief who escaped the Last Battle and dwells still in dark places, and perverts Men to his dreadful worship. When the world is much older, and the Gods weary, Morgoth will come back through the Door, and the last battle of all will be fought. Fionwë will fight Morgoth on the plain of Valinor, and the spirit of Túrin shall be beside him; it shall be Túrin who with his black sword will slay Morgoth, and thus the children of Húrin shall be avenged.

In those days the Silmarils shall be recovered from sea and earth and air, and Maidros shall break them and Palúrien with their fire rekindle the Two Trees, and the great light shall come forth again, and the Mountains of Valinor shall be levelled so that it goes out over the world, and Gods and

Elves shall grow young again, and all their dead awake. But of Men in that Day the prophecy speaks not.

And thus it was that the last Silmaril came into the air. The Gods adjudged the last Silmaril to Eärendel – 'until many things shall come to pass' – because of the deeds of the sons of Fëanor. Maidros is sent to Eärendel and with the aid of the Silmaril Elwing is found and restored. Eärendel's boat is drawn over Valinor to the Outer Seas, and Eärendel launches it into the outer darkness high above Sun and Moon. There he sails with the Silmaril upon his brow and Elwing at his side, the brightest of all stars, keeping watch upon Morgoth and the Door of Night. So he shall sail until he sees the last battle gathering upon the plains of Valinor. Then he will descend.

And this is the last end of the tales of the days before the days, in the Northern regions of the Western world.

It would take this story very much too far afield to enter into any general discussion of this most complex and obscure part of the history of the 'First Age': its end. I will only mention a few aspects of the narrative in the *Sketch of the Mythology* given here. What little writing on the subject that survives from the earliest period of my father's work had very largely been abandoned, and the account in the *Sketch* is effectively the first witness to wholly new features, among which is the emergence of the fate of the Silmarils as a central element in the story of the final war. This is borne out by a question that my father asked himself in a very early, isolated note: 'What became of the

Silmarils after the capture of Melko?' (Indeed, it may well be said that the very existence of the Silmarils was of far less radical significance in the original conception of the mythology than it was to become.)

In the account in the *Sketch* Maglor says to Maidros (p.244) that 'there are two sons of Fëanor left, and two Silmarils; one is his'. The third is lost, because it has been told in the *Sketch* (p.243) that 'Elwing cast the Nauglafring into the sea and leapt after it'. That was the Silmaril of Beren and Lúthien. When Maglor cast into a fiery pit the Silmaril from the Iron Crown that he had stolen from the keeping of Fionwë 'one Silmaril was now in the sea and one in the earth' (pp.244–5). The third was the other from the Iron Crown; and it was this that the Gods adjudged to Eärendel, who wearing it upon his brow 'launched it into the outer darkness high above Sun and Moon'.

That it was the Silmaril wrested by Beren and Lúthien from Morgoth in Angband that Eärendel wore and became the Morning and Evening Star had not been achieved at this stage, though when achieved it seems a necessity of the myth.

It is also very striking that Eärendel Half-elven is not as yet the voice that interceded before the Valar on behalf of Men and Elves.

THE CONCLUSION OF THE
QUENTA NOLDORINWA

I take up this second citation of the *Quenta* from the point at which the first citation ended (p.143), where it was told that the Elves who survived the destruction of Doriath and of Gondolin became a small people of shipbuilders at the mouths of Sirion, where they dwelt 'ever nigh unto the shores and under the shadow of Ulmo's hand.' I give now the *Quenta* to its end, following as before (see p.129) the rewritten text 'Q II'.

In Valinor Ulmo spoke unto the Valar of the need of the Elves, and he called on them to forgive and send succour unto them and rescue them from the overmastering might of Morgoth, and win back the Silmarils wherein alone now bloomed the light of the days of bliss when the Two Trees still were shining. Or so it is said, among the Gnomes, who after had tidings of many things from their kinsfolk the Quendi, the Light-elves beloved of Manwë, who ever knew something of the mind of the Lord of the Gods. But as yet Manwë moved not, and the counsels of his heart what tale shall tell? The Quendi have said that the hour was not yet come, and that only one speaking in person for the cause of both Elves and Men, pleading for pardon upon their misdeeds and pity on their woes, might move the counsels of the Powers; and the oath of Fëanor perchance even Manwë could not loose, until it found its end, and the sons of Fëanor relinquished the Silmarils, upon which they had laid their ruthless claim. For the light which lit the Silmarils the Gods had made.

In those days Tuor felt old age creep upon him, and ever a longing for the deeps of the sea grew stronger in his heart. Wherefore he built a great ship, Eärámë, Eagle's Pinion, and with Idril he set sail into the sunset and the West, and came no more into any tale or song. [*Later addition*: But Tuor alone of mortal Men was numbered among the elder race, and joined with the Noldoli whom he loved, and in aftertime dwelt still, or so it hath been said, ever upon his ship voyaging the seas of the Elven-lands, or resting a while in the harbours of the Gnomes of Tol Eressëa, and his fate is sundered from the fate of Men.] Bright Eärendel was then lord of the folk of Sirion and their many ships; and he took to wife Elwing the fair, and she bore him Elrond Half-elven [> Elrond and Elros who are called the Half-elven]. Yet Eärendel could not rest, and his voyages about the shores of the Hither Lands [Middle-earth] eased not his unquiet. Two purposes grew in his heart, blended as one in longing for the wide sea: he sought to sail thereon, seeking after Tuor and

Idril Celebrindal who returned not; and he thought to find perhaps the last shore and bring ere he died the message of Elves and Men unto the Valar of the West, that should move the hearts of Valinor and of the Elves of Tûn to pity on the world and the sorrows of Mankind.

Wingelot he built, fairest of the ships of song, the Foam-flower; white were its timbers as the argent moon, golden were its oars, silver were its shrouds, its masts were crowned with jewels like stars. In the Lay of Eärendel is many a thing sung of his adventures in the deep and in lands untrodden, and in many seas and many isles. Ungoliant in the South he slew, and her darkness was destroyed, and light came to many regions which had yet long been hid. But Elwing sat sorrowing at home.

Eärendel found not Tuor nor Idril, nor came he ever on that journey to the shores of Valinor, defeated by shadows and enchantment, driven by repelling winds, until in longing for Elwing he turned him homeward toward the East. And his heart bade him haste, for a sudden fear was fallen on him out of dreams, and the winds that before he had striven with might not now bear him back as swift as his desire.

Upon the havens of Sirion new woe had fallen. The dwelling of Elwing there, where she still possessed the Nauglamír and the glorious Silmaril, became known unto the remaining sons of Fëanor, Maidros and Maglor and Damrod and Díriel; and they gathered together from their wandering hunting-paths, and messages of friendship and yet stern demand they sent unto Sirion. But Elwing and the folk of

Sirion would not yield that jewel which Beren had won and Lúthien had worn, and for which Dior the Fair was slain; and least of all while Eärendel their lord was in the sea, for it seemed to them that in that jewel lay the gift of bliss and healing that had come upon their houses and their ships.

And so came in the end to pass the last and cruellest of the slayings of Elf by Elf; and that was the third of the great wrongs achieved by the accursed oath. For the sons of Fëanor came down upon the exiles of Gondolin and the remnant of Doriath and destroyed them. Though some of their folk stood aside, and some few rebelled and were slain upon the other part aiding Elwing against their own lords (for such was the sorrow and confusion of the hearts of Elfinesse in those days), yet Maidros and Maglor won the day. Alone they now remained of the sons of Fëanor, for in that battle Damrod and Díriel were slain; but the folk of Sirion perished or fled away, or departed of need to join the people of Maidros, who claimed now the lordship of all the Elves of the Hither Lands. And yet Maidros gained not the Silmaril, for Elwing seeing that all was lost and her child Elrond taken captive, eluded the host of Maidros, and with the Nauglamír upon her breast she cast herself into the sea and perished, as folk thought.

But Ulmo bore her up and he gave unto her the likeness of a great white bird, and upon her breast there shone as a star the shining Silmaril, as she flew over the water to seek Eärendel her beloved. And on a time of night Eärendel at the helm saw her come towards him, as a white cloud under moon exceeding swift, as a star over the sea moving in strange course, a pale flame on wings of storm. And it is sung that she fell from the air upon the timbers of Wingelot, in a swoon, nigh unto death for the urgency of her speed, and Eärendel took her unto his bosom. And in the morn with marvelling eyes he beheld his wife in her own form beside him with her hair upon his face; and she slept.

But great was the sorrow of Eärendel and Elwing for the ruin of the havens of Sirion, and the captivity of their son, for whom they feared death, and yet it was not so. For Maidros took pity on Elrond, and he cherished him, and love grew after between them, as little might be thought; but Maidros' heart was sick and weary with the burden of the dreadful oath.

> [*This passage was rewritten thus*:
> But great was the sorrow of Eärendel and Elwing for
> the ruin of the havens of Sirion, and the captivity of
> their sons; and they feared that they would be slain.
> But it was not so. For Maglor took pity on Elros and
> Elrond, and he cherished them, and love grew after
> between them, as little might be thought; but Maglor's
> heart was sick and weary, &c.]

Yet Eärendel saw now no help left in the lands of Sirion, and he turned again in despair and came not home, but sought back once more to Valinor with Elwing at his side. He stood now most often at the prow, and the Silmaril he bound upon his forehead; and ever its light grew greater as they drew unto the West. Maybe it was due in part to the puissance of that holy jewel that they came in time to the waters that as yet no vessels save those of the Teleri had known; and they came unto the Magic Isles and escaped their magic, and they came into the Shadowy Seas and passed their shadows; and they looked upon the Lonely Isle and they tarried not there, and they cast anchor in the Bay of Faërie [> Bay of Elvenhome] upon the borders of the world. And the Teleri saw the coming of that ship and were amazed, gazing from afar upon the light of the Silmaril, and it was very great.

But Eärendel landed on the immortal shores alone of living Men; and neither Elwing nor any of his small company would he suffer to go with him, lest they fell beneath the wrath of the Gods, and he came at a time of festival even as Morgoth and Ungoliant had in ages past, and the watchers upon the hill of Tûn were few, for the Quendi were most in the halls of Manwë on Tindbrenting's height.

The watchers rode therefore in haste to Valmar, or hid them in the passes of the hills; and all the bells of Valmar pealed; but Eärendel climbed the marvellous hill of Kôr and found it bare, and he entered into the streets of Tûn and they were empty; and his heart sank. He walked now in the deserted ways of Tûn and the dust upon his raiment and his shoes was a dust of diamonds, yet no one heard his call. Wherefore he went back unto the shores and would climb once more upon Wingelot his ship; but one came unto the strand and cried unto him: 'Hail Eärendel, star most radiant, messenger most fair! Hail thou bearer of light before the Sun and Moon, the looked-for that comest unawares, the

longed-for that comest beyond hope! Hail thou splendour of
the children of the world, thou slayer of the dark! Star of the
sunset, hail! Hail herald of the morn!'

And that was Fionwë the son of Manwë, and he summoned Eärendel before the Gods; and Eärendel went unto
Valinor and to the halls of Valmar, and came never again
back into the lands of Men. But Eärendel spoke the embassy
of the two kindreds before the faces of the Gods, and asked
for pardon upon the Gnomes and pity for the exiled Elves
and for unhappy Men, and succour in their need.

Then the sons of the Valar prepared for battle, and the
captain of their host was Fionwë son of Manwë. Beneath
his white banner marched also the host of the Quendi, the
Light-elves, the folk of Ingwë, and among them such of
the Gnomes of old as had never departed from Valinor; but
remembering Swan Haven the Teleri went not forth save
very few, and these manned the ships wherewith the most of
that army came into the Northern lands; but they themselves
would set foot never on those shores.'

*Eärendel was their guide; but the Gods would not suffer
him to return again, and he built him a white tower upon the
confines of the outer world in the Northern regions of the
Sundering Seas; and there all the sea-birds of the earth at
times repaired. And often was Elwing in the form and likeness of a bird; and she devised wings for the ship of Eärendel,
and it was lifted even into the oceans of the air. Marvellous
and magical was that ship, a starlit flower in the sky, bearing
a wavering and holy flame; and the folk of Earth beheld it
from afar and wondered, and looked up from despair, saying

surely a Silmaril is in the sky, a new star is risen in the West.
Maidros said unto Maglor:

[*This passage, from the asterisk, was rewritten thus*:
In those days the ship of Eärendel was drawn by the
Gods beyond the edge of the world, and it was lifted
even into the oceans of the air. Marvellous and magical
was that ship ... [*&c. as first written*] ... a new star is
risen in the West. But Elwing mourned for Eärendel
yet found him never again, and they are sundered till
the world endeth. Therefore she built a white tower
upon the confines of the outer world in the Northern
regions of the Sundering Seas; and there all the sea-
birds of the earth at times repaired. And Elwing
devised wings for herself, and desired to fly to Eärendel's ship. But [*illegible: ?she fell back* ....] But
when the flame of it appeared on high Maglor said unto
Maidros:]

'If that be the Silmaril that riseth by some power divine
out of the sea into which we saw it fall, then let us be glad,
that its glory is seen now by many.' Thus hope arose and a
promise of betterment; but Morgoth was filled with doubt.

Yet it is said that he looked not for the assault that came
upon him from the West. So great was his pride become that
he deemed none would ever again come against him in open
war; moreover he thought that he had estranged for ever the
Gnomes from the Gods and from their kin, and that content
in their Blissful Realm the Valar would heed no more his

kingdom in the world without. For heart that is pitiless counteth not the power that pity hath, of which stern anger may be forged and a lightning kindled before which mountains fall.

Of the march of the host of Fionwë to the North little is said, for in his armies came none of those Elves who had dwelt and suffered in the Hither Lands, and who made these tales; and tidings only long after did they learn of these things from their kinsfolk the Light-elves of Valinor. But Fionwë came, and the challenge of his trumpets filled the sky, and he summoned unto him all Men and Elves from Hithlum unto the East; and Beleriand was ablaze with the glory of his arms, and the mountains rang.

The meeting of the hosts of the West and of the North is named the Great Battle, the Battle Terrible, the Battle of Wrath and Thunder. There was marshalled the whole power of the Throne of Hate, and well nigh measureless had it become, so that Dor-na-Fauglith could not contain it, and all the North was aflame with war. But it availed not. All the Balrogs were destroyed, and the uncounted hosts of the Orcs perished like straw in fire, or were swept like shrivelled leaves before a burning wind. Few remained to trouble the world thereafter. And it is said that there many Men of Hithlum repentant of their evil servitude did deeds of valour, and many beside of Men new come out of the East; and so were fulfilled in part the words of Ulmo; for by Eärendel son of Tuor was help brought unto the Elves, and by the swords of Men were they strengthened on the fields of war.

[*Later addition*: But most Men, and especially those new come out of the East, were on the side of the Enemy.] But Morgoth quailed and he came not forth; and he loosed his last assault, and that was the winged dragons [*Later addition*: for as yet had none of these creatures of his cruel thought assailed the air]. So sudden and so swift and ruinous was the onset of that fleet, as a tempest of a hundred thunders winged with steel, that Fionwë was driven back; but Eärendel came and a myriad of birds were about him, and the battle lasted all through the night of doubt. And Eärendel slew Ancalagon the black and the mightiest of all the dragon-horde, and cast him from the sky, and in his fall the towers of Thangorodrim were thrown down. Then the sun rose of the second day and the sons of the Valar prevailed, and all the dragons were destroyed save two alone; and they fled into the East. Then were all the pits of Morgoth broken and unroofed, and the might of Fionwë descended into the deeps of the Earth, and there Morgoth was thrown down.

[*The words* and there Morgoth was thrown down were *rejected and replaced by this passage*:
and there Morgoth stood at last at bay; and yet not valiant. He fled unto the deepest of his mines and sued for peace and pardon. But his feet were hewn from under him, and he was hurled upon his face.]

He was bound with the chain Angainor, which long had been prepared, and his iron crown they beat into a collar for his neck, and his head was bowed unto his knees. But Fionwë took the two Silmarils that remained and guarded them.

Thus perished the power and woe of Angband in the North, and its multitude of thralls came forth beyond all hope into the light of day, and they looked upon a world all changed; for so great was the fury of those adversaries that the Northern regions of the Western world were rent and riven, and the sea roared in through many chasms, and there was confusion and great noise; and the rivers perished or found new paths, and the valleys were upheaved and the hills trod down; and Sirion was no more. Then Men fled away, such as perished not in the ruin of those days, and long was it ere they came back over the mountains to where Beleriand once had been, and not until the tale of those wars had faded to an echo seldom heard.

But Fionwë marched through the Western lands summoning the remnants of the Gnomes, and the Dark-elves that had yet not looked on Valinor, to join with the thralls released and to depart. But Maidros would not harken, and he prepared, though with weary loathing and despair, to perform even yet the obligation of his oath. For Maidros and Maglor would have given battle for the Silmarils, were they withheld, even against the victorious host of Valinor, and though they stood alone in all the world. And they sent unto Fionwë and bade him yield now up those jewels which of old Morgoth stole from Fëanor. But Fionwë said that the right to the work of their hands which Fëanor and his sons had formerly possessed now had perished, because of their many and evil deeds blinded by their oath, and most of all the slaying of Dior and the assault upon Elwing; the light of the Silmarils should go now to the Gods whence it came, and to Valinor must Maidros and Maglor return and there abide the judgement of the Gods, by whose decree alone would Fionwë yield the jewels from his charge.

Maglor was minded to submit, for he was sad at heart, and he said: 'The oath says not that we may not bide our time, and maybe in Valinor all shall be forgiven and forgot, and we shall come into our own.' But Maidros said that if once they returned and the favour of the Gods were withheld from them, then would their oath still remain, to be fulfilled in despair yet greater; 'and who can tell to what dreadful doom we shall come, if we disobey the Powers in their own land, or purpose ever to bring war again into their Guarded Realm?' And so it came that Maidros and Maglor crept into the camps of Fionwë, and laid hands on the Silmarils, and slew the guards; and there they prepared to defend themselves to the death. But Fionwë stayed his folk; and the brethren departed and fled far away.

Each took a single Silmaril, saying that one was lost unto them and two remained, and but two brethren. But the jewel burned the hand of Maidros in pain unbearable (and he had but one hand as has before been told); and he perceived that it was as Fionwë had said, and that his right thereto had become void, and that the oath was vain. And being in anguish and despair he cast himself into a gaping chasm filled with fire, and so ended; and his Silmaril was taken into the bosom of the Earth.

And it is told also of Maglor that he could not bear the pain with which the Silmaril tormented him; and he cast it at last into the sea, and thereafter wandered ever upon the shore singing in pain and regret beside the waves; for Maglor was the mightiest of the singers of old, but he came never back among the folk of Elfinesse.

In those days there was a mighty building of ships on the shores of the Western Sea, and especially upon the great isles, which in the disruption of the Northern world were fashioned of ancient Beleriand. Thence in many a fleet the survivors of the Gnomes and of the Western companies of the Dark-elves set sail into the West and came not again into the lands of weeping and of war; but the Light-elves marched back beneath the banners of their king following in the train of Fionwë's victory, and they were borne back in triumph unto Valinor. [*Later addition*: Yet little joy had they in their return, for they came without the Silmarils, and these could not be again found, unless the world was broken and remade anew.] But in the West the Gnomes and Dark-elves rehabited for the most part the Lonely Isle, that looks both East and West; and very fair did that land become, and so remains. But some returned even unto Valinor, as all were free to do who willed; and the Gnomes were admitted again to the love of Manwë and the pardon of the Valar, and the Teleri forgave their ancient grief, and the curse was laid to rest.

Yet not all would forsake the Outer Lands where they had long suffered and long dwelt; and some lingered many an age in the West and North, and especially in the western isles. And among these were Maglor as has been told; and with him Elrond the Half-elven, who after went among mortal Men again, and from whom alone the blood of the Firstborn and the seed divine of Valinor have come among Mankind (for he was son of Elwing, daughter of Dior, son of Lúthien, child of Thingol and Melian; and Eärendel his sire was son of Idril Celebrindal, the fair maid of Gondolin). But ever as the ages drew on and the Elf-folk faded on the Earth, they would still set sail at eve from our Western shores; as still they do, when now there linger few anywhere of their lonely companies.

This was the judgement of the Gods, when Fionwë and the sons of the Valar had returned unto Valmar: thereafter the Outer Lands should be for Mankind, the younger children of the world; but to the Elves alone should the gateways of the West stand ever open; and if they would not come thither and tarried in the world of Men, then they should slowly fade and fail. This is the most grievous of the fruits of the lies and works that Morgoth wrought, that the Eldalië should be sundered and estranged from Men. For a while his Orcs and his Dragons breeding again in dark places affrighted the world, and in sundry regions do so yet; but ere the End all shall perish by the valour of mortal Men.

But Morgoth the Gods thrust through the Door of Timeless Night into the Void, beyond the Walls of the World, and a guard is set for ever on that door, and Eärendel keeps watch upon the ramparts of the sky. Yet the lies that Melko, Moeleg the mighty and accursed, Morgoth Bauglir the Dark Power Terrible, sowed in the hearts of Elves and Men have not all died and cannot by the Gods be slain, and they live to work much evil even to this later day. Some say also that Morgoth at whiles secretly as a cloud that cannot be seen or felt, and yet is venomous, creeps back surmounting the Walls and visiteth the world; *but others say that this is the black shadow of Thû, whom Morgoth made, and who escaped from the Battle Terrible, and dwells in dark places and perverts Men to his dreadful allegiance and his foul worship.

[*This passage, from the asterisk, was rewritten thus*:
but others say that this is the black shadow of Sauron, who served Morgoth and became the greatest and most evil of his underlings; and Sauron escaped from the Great Battle, and dwelt in dark places and perverted Men to his dreadful allegiance and his foul worship.]

After the triumph of the Gods Eärendel sailed still in the seas of heaven, but the Sun scorched him and the Moon hunted him in the sky. Then the Valar drew his white ship Wingelot over the land of Valinor, and they filled it with radiance and hallowed it, and launched it through the Door of Night. And long Eärendel set sail into the starless vast, [*struck out*: Elwing at his side, *see the rewritten passage on p.255*] the Silmaril upon his brow voyaging the Dark behind the world, a glimmering and fugitive star. And ever and anon he returns and shines behind the courses of the Sun and Moon above the ramparts of the Gods, brighter than all other stars, the mariner of the sky, keeping watch against Morgoth upon the confines of the world. Thus shall he sail until he sees the Last Battle fought upon the plains of Valinor.

Thus spoke the prophecy of Mandos, which he declared in Valmar at the judgement of the Gods, and the rumour of it was whispered among all the Elves of the West: when the world is old and the Powers grow weary, then Morgoth shall come back through the Door out of the Timeless Night; and he shall destroy the Sun and the Moon, but Eärendel shall come upon him as a white flame and drive him from the airs. Then shall the last battle be gathered on the fields of Valinor. In that day Tulkas shall strive with Melko, and on his right shall stand Fionwë and on his left Túrin Turambar, son of Húrin, Conqueror of Fate; and it shall be the black sword of Túrin that deals unto Melko his death and final end; and so shall the children of Húrin and all Men be avenged.

Thereafter shall the Silmarils be recovered out of sea and earth and air; for Eärendel shall descend and yield up that flame that he hath had in keeping. Then Fëanor shall bear the Three and yield them unto Yavanna Palúrien; and she will break them and with their fire rekindle the Two Trees, and a great light shall come forth; and the Mountains of Valinor shall be levelled, so that the light goes out over all the world. In that light the Gods will again grow young, and the Elves awake and all their dead arise, and the purpose of Ilúvatar be fulfilled concerning them.

Such is the end of the tales of the days before the days
in the Northern regions of the Western world.

*

My history of a history thus ends with a prophecy, the prophecy of Mandos. I will end the book with a repetition of what I wrote in my edition of the Great Tale of *The Children of Húrin*. 'It is to be borne in mind that at that time the *Quenta Noldorinwa* represented (if only in a somewhat bare structure) the full extent of my father's "imagined world". It was not the history of the First Age, as it afterwards became, for there was as yet no Second Age, nor Third Age; there was no Númenor, no hobbits, and of course no Ring.'

LIST OF NAMES

At the end of the main list that follows here are listed the seven longer additional notes to which a few of the names in the main list are extended. Names that appear in the map of Beleriand are followed by an asterisk.

Ainairos   An Elf of Alqualondë.

Ainur   See the additional note on p.287.

Almaren   The isle of Almaren was the first dwelling of the Valar in Arda.

Alqualondë   See *Swanhaven*.

Aman   The land in the West beyond the Great Sea in which was Valinor.

Amnon   The words of the Prophecy of Amnon, 'Great is the fall of Gondolin', uttered by Turgon in the midst of the battle for the city, are cited in two closely similar forms in isolated jottings under this title. Both begin with the words under the title 'Great is the fall of Gondolin', and then follow in the one case 'Turgon shall not fade till the lily of the valley fadeth' and in the other 'When the lily of the valley withers then shall Turgon fade'.

    The lily of the valley is Gondolin, one of the seven names of the city, the Flower of the Plain. There are references also in notes to the prophecies of Amnon, and to the places of the prophecies; but nowhere, it seems, is there any explanation of who Amnon was or when he uttered these words.

Amon Gwareth   'The Hill of Watch', or 'The Hill of Defence', a tall and isolated rocky height in the Guarded Plain of Gondolin, on which the city was built.

Anar   The Sun.

Ancalagon the black   The greatest of Morgoth's winged dragons, destroyed by Eärendel in the Great Battle.

Androth   Caves in the hills of Mithrim where Tuor dwelt with Annael and the Grey-elves, and afterwards as a solitary outlaw.

*Anfauglith**   Once the great grassy plain of Ard-galen north of Taur-na-Fuin before its desolation by Morgoth.

Angainor   The name of the chain, wrought by Aulë, with which Morgoth was twice bound: for he had been forced to wear it when imprisoned by the Valar in a very remote age, and again in his final defeat.

Angband   The great dungeon-fortress of Morgoth in the North-west of Middle-earth.

Annael   Grey-elf of Mithrim, fosterfather of Tuor.

Annon-in-Gelydh   'Gate of the Noldor': the entrance to the subterranean river rising in the lake of Mithrim and leading to the Rainbow Cleft.

Aranwë   Elf of Gondolin, father of Voronwë.

Aranwion   'Son of Aranwë'. See *Voronwë*.

Arlisgion   A region, translated 'the place of reeds', through which Tuor passed on his great southward journey; but the name is not found on any map. It seems impossible to trace the way that Tuor took until he reached the Land of Willows after many days; but it is clear that in this account Arlisgion was somewhere to the north of that land. The only other reference to this place seems to be in the Last Version (p.173), where Voronwë spoke to Tuor of the Lisgardh, 'the land of reeds at the Mouths

of Sirion'. Arlisgion 'place of reeds' is clearly the same as
Lisgardh 'land of reeds'; but the geography of this region at this
time is very unclear.

Arvalin   A desolate region of wide and misty plains between the
Pelóri (the Mountains of Valinor) and the sea. Its name, meaning
'near Valinor', was later replaced by *Avathar*, 'the shadows'. It
was here that Morgoth met with Ungoliant, and it was said that
the Doom of Mandos was spoken in Arvalin. See *Ungoliant*.

Aulë   He is one of the great Valar, called 'the Smith', of might
little less than Ulmo. The following is taken from the portrait
of him, in the text named *Valaquenta*:

> His lordship is over all the substances of which Arda is made.
> In the beginning he wrought much in fellowship with Manwë
> and Ulmo; and the fashioning of all lands was his labour. He
> is a smith and a master of all crafts, and he delights in works of
> skill, however small, as much as in the mighty building of old.
> His are the gems that lie deep in the Earth and the gold that is
> fair in the hand, no less than the walls of the mountains and
> the basins of the sea.

Bablon, Ninwi, Trui, Rûm   Babylon, Nineveh, Troy, Rome. A note
on *Bablon* reads: '*Bablon* was a city of Men, and more rightly
Babylon, but such is the Gnomes' name as they now shape it,
and they got it from aforetime.'

Bad Uthwen   See *The Way of Escape*.

Balar, Isle of   An island far out in the Bay of Balar. See *Círdan
the Shipwright*.

Balcmeg   An Orc slain by Tuor.

Balrogs   'Demons with whips of flame and claws of steel'.

Battle of Unnumbered Tears   See the note on p.295.

Bauglir   A name frequently added to *Morgoth*; translated 'The
Constrainer'.

Bay of Faërie   A great bay in the eastern face of Aman.

Beleg   A great archer of Doriath and close friend of Túrin, whom
he slew in darkness thinking him a foe.

267

Belegaer See *Great Sea*.

Beleriand* The great north-western region of Middle-earth, extending from the Blue Mountains in the East to include all the inner lands south of Hithlum and the coasts south of Drengist.

Beren Man of the House of Bëor, lover of Lúthien, who cut the Silmaril from Morgoth's crown. Slain by Carcharoth the wolf of Angband; he alone of mortal Men returned from the dead.

The Blacksword (Mormegil) A name given to Túrin on account of his sword Gurthang ('Iron of Death').

The Blessed Realm See *Aman*.

Bragollach Short form of *Dagor Bragollach*, 'The Battle of Sudden Flame', in which the Siege of Angband was ended.

Bredhil Gnomish name of Varda (also Bridhil).

Brethil* The forest between the rivers Teiglin and Sirion.

Brithiach* The ford over Sirion leading into Dimbar.

Brithombar* The northernmost of the Havens of the Falas.

Bronweg The Gnomish name of *Voronwë*.

Celegorm Son of Fëanor; called the Fair.

Círdan the Shipwright Lord of the Falas (the western coasts of Beleriand); at the destruction of the Havens in that region by Morgoth after the Battle of Unnumbered Tears Círdan escaped to the Isle of Balar and the region of the Mouths of Sirion, and continued the building of ships. This is the Círdan the Shipwright who appears in *The Lord of the Rings* as the lord of the Grey Havens at the end of the Third Age.

Cirith Ninniach The 'Rainbow Cleft'; see *Cris-Ilfing*.

City of Stone Gondolin; see *Gondothlim*.

Cleft of Eagles In the southernmost of the Encircling Mountains about Gondolin. Elvish name *Cristhorn*.

Cranthir Son of Fëanor, called the Dark; changed to Caranthir.

Cris-Ilfing 'Rainbow Cleft': the ravine in which flowed the river from Lake Mithrim. Replaced by the name *Kirith Helvin*, and finally *Cirith Ninniach*.

Crissaegrim* The mountain-peaks south of Gondolin, where were the eyries of Thorondor, the Lord of the Eagles.

Cristhorn Elvish name of the *Cleft of Eagles*. Replaced by the name *Kirith-thoronath*.

Cuiviénen The 'waters of awakening' of the Elves in the far distant East of Middle-earth: 'a dark lake amid mighty rocks, and the stream that feeds that water falls therein down a deep cleft, a pale and slender thread'.

Curufin Son of Fëanor; called the Crafty.

Damrod and Díriel Twin brothers, youngest of the sons of Fëanor; later changed to Amrod and Amras.

Deep-elves A name of the second host of the Elves on the great journey. See *Noldoli, Noldor,* and the note on p.300.

Dimbar* The land between the rivers Sirion and Mindeb.

Dior The son of Beren and Lúthien and possessor of their Silmaril; known as 'Thingol's Heir'. He was the father of Elwing; and was slain by the sons of Fëanor.

Doom of Mandos See note on p.299.

The Door of Night See the entry *Outer Seas*. In the text named *Ambarkanta* that I have cited there, concerning *Ilurambar*, the Walls of the World, and *Vaiya*, the Enfolding Ocean or Outer Sea, it is further said:

> In the midst of Valinor is Ando Lómen, the Door of Timeless Night that pierces the Walls and opens upon the Void. For the World is set amid Kúma, the Void, the Night without form or time. But none can pass the chasm and the belt of Vaiya and come to that Door, save the great Valar only. And they made that Door when Melko was overcome and put forth into the Outer Dark, and it is guarded by Eärendel.

Doriath* The great forested region of Beleriand, ruled by Thingol and Melian. The Girdle of Melian gave rise to the later name *Doriath* (*Dor-iâth* 'Land of the Fence').

Dor-lómin* 'The Land of Shadows': region in the south of Hithlum.

Dor-na-Fauglith The great northern grassy plain named Ard-galen; utterly destroyed by Morgoth it was named Dor-na-Fauglith, translated as 'the land under choking ash'.

Dramborleg Tuor's axe. A note on this name says: '*Dramborleg* means "Thudder-sharp", and was the axe of Tuor that smote both a heavy dint as of a club and cleft as a sword'.

Drengist A long firth of the sea penetrating the Echoing Mountains. The river from Mithrim that Tuor followed through the Rainbow Cleft would have brought him to the sea by that route, 'but he was dismayed by the fury of the strange waters, and he turned aside and went away southward, and so came not to the long shores of the Firth of Drengist' (p. 158).

The Dry River The bed of the river that once flowed out from the Encircling Mountains to join Sirion; forming the entrance to Gondolin.

Duilin Lord of the people of the Swallow in Gondolin.

Dungortheb Shortened form of *Nan Dungortheb*, 'the valley of dreadful death', between Ered Gorgoroth, the Mountains of Terror, and the Girdle of Melian protecting Doriath from the north.

The Dweller in the Deep Ulmo.

Eagle-stream See *Thorn Sir*.

Eärámë 'Eagle's Pinion', Tuor's ship.

Eärendel (later form *Eärendil*) 'Halfelven': the son of Tuor and Idril Turgon's daughter; the father of Elrond and Elros. See the note on p.296.

Easterlings Name given to Men who followed the Edain into Beleriand; they fought on both sides in the Battle of Unnumbered Tears, and were given Hithlum by Morgoth, where they oppressed the remnant of the People of Hador.

*Echoing Mountains of Lammoth** The Echoing Mountains (Ered Lómin) formed the 'west wall' of Hithlum; Lammoth was the region between those mountains and the sea.

Echoriath See *Encircling Mountains*.

Ecthelion   Lord of the people of the Fountain in Gondolin.

Edain   The Men of the Three Houses of the Elf-friends.

Egalmoth   Lord of the people of the Heavenly Arch in Gondolin.

Eglarest*   The southern Haven of the Falas.

Eldalië   'Elven folk', a name used interchangeably with *Eldar.*

Eldar   In early writings the name *Eldar* meant the Elves of the great journey from Cuiviénen, which was divided into three hosts: see *Light-elves, Deep-elves, and Sea-elves*: on these names see the remarkable passage in *The Hobbit* given in the note on p.300. Subsequently it could be used as distinct from *Noldoli*, and of the language of the Eldar as opposed to Gnomish (the language of the Noldoli).

Elemmakil   Elf of Gondolin, captain of the guard of the outer gate.

Elfinesse   An inclusive name for all the lands of the Elves.

Elrond and Elros   The sons of Eärendel and Elwing. Elrond elected to belong to the Firstborn; he was the master of Rivendell and keeper of the ring Vilya. Elros was numbered among Men and became the first King of Númenor.

Elwing   Daughter of Dior, wedded Eärendel; mother of Elrond and Elros.

Encircling Mountains, ~Hills   The mountains encircling the plain of Gondolin. Elvish name *Echoriath.*

Eöl   The 'dark Elf' of the forest who ensnared Isfin; father of Maeglin.

Ered Wethrin   (earlier form *Eredwethion*) Mountains of Shadow ('The walls of Hithlum'). See the note on *Iron Mountains*, p.293.

Evermind   White flower that was continuously in bloom.

The Exiles   The rebellious Noldor who returned to Middle-earth from Aman.

Falas*   The western coastlands of Beleriand, south of Nevrast.

Falasquil   A cove of the sea-coast where Tuor dwelt for a time. This was clearly a small bay, marked without a name on a map made by my father, on the long firth (named Drengist) running east to Hithlum and Dor-lómin. The wood for Eärendel's ship Wingilot ('Foam-flower') was said to have come from Falasquil.

Falathrim The Telerin Elves of the Falas.

Fëanor The eldest son of Finwë; maker of the Silmarils.

Finarfin The third son of Finwë; father of Finrod Felagund and Galadriel. He remained in Aman after the flight of the Noldor.

Finduilas Daughter of Orodreth, King of Nargothrond after Finrod Felagund. *Faelivrin* was a name given to her; the meaning is 'the gleam of the sun on the pools of Ivrin'.

Fingolfin The second son of Finwë; father of Fingon and Turgon; High King of the Noldor in Beleriand; slain by Morgoth in single combat at the gates of Angband (described in *The Lay of Leithian, Beren and Lúthien* pp.190 ff.).

Fingolma Early name of Finwë.

Fingon The elder son of Fingolfin; brother of Turgon; High King of the Noldor after the death of Fingolfin; slain in the Battle of Unnumbered Tears.

Finn Gnomish form of Finwë.

Finrod Felagund Eldest son of Finarfin; founder and King of Nargothrond, whence his name *Felagund* 'cave-hewer'. See *Inglor*.

Finwë Leader of the second host (Noldoli) on the great journey from Cuiviénen; father of Fëanor, Fingolfin and Finarfin.

Fionwë Son of Manwë; captain of the host of the Valar in the Great Battle.

The Fountain Name of one of the kindreds of the Gondothlim. See *Ecthelion*.

Galdor The father of Húrin and Huor; see *Tuor*.

Galdor Lord of the people of the Tree in Gondolin.

Gar Ainion 'The Place of the Gods' (*Ainur*) in Gondolin.

Gate of the Noldor See *Annon-in-Gelydh*.

Gates of Summer See *Tarnin Austa*.

Gelmir and Arminas Noldorin Elves who came upon Tuor at the Gate of the Noldor when on their way to Nargothrond to warn

Orodreth (the second king, following Felagund) of its peril, of which they did not speak to Tuor.

Girdle of Melian See *Melian.*

Glamhoth Orcs; translated 'the barbaric host', 'hosts of hate'.

Glaurung The most celebrated of all the dragons of Morgoth.

Glingol and Bansil The gold and silver trees at the doors of the King's palace in Gondolin. Originally these were shoots of old from the Two Trees of Valinor before Melko and Gloomweaver withered them, but later the story was that they were images made by Turgon in Gondolin.

Glithui* A river flowing down from Ered Wethrin, a tributary of Teiglin.

Gloomweaver See *Ungoliant.*

Glorfalc 'Golden Cleft': Tuor's name for the ravine through which flowed the river that rose in Lake Mithrim.

Glorfindel Lord of the people of the Golden Flower in Gondolin.

Gnomes This was the early translation of the name of the Elves called *Noldoli* (later *Noldor*). For explanation of this use of 'Gnomes' see *Beren and Lúthien* pp.32–3. Their language was Gnomish.

The Golden Flower Name of one of the kindreds of the Gondothlim.

Gondolin* For the name see *Gondothlim.* For the other names see p.51.

Gondothlim The people of Gondolin; translated 'the dwellers in stone'. Other names of related form are *Gondobar* meaning 'City of Stone' and *Gondothlimbar* ' City of the Dwellers in Stone'. Both these names are included in the Seven Names of the city cited to Tuor by the guard at the gate of Gondolin (p.51). The element *gond* meant 'stone', as in *Gondor. Gondolin* was interpreted at the time of writing the *Lost Tales* as 'Stone of Song', which was said to mean 'stone carved and wrought to great beauty.' A later interpretation was 'the Hidden Rock'.

Gondothlimbar See *Gondothlim.*

Gorgoroth   Shortened form of *Ered Gorgoroth*, the Mountains of
Terror; see *Dungortheb*.

Gothmog   Lord of Balrogs, captain of the hosts of Melkor; son
of Melkor, slain by Ecthelion.

The Great Battle   The world-changing battle that finally over-
threw Morgoth and brought the First Age of the World to its
end. It may also be said to have ended the Elder Days, for 'in
the Fourth Age the earlier Ages were often called the *Elder
Days*; but that name was properly given only to the days before
the casting out of Morgoth' (*The Tale of Years*, appendix to *The
Lord of the Rings*). That is why Elrond said at the great council
in Rivendell: 'My memory reaches back *even to the Elder Days*.
Eärendil was my sire, who was born in Gondolin before its
fall.'

Great Sea*   The Great Sea of the West, whose name was *Belegaer*,
extended from the western coasts of Middle-earth to the coasts
of Aman.

Great Worm of Angband   See *Glaurung*.

Grey Annals   See p.220.

Grey-elves   The Sindar. This name was given to the Eldar who
remained in Beleriand and did not go further into the West.

The Grinding Ice   In the far north of Arda there was a strait
between the 'western world' and the coast of Middle-earth, and
in one of the accounts of the 'Grinding Ice' it is described thus:

> Through these narrows the chill waters of the Encircling Sea
> [see *Outer Seas*] and the waves of the Great Sea of the West
> flow together, and there are vast mists of deathly cold, and the
> sea-streams are filled with clashing hills of ice and the grind-
> ing of ice submerged. This strait was named *Helkaraksë*.

Guarded Plain   Tumladen, the plain of Gondolin.

Gwindor   Elf of Nargothrond, lover of Finduilas.

Hador   See *Tuor*. The House of Hador was called The Third
House of the Edain. His son Galdor was the father of Húrin
and Huor.

The Hammer of Wrath   Name of one of the kindreds of the Gondothlim.

The Harp   Name of one of the kindreds of the Gondothlim.

Haudh-en-Ndengin   'The Hill of Slain': a great mound in which
were laid all the Elves and Men who died in the Battle of
Unnumbered Tears. This was in the desert of Anfauglith.

Heavenly Arch   Name of one of the kindreds of the Gondothlim.

Hells of Iron   Angband. See the note on *Iron Mountains*, p.293.

Hendor   A servant of Idril who carried Eärendel in the flight
from Gondolin.

The Hidden King   Turgon.

The Hidden Kingdom   Gondolin.

The Hidden People   See *Gondothlim*.

Hill of Watch   See *Amon Gwareth*.

Hisilómë   The Gnomish form of the name *Hithlum*.

Hísimë   The eleventh month, corresponding to November.

Hither Lands   Middle-earth.

*Hithlum**   The great region, translated 'Land of Mist', 'Twilit
Mist', extending northward from the great wall of Ered Wethrin,
the Mountains of Shadow; in the south of the region lay Dor-
lómin and Mithrim. See *Hisilómë*.

Huor   The brother of Húrin, husband of Rían, and father of
Tuor; slain in the Battle of Unnumbered Tears. See the note on
Húrin and Gondolin, p.290.

Húrin   The father of Túrin Turambar and brother of Huor father
of Tuor; see the note *Húrin and Gondolin*, p.290.

Idril   Called *Celebrindal* 'Silverfoot', the daughter of Turgon.
Her mother was Elenwë, who perished in the crossing of the
Helcaraxë, the Grinding Ice. It is told in a very late note that
'Turgon had himself come near to death in the bitter waters
when he attempted to save her and his daughter Idril, whom
the breaking of treacherous ice had cast into the cruel sea. Idril
he saved; but the body of Elenwë was covered in fallen ice.'
She was the wife of Tuor and the mother of Eärendel.

Ilfiniol   Elvish name of *Littleheart*.

Ilkorindi, Ilkorins   Elves who never dwelt in Kôr in Valinor.

Ilúvatar   The Creator. The elements are *Ilu* 'the Whole, the Universe'; and *atar* 'father'.

Inglor   Earlier name for Finrod Felagund.

Ingwë   Leader of the Light-elves on the great journey from Cuiviénen. It is told in the *Quenta Noldorinwa* that 'he entered into Valinor and sits at the feet of the Powers, and all Elves revere his name, but he has come never back to the Outer Lands.'

Iron Mountains   'Morgoth's mountains' in the far North. But the occurrence of the name in the text of the original *Tale* on p.43 derives from an earlier time when *Iron Mountains* was applied to the range later named *Shadowy Mountains* (*Ered Wethrin*): see the note on *Iron Mountains* on p.293. I have emended the text on p.43 at this point.

Isfin   Sister of King Turgon; mother of Maeglin, wife of Eöl.

Ivrin   The lake and falls beneath Ered Wethrin where the river Narog rose.

Kôr   The hill in Valinor overlooking the Bay of Faërie on which was built the Elvish city of Tûn, later Tirion; also as the name of the city itself. See *Ilkorindi*.

Land of Shadows   See *Dor-lómin*.

*Land of Willows**   The beautiful land where the river Narog flowed into the Sirion, south of Nargothrond. Its Elvish names were *Nan-tathrin* 'Willow-vale' and *Tasarinan*. In *The Two Towers* (Book 3, chapter 4), when Treebeard was carrying Merry and Pippin in the forest of Fangorn he chanted to them, and the first words were

In the willow-meads of Tasarinan I walked in the Spring.

Ah! the sight and the smell of the Spring in Nan-tasarion!

Laurelin   Name of the Golden Tree of Valinor.

Legolas Greenleaf   An Elf of the House of the Tree in Gondolin, gifted with extraordinary night-sight.

Light-elves   A name of the first host of the Elves on the great journey from Cuiviénen. See *Quendi*, and the note on p.300.

Linaewen   The great mere in Nevrast 'in the midst of the hollow land'.

Lisgardh   'The land of reeds at the Mouths of Sirion'. See *Arlisgion*.

Littleheart   Elf of Tol Eressëa who told the original tale of *The Fall of Gondolin*. He is described thus in the *Lost Tales*: 'He had a weatherworn face and blue eyes of great merriment, and was very slender and small, nor might one say if he were fifty or ten thousand'; and it is also said that he owed his name to 'the youth and wonder of his heart'. In the *Lost Tales* he has many Elvish names, but *Ilfiniol* is the only one that appears in this book.

Lonely Isle   *Tol Eressëa*: a large island in the Western Ocean, within remote sight of the coasts of Aman. For its early history see p.26.

Lord of Waters   See *Ulmo*.

Lords of the West   The Valar.

Lorgan   Easterling chief in Hithlum who enslaved Tuor.

Lórien   The Valar Mandos and Lórien were called brothers, and bore the name *Fanturi*. Mandos was *Nefantur* and Lórien was *Olofantur*. Like Mandos, Lórien was the name of his dwelling but was also used as his own name. He was 'the master of visions and dreams'.

Lothlim   'People of the Flower': the name taken by the survivors of Gondolin in their dwellings at the Mouths of Sirion.

Lug   An Orc slain by Tuor.

Maglor   Son of Fëanor, called the Mighty; a great singer and minstrel.

Maidros   Eldest son of Fëanor, called the Tall.

*Malduin**   A tributary of the Teiglin.

Malkarauki   Elvish name for *Balrogs*.

Mandos   The dwelling, by which he himself is always named, of the great Vala Namo. I give here the portrait of Mandos in the brief text *Valaquenta*:

> [Mandos] is the keeper of the Houses of the Dead, and the summoner of the spirits of the slain. He forgets nothing; and he knows all things that shall be, save only those that lie still in the freedom of Ilúvatar. He is the Doomsman of the Valar; but he pronounces his dooms and his judgements only at the bidding of Manwë. Vairë the Weaver is his spouse, who weaves all things that have ever been in Time into her storied webs, and the halls of Mandos that ever widen as the ages pass are clothed with them.

See *Lórien*.

Manwë　The chief of the Valar and the spouse of Varda; Lord of the realm of Arda. See *Súlimo*.

Meglin (and later *Maeglin*)　Son of Eöl and Isfin sister of King Turgon; he betrayed Gondolin to Morgoth, the most infamous treachery in the history of Middle-earth; slain by Tuor.

Meleth　The nurse of Eärendel.

Melian　A Maia from the company of the Vala Lórien in Valinor, who came to Middle-earth and became the Queen of Doriath. 'She put forth her power' [as told in the *Grey Annals*, see p.220] 'and fenced all that region about with an unseen wall of shadow and bewilderment: the Girdle of Melian, that none thereafter could pass against her will or the will of King Thingol'. See *Thingol* and *Doriath*.

Melko (later form *Melkor*)　'He who arises in might'; the name of the great evil Ainu before he became 'Morgoth'. 'The mightiest of those Ainur who came into the World was in his beginning Melkor. [He] is counted no longer among the Valar, and his name is not spoken upon Earth.' (From the text named *Valaquenta*.)

Menegroth*　See *Thousand Caves*.

Meres of Twilight　Aelin-uial, a region of great pools and marshes, wrapped in mists, where Aros, flowing out of Doriath, met Sirion.

Mighty of the West   The Valar.

Minas of King Finrod   The tower (Minas Tirith) built by Finrod Felagund. This was a great watch-tower that he built on Tol Sirion, the isle in the Pass of Sirion that became after its capture by Sauron *Tol-in-Gaurhoth*, the Isle of Werewolves.

*Mithrim**   The great lake in the south of Hithlum, and also the region in which it lay and the mountains to the west.

Moeleg   The Gnomish form of Melko, which the Gnomes would not speak, calling him Morgoth Bauglir, the Dark Power Terrible.

The Mole   A sable Mole was the sign of Meglin and his house.

Morgoth   This name ('the Black Foe' and other translations) only occurs once in the *Lost Tales*. It was first given by Fëanor after the rape of the Silmarils. See *Melko* and *Bauglir*.

Mountains of Darkness   The Iron Mountains.

*Mountains of Shadow**   See *Ered Wethrin*.

Mountains of Turgon   See *Echoriath*.

Mountains of Valinor   The great range of mountains that were raised by the Valar when they came to Aman. Called also the *Pelóri*, they extended in a vast crescent from north to south not far from the eastern shores of Aman.

*Nan-tathrin**   Elvish name of the *Land of Willows*.

*Nargothrond**   The great underground fortress city on the river Narog in West Beleriand, founded by Finrod Felagund and destroyed by the dragon Glaurung.

*Narog**   The river that rose in the lake of Ivrin under Ered Wethrin and flowed into Sirion in the Land of Willows.

Narquelië   The tenth month, corresponding to October.

Nessa   A 'Queen of the Valar', the sister of Vána and spouse of Tulkas.

*Nevrast**   The region south-west of Dor-lómin where Turgon dwelt before his departure to Gondolin.

Ninniach, Vale of   The site of the Battle of Unnumbered Tears, but found only here under this name.

Nirnaeth Arnoediad The Battle of Unnumbered Tears. Often referred to as 'the Nirnaeth'. See the note on p.295.

Noldoli, Noldor The earlier and later forms of the name of the second host of the Elves on the great journey from Cuiviénen. See *Gnomes, Deep-elves*.

Nost-na-Lothion 'The Birth of Flowers', a festival of spring in Gondolin.

Orcobal A great champion of Orcs, slain by Ecthelion.

Orcs In a note on the word my father wrote: 'A folk devised and brought into being by Morgoth to make war on Elves and Men; sometimes translated "Goblins", but they were of nearly human stature.' See *Glamhoth*.

Orfalch Echor The great ravine in the Encircling Mountains by which Gondolin was approached.

Oromë Vala, the son of Yavanna, renowned as the greatest of all hunters; he and Yavanna alone of the Valar came at times to Middle-earth in the Elder Days. On Nahar his white horse he led the Elves on the great journey from Cuiviénen.

Ossë He is a Maia, a vassal of Ulmo, and is thus described in the *Valaquenta*:

> He is master of the seas that wash the shores of Middle-earth.
> He does not go in the deeps, but loves the coasts and the isles,
> and rejoices in the winds of Manwë; for in storm he delights,
> and laughs amid the roaring of the waves.

Othrod A lord of Orcs, slain by Tuor.

Outer Lands The lands east of the Great Sea (Middle-earth).

Outer Seas I quote from a passage in a text named *Ambarkanta* ('Shape of the World') of the 1930s, probably later than the *Quenta Noldorinwa*: 'About all the world are the Ilurambar, or Walls of the World ['the final Wall' in the *Prologue*, p.24] ... They cannot be seen, nor can they be passed, save by the Door of Night. Within these Walls the Earth is globed: above, below, and upon all sides is *Vaiya*, the Enfolding Ocean [which is the *Outer Sea*]. But this is more like to sea below the Earth and more like to air above the Earth. In *Vaiya* below the Earth dwells Ulmo.'

In the *Lost Tale* of *The Coming of the Valar* Rúmil, who tells the tale, says: 'Beyond Valinor I have never seen or heard, save that of a surety there are the dark waters of the Outer Seas, that have no tides, and they are very cool and thin, that no boat can sail upon their bosom or fish swim within their depths, save the enchanted fish of Ulmo and his magic car.'

Outer World, Outer Earth The lands east of the Great Sea (Middle-earth).

Palisor The distant land in the East of Middle-earth where the Elves awoke.

Palúrien A name of Yavanna; both names are often conjoined. *Palúrien* was replaced later by *Kementári*; both names bear such meanings as 'Queen of the Earth', 'Lady of the Wide Earth'.

Peleg son of Indor son of Fengel Peleg was the father of Tuor in the first genealogy. (See *Tunglin*)

Pelóri See *Mountains of Valinor*.

Penlod Lord of the peoples of the Pillar and the Tower of Snow in Gondolin.

The Pillar Name of one of the kindreds of the Gondothlim. See *Penlod*.

Prophecy of Mandos See note on p.299.

Quendi An early name for all Elves, meaning 'Those who have voices'; later, the name of the first of the three hosts on the great journey from Cuiviénen. See *Light-elves*.

Rían Wife of Huor, mother of Tuor; died in Anfauglith after the death of Huor.

Rog Lord of the people of the Hammer of Wrath in Gondolin.

Salgant   Lord of the people of the Harp in Gondolin. Described as 'a craven'.

Sea-elves   A name of the third host of the Elves on the great journey from Cuiviénen. See *Teleri*, and the note on p.300.

Silpion   The White Tree; see *Trees of Valinor* and *Telperion*.

Sindar   See *Grey-elves*.

*Sirion**   The Great River that rose at Eithel Sirion ('Sirion's Well') and dividing West from East Beleriand flowed into the Great Sea in the Bay of Balar.

Sorontur   'King of Eagles'. See *Thorondor*.

The Stricken Anvil   Emblem of the people of the Hammer of Wrath in Gondolin.

Súlimë   The third month, corresponding to March.

Súlimo   This name, referring to Manwë as a wind-god, is very frequently attached to his name. He is called 'Lord of the Airs'; but only once does there seem to be a translation specifically of *Súlimo*: 'Lord of the Breath of Arda'. Related words are *súya* 'breath' and *súle* 'breathe'.

The Swallow   Name of one of the kindreds of the Gondothlim.

Swanhaven   The chief city of the Teleri (Sea-elves), on the coast north of Kôr. Elvish *Alqualondë*.

Taniquetil   The highest of the Pelóri (the Mountains of Valinor) and the highest mountain of Arda, on which Manwë and Varda had their dwelling (Ilmarin).

Taras   A great mountain on the western headland of Nevrast, beyond which was Vinyamar.

Tarnin Austa   'The Gates of Summer', a festival in Gondolin.

*Taur-na-Fuin**   'Forest of Night', previously called *Dorthonion* 'Land of Pines', the great forested highlands to the north of Beleriand.

*Teiglin**   A tributary of Sirion, rising in Ered Wethrin.

Teleri   The third host of the Elves on the great journey from Cuiviénen.

Telperion   Name of the White Tree of Valinor.

Thangorodrim The three-peaked mountain raised by Melko above his great dungeon-fortress of Angband.

Thingol A leader of the third host (Teleri) on the great journey from Cuiviénen; his earlier name *Tinwelint*. He never came to Kôr, but became the King of Doriath in Beleriand.

Thorn Sir Falling stream below Cristhorn.

Thornhoth 'The people of the Eagles'.

Thorondor 'King of Eagles', Gnomish name of Eldarin *Sorontur*; earlier form *Thorndor*.

Thousand Caves *Menegroth*, the hidden halls of Thingol and Melian.

Thû (later form *Sauron*) Great chief of Melko who escaped the Last Battle.

Timbrenting The Old English name of Taniquetil.

The Tower of Snow Name of one of the kindreds of the Gondothlim. See *Penlod*.

The Tree Name of one of the kindreds of the Gondothlim. See *Galdor*.

Trees of Valinor *Silpion* the White Tree and *Laurelin* the Golden Tree; see p.24, where they are described, and *Glingol and Bansil*.

Tulkas Of this Vala, 'the greatest in strength and deeds of prowess', it is said in the *Valaquenta*:

> He came last to Arda, to aid the Valar in the first battles with Melkor. He delights in wrestling and in contests of strength; and he rides no steed, for he can outrun all things that go on feet, and he is tireless. He has little heed for either the past or the future, and is of no avail as a counsellor, but is a hardy friend.

Tumladen 'Valley of smoothness', the 'Guarded Plain' of Gondolin.

Tûn The Elvish city in Valinor; see *Kôr*.

Tunglin 'The folk of the Harp': in an early and soon abandoned text of *The Fall of Gondolin* a name given to the people living in Hithlum after the Battle of Unnumbered Tears. Tuor was of that people (see *Peleg*).

Tuor Tuor was a descendant (great-grandson) of the renowned Hador Lórindol ('Hador Goldenhead'). In *The Lay of Leithian* it is said of Beren:

> As fearless Beren was renowned:
> when men most hardy upon ground
> were reckoned folk would speak his name,
> foretelling that his after-fame
> *would even golden Hador pass ...*

To Hador was given the lordship of Dor-lómin by Fingolfin, and his successors were the House of Hador. Tuor's father Huor was slain in the Battle of Unnumbered Tears, and his mother, Rían, died of grief. Huor and Húrin were brothers, the sons of Galdor of Dor-lómin, son of Hador; and Húrin was the father of Túrin Turambar; thus Tuor and Túrin were first cousins. But only once did they meet, and they did not know each other as they passed: this is told in *The Fall of Gondolin*.

Turgon The second son of Fingolfin, founder and king of Gondolin, father of Idril.

Turlin A name briefly preceding *Tuor*.

Uinen 'Lady of the Seas'; a Maia, the spouse of Ossë. This is said of her in the text named *Valaquenta*:

> [Her] hair lies spread through all waters under sky. All creatures she loves that live in the salt streams, and all weeds that grow there; to her mariners cry, for she can lay calm upon the waves, restraining the wildness of Ossë.

Uldor the accursed He was a leader among certain Men moving into the West of Middle-earth who treacherously allied themselves with Morgoth in the Battle of Unnumbered Tears.

Ulmo The following text is taken from the portrait of the great Vala, who was 'next in might to Manwë', from the text named *Valaquenta*, an account of each individual Vala.

> [Ulmo] kept all Arda in thought, and he has no need of any resting-place. Moreover he does not love to walk upon land, and will seldom clothe himself in a body after the manner of

his peers. If [Men or Elves] beheld him they were filled with a great dread; for the arising of the King of the Sea was terrible, as a mounting wave that strides to the land, with dark helm foam-crested and raiment of mail shimmering from silver down into shadows of green. The trumpets of Manwë are loud, but Ulmo's voice is deep as the deeps of the ocean which he only has seen.

Nonetheless Ulmo loves both Elves and Men, and never abandoned them, not even when they lay under the wrath of the Valar. At times he will come unseen to the shores of Middle-earth, or pass far inland up firths of the sea, and there make music upon his great horns, the Ulumúri, that are wrought of white shell; and those to whom that music comes hear it ever after in their hearts, and longing for the sea never leaves them again. But mostly Ulmo speaks to those who dwell in Middle-earth with voices that are heard only as the music of water. For all seas, lakes, rivers, fountains and springs are in his government; so that the Elves say that the spirit of Ulmo runs in all the veins of the world. Thus news comes to Ulmo, even in the deeps, of all the needs and griefs of Arda.

Ulmonan Ulmo's halls in the Outer Sea.

Ungoliant The great spider, called Gloomweaver, who dwelt in Arvalin. This is said of Ungoliant in the *Quenta Noldorinwa*: There [in Arvalin] secret and unknown dwelt Ungoliant, Gloomweaver, in spider's form. It is not told whence she is, from the outer darkness, maybe, that lies beyond the Walls of the World [see *Outer Seas*].

Valar The ruling powers of Arda; sometimes referred to as 'the Powers'. In the beginning there were nine Valar, as stated in the *Sketch*, but Melkor (Morgoth) ceased to be numbered among them.

Valinor The land of the Valar in Aman. See *Mountains of Valinor*.

Valmar The city of the Valar in Valinor.

Vána   A 'Queen of the Valar', spouse of Oromë; called 'the Ever-Young'.

Varda   Spouse of Manwë, with whom she dwelt on Taniquetil; greatest of the Queens of the Valar; maker of the stars. In Gnomish her name was *Bredhil* or *Bridhil*.

*Vinyamar**   The house of Turgon in Nevrast under Mount Taras before his departure to Gondolin.

Voronwë   Elf of Gondolin, the only mariner to survive from the seven ships sent into the West by Turgon after the Nirnaeth Arnoediad, who guided Tuor to the hidden city. The name means 'steadfast'.

The Way of Escape   The tunnel under the Encircling Mountains leading into the plain of Gondolin. Elvish name *Bad Uthwen*.

The Western Sea(s)   See *Great Sea*.

The Wing   Emblem of Tuor and his followers.

Wingelot   'Foam-flower', the ship of Eärendel.

Yavanna   After Varda, Yavanna was the greatest of the Queens of the Valar. She was 'the Giver of Fruits' (the meaning of her name) and 'the lover of all things that grow in the earth'. Yavanna brought into being the Trees that gave light to Valinor, growing near the gates of Valmar. See *Palúrien*.

Ylmir   Gnomish form for *Ulmo*.

ADDITIONAL NOTES

Ainur

The name *Ainur*, translated 'the Holy Ones', derives from my father's myth of the Creation of the World. He set down the original conception, according to a letter of 1964 (from which I have cited a passage on p.21), when at Oxford he was 'employed on the staff of the then still incomplete great Dictionary' from 1918–20. 'In Oxford', the letter continues, 'I wrote a cosmogonical myth, "The Music of the Ainur", defining the relation of The One, the transcendental Creator, to the Valar, the "Powers", the angelical First-created, and their part in ordering and carrying out the Primeval Design.'

It may seem an excessive departure from the tale of the Fall of Gondolin to his myth of the Creation of the World, but I hope it will soon be apparent why I have made it.

The central conception of the 'cosmogonical myth' is

declared in the title: *The Music of the Ainur.* It was not until the 1930s that my father composed a further version, the *Ainulindalë* (The Music of the Ainur), in substance closely following the original text. It is from this version that I have taken the quotations in the very brief account that follows.

The Creator is Eru, the One, also and more frequently named Ilúvatar, meaning 'the Father of All', of the Universe. It is told in this work that before all else Eru made the Ainur 'that were the offspring of his thought, and they were with him before Time. And he spoke to them, propounding to them themes of music. And they sang before him, each one alone, while the rest hearkened.' This was the beginning of the Music of the Ainur: for Ilúvatar summoned them all, and he declared to them a mighty theme, of which they must make in harmony together 'a Great Music'.

When Ilúvatar brought this great music to an end he made it known to the Ainur that he being the Lord of All had transformed all that they had sung and played: he had caused them to be: to have shape and reality, as had the Ainur themselves. He led them then out into the darkness.

But when they came into the midmost Void they beheld a sight of surpassing beauty, where before had been emptiness. And Ilúvatar said: 'Behold your music! For of my will it has taken shape, and even now the history of the world is beginning.'

I conclude this account with a passage of great significance in this book. There is speech between Ilúvatar and Ulmo concerning the realm of the Lord of Waters. Then follows:

And even as Ilúvatar spoke to Ulmo, the Ainur beheld the unfolding of the world, and the beginning of that history which Ilúvatar had propounded to them as a theme of song. Because of their memory of the speech of Ilúvatar, and the knowledge that each has of the music which he played, the Ainur know much of what is to come, and few things are unforeseen by them.

If we set this passage beside the foresight of Ulmo concerning Eärendel, which I have characterised (p.230) as 'miraculous', it seems that Ulmo was looking very far back in time to know for a certainty what the near future was portending.

There remains a further aspect of the Ainur to notice. To quote the *Ainulindalë* once more, it is told that

Even as they gazed, many became enamoured of the beauty of the world and engrossed in the history which came there to being, and there was unrest among them. Thus it came to pass that some abode still with Ilúvatar beyond the world ... But others, and among them were many of the wisest and fairest of the Ainur, craved leave of Ilúvatar to enter into the world and dwell there, and put on the form and raiment of Time ...

Then those that wished descended, and entered into the world. But this condition Ilúvatar made, that their power should thenceforth be contained and bounded by the world, and fail with it; and his purpose with them afterward Ilúvatar has not revealed.

Thus the Ainur came into the world, whom we call the Valar, or the Powers, and they dwelt in many places: in the firmament, or in the deeps of the sea, or upon Earth, or in Valinor upon the borders of Earth. And the four greatest were Melko and Manwë and Ulmo and Aulë.

This is followed by the portrait of Ulmo that is given in *The Music of the Ainur* (p.234).

It follows from the foregoing that the term *Ainur*, singular *Ainu*, may be used in the place of *Valar*, *Vala* now and again: so for example 'but the Ainur put it into his heart', p.40.

I must add finally that in this sketch of the Music of the Ainur I have deliberately omitted a major strand in the story of the Creation: the huge and destructive part played by Melko/Morgoth.

Húrin and Gondolin

This story is found in the relatively late text which my father called the *Grey Annals* (see p.220). It tells that Húrin and his brother Huor (the father of Tuor) 'went both to battle with the Orcs, even Huor, for he would not be restrained, though he was but thirteen years of age. And being with a company that was cut off from the rest, they were pursued to the ford of Brithiach; and there they would have been taken or slain, but for the power of Ulmo, which was still strong in Sirion. Therefore a mist arose from the river and hid them from their enemies, and they escaped into Dimbar, and wandered in the hills beneath the sheer walls of the Crissaegrim. There Thorondor espied them, and sent two Eagles that took them and bore them up and brought them beyond the mountains to the secret vale of Tumladen and the hidden city of Gondolin, which no man else yet had seen.'

King Turgon welcomed them, for Ulmo had counselled him to deal kindly with the house of Hador whence help should come at need. They dwelt in Gondor a year, and it is said that at this time Húrin learned something of the counsels and purposes of Turgon; for he had great liking for them, and wished to keep them in Gondolin. But they desired to return to their own kin, and share in the wars and griefs that now beset them. Turgon yielded to their wish and he said: 'By the way that you came you have leave to depart, if Thorondor is willing. I grieve at this parting, yet in a little while, as the Eldar account it, we may meet again.'

The story ends with the hostile words of Maeglin, who greatly opposed the king's generosity towards them. 'The law is become less stern than aforetime,' he said, 'or else no choice would be given you but to abide here to your life's end.' To this Húrin replied that if Maeglin did not trust them, they would take oaths; and they swore never to reveal the counsels of Turgon and to keep secret all that they had seen in his realm.

Years later Tuor would say to Voronwë, as they stood beside the sea at Vinyamar (p.171): 'But as for my right to seek Turgon: I am Tuor son of Huor and kin to Húrin, whose names Turgon will not forget.'

*

Húrin was taken alive in the Battle of Unnumbered Tears. Morgoth offered him his freedom, or else power as the greatest of Morgoth's captains, 'if he would but reveal where Turgon had his stronghold'. This proposal Húrin refused to Morgoth's face with the utmost boldness and scorn. Then Morgoth set him in a high place of Thangorodrim, to sit there upon a chair of stone; and he said to Húrin that seeing with the eyes of Morgoth he should look out upon the evil fates of those he loved and nothing would escape him. Húrin endured this for twenty-eight years. At the end of that time Morgoth released him. He feigned that he was moved by pity for an enemy utterly defeated, but he lied. He had further evil purpose; and Húrin knew that Morgoth was without pity. But he took his freedom. In the extension of the *Grey Annals* in which this story is told, 'The Wanderings of Húrin', he came at length to the Echoriath, the Encircling Mountains of Gondolin. But he could find no way further, and he stood at last in despair 'before the stern silence of the mountains ... He stood at last upon a great stone, and spreading wide his arms, looking towards Gondolin, he called in a great voice: "Turgon! Húrin calls you. O Turgon, will you not hear in your hidden halls?" But there was no answer, and all that he heard was wind in the dry grasses ... Yet there were ears that had heard the words that Húrin spoke, and eyes that marked well his gestures; and report of all came soon to the Dark Throne in the North. Then Morgoth smiled, and knew now clearly in what region Turgon dwelt, though because of the Eagles no spy of his could yet come within sight of the land behind the encircling mountains.'

So here again we meet my father's shifting perception of how Morgoth discovered where the Hidden Kingdom lay (see pp.126–7). The story in the present text is clearly at odds with the passage in the *Quenta Noldorinwa* (p.140), where the treachery of Maeglin, taken prisoner by the Orcs, is told in this clear form: 'he purchased his life and freedom by revealing unto Morgoth the place of Gondolin and the ways whereby it might be found and assailed. Great indeed was the joy of Morgoth...'

The story was in fact, I think, now taking a further step in the light of the end of the passage given above, where Húrin's cries revealed the place of Gondolin 'to the joy of Morgoth'. This is seen from what my father added at this point in the manuscript:

Later when captured and Maeglin wished to buy his release with treachery, Morgoth must answer laughing, saying: 'Stale news will buy nothing. I know this already, I am not easily blinded!' So Maeglin was obliged to offer more - to undermine resistance in Gondolin.

Iron Mountains

At first sight it appeared from early texts that *Hisilómë* (*Hithlum*) was a region distinct from the later Hithlum, since it was placed *beyond* the Iron Mountains. I concluded however that what was involved was simply a change of names, and this is certainly the truth of the matter. It is told elsewhere in the *Lost Tales* that after the escape of Melko from his imprisonment in Valinor he made for himself 'new dwellings in that region of the North where stand the Iron Mountains very high and terrible to see'; and also that Angband lay beneath the roots of the northernmost fortresses of the Iron Mountains: those mountains were so named from 'the Hells of Iron' beneath them.

The explanation is that the name 'Mountains of Iron' was originally applied to the range later called 'Shadowy Mountains' or 'Mountains of Shadow', *Ered Wethrin.* (It might be that while these mountains were regarded as a continuous range, the southern extension, the southern and eastern walls of Hithlum, came to be distinguished in name from the terrible northern peaks above Angband, the mightiest of them being Thangorodrim.)

Unhappily I failed to alter the List of Names in the entry *Hisilómë* in *Beren and Lúthien*, which states that that region owes its name to 'the scanty sun which peeps over the Iron Mountains to the east and south of it.' At p.43 in the present text I have replaced 'Iron' by 'Shadowy'.

Nirnaeth Arnoediad: The Battle of
Unnumbered Tears

It is said in the *Quenta Noldorinwa*:

Now it must be told that Maidros, son of Fëanor, perceived
that Morgoth was not unassailable after the deeds of Huan
and Lúthien and the breaking of the towers of Thû [Tol
Sirion, Isle of Werewolves; later > Sauron's tower], but that
he would destroy them all, one by one, if they did not form
again a league and council. This was the Union of Maidros
and wisely planned.

The gigantic battle that ensued was the most disastrous
in the history of the wars of Beleriand. References to the
Nirnaeth Arnoediad abound in the texts, for Elves and
Men were utterly defeated and the ruin of the Noldor was
achieved. Fingon, king of the Noldor, a son of Fingolfin and
brother of Turgon was slain, and his realm was no more. But
a very notable event, early in the battle, was the intervention
of Turgon, breaking the leaguer of Gondolin: this event is
told thus in the *Grey Annals* (on which see *The Evolution of
the Story* p.220):

To the joy and wonder of all there was a sounding of great
trumpets, and there marched up to war a host unlooked
for. This was the army of Turgon that issued from Gondolin, ten thousand strong, with bright mail and long swords,

and they were stationed southwards guarding the passes of
Sirion.

There is also in the *Grey Annals* a very noteworthy passage
on the subject of Turgon and Morgoth.

But one thought troubled Morgoth deeply, and marred
his triumph; Turgon had escaped the net, whom he most
desired to take. For Turgon came of the great house of
Fingolfin, and was now by right King of all the Noldor,
and Morgoth feared and hated most the house of Fingolfin,
because they had scorned him in Valinor, and had the
friendship of Ulmo, and because of the wounds that Fingolfin gave him in battle. Moreover of old his eye had
lighted on Turgon, and a dark shadow fell on his heart,
foreboding that, in some time that lay yet hidden in doom,
from Turgon ruin should come to him.

The Origins of Eärendel

The text that follows here is derived from a lengthy letter
written by my father in 1967 on the subject of his construc-
tion of names within his history and his adoption of names
exterior to his history.

He remarked at the outset that the name *Eärendil* (the
later form) was very plainly derived from the Old English
word *Éarendel* – a word that he felt to be of peculiar beauty

in that language. 'Also' (he continued) 'its form strongly suggests that it is in origin a proper name and not a common noun.' From related forms in other languages he thought it certain that it belonged to astronomical myth, and was the name of a star or star-group.

'To my mind', he wrote, 'the Old English uses seem plainly to indicate that it was a star presaging the dawn (at any rate in English tradition): that is what we call *Venus*: the morning star as it may be seen shining brilliantly in the dawn, before the actual rising of the Sun. That is at any rate how I took it. Before 1914 I wrote a "poem" upon Eärendel who launched his ship like a bright spark from the havens of the Sun. I adopted him into my mythology – in which he became a prime figure as a mariner, eventually as a herald star, and a sign of hope to men. *Aiya Eärendil Elenion Ancalima* "hail Eärendel brightest of Stars" is derived at long remove from *Éala Éarendel engla beorhtast*.'

It was indeed a long remove. These Old English words are taken from the poem *Crist*, which reads at this point *Éala! Éarendel engla beorhtast ofer middangeard monnum sended.* But, extraordinary as it seems at first sight, in the Elvish words *Aiya Eärendil Elenion Ancalima* cited by my father in this letter he was referring to a passage in the chapter *Shelob's Lair* in *The Lord of the Rings*. As Shelob approached Sam and Frodo in the darkness Sam cried out 'The Lady's gift! The star-glass! A light to you in dark places, she said it was to be. The star-glass!' In amazement at his forgetfulness 'slowly Frodo's hand went to his bosom, and slowly he held aloft the Phial of Galadriel' ... 'The darkness receded from it, until it seemed to shine in the centre of a globe of airy crystal, and the hand that held it sparkled with white fire.

'Frodo gazed in wonder at this marvellous gift that he had so long carried, not guessing its full worth and potency. Seldom had he remembered it on the road, until they came to Morgul Vale, and never had he used it for fear of its revealing light. *Aiya Eärendil Elenion Ancalima!* he cried, and knew not what he had spoken; for it seemed that another voice spoke through his, clear, untroubled by the foul air of the pit.'

In the letter of 1967 my father went on to say that 'the name could not be adopted just like that: it had to be accommodated to the Elvish linguistic situation, at the same time as a place for this person was made in legend. From this, far back in the history of "Elvish", which was beginning, after many tentative starts in boyhood, to take definite shape at the time of the name's adoption, arose eventually the Common Elvish stem AYAR "sea", primarily applied to the Great Sea of the West and the verbal element (N)DIL, meaning "to love, be devoted to". Eärendil became a character in the earliest written (1916–17) of the major legends ... Tuor had been visited by Ulmo one of the greatest Valar, the lord of seas and waters, and sent by him to Gondolin. The visitation had set in Tuor's heart an insatiable sea-longing, hence the choice of name for his son, to whom this longing was transmitted.'

The Prophecy of Mandos

In the extract from the *Sketch of the Mythology* given in the Prologue it is told (p.32) that as the Noldoli sailed from Valinor in their rebellion against the Valar Mandos sent an emissary, who speaking from a high cliff as they sailed by warned them to return, and when they refused he spoke the Prophecy of Mandos concerning their fate in afterdays. I give here a passage that gives an account of it. The text is the first version of *The Annals of Valinor* – the last version being the *Grey Annals* (see *The Evolution of the Story* p.220). This earliest version belongs to the same period as the *Quenta Noldorinwa*.

They [the departing Noldoli] came to a place where a high rock stands above the shores, and there stood either Mandos or his messenger and spoke the Doom of Mandos. For the kin-slaying he cursed the house of Fëanor, and to a less degree all who followed them, or shared in their emprise, unless they would return to abide the doom and pardon of the Valar. But if they would not, then should evil fortune and disaster befall them, and ever from treachery of kin towards kin; and their oath should turn against them; and a measure of mortality should visit them, that they should be lightly slain with weapons, or torments, or sorrow, and in the end fade and wane before the younger race. And much else he foretold darkly that after befell, warning them that the Valar would fence Valinor against their return.

But Fëanor hardened his heart and held on, and so also but reluctantly did Fingolfin's folk, feeling the constraint of their kindred and fearing for the doom of the Gods (for not all of Fingolfin's house had been guiltless of the kin-slaying).

See also the words of Ulmo to Tuor at Vinyamar, LV p.166.

The Three Kindreds of the Elves in The Hobbit

In *The Hobbit*, not far from the end of Chapter 8, *Flies and Spiders*, occurs this passage.

The feasting people were Wood-elves, of course ... They differed from the High Elves of the West, and were more dangerous and less wise. For most of them (together with their scattered relations in the hills and mountains) were descended from the ancient tribes that never went to Faerie in the West. There the Light-elves and the Deep-elves and the Sea-elves went and lived for ages, and grew fairer and wiser and more learned, and invented their magic and their cunning craft in the making of beautiful and marvellous things, before some came back into the Wide World.

These last words refer to the rebellious Noldor who left Valinor and in Middle-earth became known as the Exiles.

SHORT GLOSSARY OF OBSOLETE, ARCHAIC AND RARE WORDS

affray attack, assault
ambuscaded placed in *ambuscade,* ambushed
ardour burning heat (of breath)
argent silver or silvery-white
astonied earlier form of *astonished*
bested beset [also spelt *bestead*]
blow bloom
boss raised centre of a shield
broidure embroidery
burg a walled town
byrnie coat of mail
car chariot
carle peasant or servant
chrysoprase a golden-green precious stone
conch shellfish used as a musical instrument or instrument of call
cravenhood cowardice [apparently unique here]
damascened etched or inlaid with gold or silver
descry catch sight of
diapered diamond-patterned
dight arrayed
drake dragon. Old English *draca.*
drolleries something amusing or funny
emprise enterprise
fain gladly, willingly
fell (1) cruel, terrible (2) mountain
glistering sparkling
greave armour for the shin
hauberk defensive armour, long tunic of chain-mail
illfavoured having an unpleasant appearance, ugly

kirtle   garment reaching to the knees or lower
lappet   small fold of a garment
leaguer/-ed [lands] besiege/-d
lealty   faithfulness, loyalty
let   allowed (if occasion let, let fashion)
malachite   a green mineral
marges   margins or edges
mattock   two-headed agricultural tool
mead   meadow
meshed   entangled inextricably
plash   splash
plenished   filled up
puissance   power, strength, force
reck   take thought of
rede   counsel
repair   go frequently to
repast   food; meal, feast
rowan   mountain ash
ruth   sorrow, distress
sable   black
scathe   harm
sojourned   stayed
sward   expanse of short grass
swart   dark-hued
tarry/-ied   linger/-ed
thrall/thralldom   slave/slavery
twain   two
vambrace   armour for the fore-arm
weird   fate
whin   gorse
whortleberry   bilberry
writhen   twisted, arranged in coils

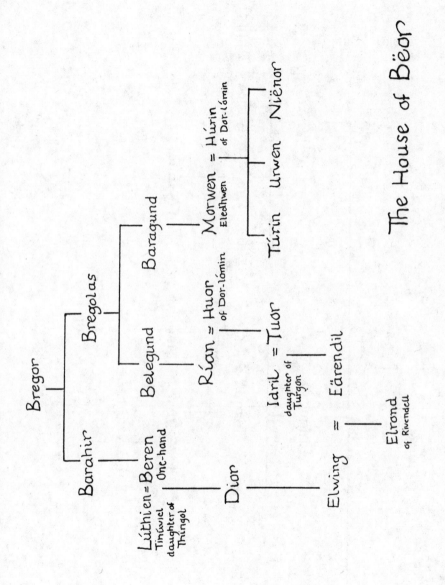

The House of Bëor

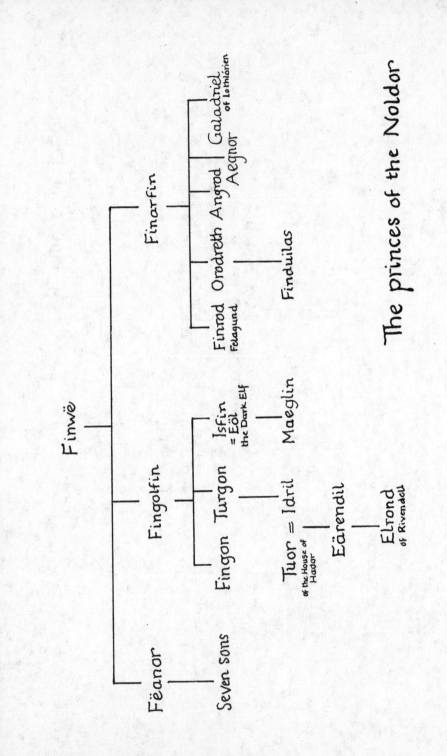

The princes of the Noldor